CHASING MIND

BRANDT LEGG

BOOKS

By Brandt Legg

Chase Malone Thriller

Chasing Rain
Chasing Fire
Chasing Wind
Chasing Dirt
Chasing Life
Chasing Kill
Chasing Risk
Chasing Mind
Chasing Time
Chasing Lies
Chasing Fear
Chasing Lost

*As always, this book is dedicated to
Teakki and Ro*

Vinci Books

vinci-books.com

Published by Vinci Books Ltd in 2025

Copyright © Brandt Legg 2021

The author has asserted their moral right to be identified as the author of this work in accordance with the Copyright, Designs and Patents Act 1988. This work is a work of fiction. Names, characters, places and incidents are the product of the author's imagination or are used fictitiously. Any resemblance to actual persons, living or dead, places and incidents is entirely coincidental.

All rights reserved. No part of this publication may be copied, reproduced, distributed, stored in any retrieval system, or transmitted in any form or by any means, including photocopying, recording, or other electronic or mechanical methods, nor used as a source for any form of machine learning including AI datasets, without the prior written permission of the publisher.

The publisher and the author have made every effort to obtain permissions for any third party material used in this book and to comply with copyright law. Any queries in this respect should be brought to the attention of the publisher and any omissions will be corrected in future editions.

A CIP catalogue record for this book is available from the British Library.

Paperback ISBN: 9781036705275

Chapter One

Nine black-clad operatives moved into position, their leader confident. "The day has finally come," he said to himself, lining up the sight of his sniper rifle, as a gentle snow fell. "The last day of Chase Malone's life."

Chase Malone sipped an earthy concoction of tea and coffee, bitter and good, gently waking up his tired brain. His thirty-second birthday not far off, he looked and felt older than that. "It's been a while since I used these parts of my mind," he said, smiling at Wen, taking in her beauty framed by a view of jagged peaks and blue skies in this gorgeous slice of Utah. It was as good as any place to hide—not that they *were* hiding, or at least that wasn't their initial objective, but in reality the pair was always on the run.

"Alpha ready," an operative said, beginning a relay of check-ins.

They were there trying to solve a problem with Chase's latest invention: OvR-sITe, a program designed to keep the government in check. Chase, a brilliant engineer and AI expert had made a series of tech breakthroughs during the prior ten years.

"Bravo ready," an operative reported.

"Charlie ready."

Chase and Wen had come to Dan Shaw's mountain estate because, like Chase, he was an expert on machine learning. The two old friends had spent the previous thirty-six hours looking for a way around the ever-changing government firewalls and writing code.

"Delta ready."

Wen, svelte, muscled, alert, checked out the window, a habit the former Chinese MSS agent couldn't seem to shake. Although no one knew where they were, someone always seemed to anyway. She made eye contact with Chase, an unspoken *all clear*.

"Echo ready."

"Foxtrot ready."

Dan Shaw, whose net worth at 7.3 billion made him almost seven times wealthier than Chase, glanced up from his computer. "I think it's in the autonomic computing," he said, excited. "If we use Heuristic search techniques, we should be able to get it to work."

Chase smiled, his rugged good looks belied his geek mind. "Let's put it in the predictive model."

"Golf ready."

"Hotel ready."

Chase started to walk toward Dan, excited that they *finally* had an answer, wondering if it would really work. The model would be critical in stopping the governments of the world from further abusing their power.

"Go," the leader said into his wrist.

The mansion erupted in gunfire.

"Down!" Wen yelled, rolling away from the window under a storm of splintering wood and shards of glass.

Chase dove under a table, where somehow Wen slid him a submachine gun.

"Dan!" Chase shouted, wondering where his friend was as the opulent room of a minute earlier was shredded by an unrelenting hail of bullets.

No answer, but moments later he appeared in the hall, wielding a shotgun.

Wen executed a man as he entered the blown-out south window. Dan got three shots off and managed to badly wound one of the intruders before a stray bullet caught him in the head.

Chase saw his friend fall, but Dan was already dead by the time he reached him. "Sorry, man," Chase wheezed painfully, sounding as if he'd been shot himself. Then he twisted in a blur and finished off the man who'd killed his longtime friend, a kind and generous man, light years ahead in technology.

"We've got to get out of the house!" Wen yelled.

"Wine cellar?" Chase replied.

"You read my mind."

They both continued shooting while retreating to the large kitchen. A sliding door, partially concealed inside the walk-in pantry, opened onto a narrow wooden staircase. Had it only been twelve hours since Dan had proudly showed them his wine cellar?

Chase closed the pantry door behind them and rushed onto the first step. Wen found the light switch as Chase slid the paneled door shut, wondering how long it would take for their escape route to be discovered.

"Where's that door?" Chase muttered as they reached the bottom of the stairs. The stone façade archways led off in three separate directions. Chase recalled Dan's enthusiasm as he'd shown them his prized six thousand bottle collection.

"Over here," Wen said, choosing the center corridor.

"Of course *you* remember," Chase said quietly, knowing Wen's first task upon entering any new place was to scope out every possible exit, anything which could be used as an advantage. "While I was looking at the bottle of 1945 Chateau Mouton-Rothschild, you were making mental maps."

Wen unbolted the heavy exterior door and opened it slowly, peering out, leading with her gun. "Come on," she said. "You go first, get the car."

As snow continued to fall, Chase darted across the driveway, knowing Wen would be covering him.

He made it into the front seat and turned over the engine before the first shots came his way. Hitting the accelerator, Chase steered the Mercedes-Benz GLS 580 SUV back toward the side of the house where he'd left his long time Jedi-like sweetheart at the entrance to the wine cellar, but she was no longer there.

Keeping the SUV moving, the submachine gun on his lap, he scanned the area, trying to find Wen. He finally spotted her on the other side of the heated outdoor swimming pool, heading for the trees. He'd have to drive around the far side of the circular drive and across a wide section of lawn to reach her.

The operatives swarmed into the open like vultures circling roadkill. Chase punched the gas, then saw what had prompted Wen to run.

Seven armed men were closing in on her.

She's going to die, he thought, an instant before a sudden burst of gunfire sprayed across his windshield.

Chapter Two

With the front and side windows blown out, Chase swerved the vehicle around a flagstone fountain and headed straight at one of Wen's pursuers, intending to mow him down, actually visualizing their bodies crunching under the Mercedes' twenty-three inch wheels. *They must be from the shadow people,* he thought angrily. The mysterious group had been trailing them relentlessly for more than two years, and they'd yet to discover why.

Blazing across the expansive lawn at close to seventy miles an hour, Chase zeroed in on his target. The man heard the 580's eight cylinder engine pumping 483 horsepower. He turned to shoot, but it was too late. The SUV steamrolled over him, bouncing over his crushed body as if it were little more than a bump in the road. Chase, whose driving skills were one of his greatest sources of pride, cranked the wheel and aimed for the next body, even though he cringed at the thought of killing another person. Grass and dirt flew as the heavy vehicle cut through the dried-out lawn, now slick with a dusting of snow.

The wintery storm suddenly picked up, flakes flying into Chase's eyes through the shattered glass, making it a trickier run at his next victim. This time the man fired quick enough to damage the grill and hood of the SUV, but not soon enough to save his life. His body broke upon impact, rolling across the bullet punctured hood, crashing through remnants of the shot-out windshield and plunging head-first into the passenger seat, his legs still dangling out onto the hood.

"You think I'm an Uber?" Chase asked, his sarcastic humor often surfaced during times of stress. He cut the wheel hard, attempting to line up with the next man when a Suburban SUV came barreling toward him.

Seeing Wen almost to the trees, and with no other choice, Chase turned wide and went heavy on the gas pedal. The Mercedes fishtailed as he tore up more of the lawn before sailing out onto a narrow dirt road lined by towering trees.

Snow and freezing rain blinded the already foggy air. The driver of the Suburban took full advantage of the tight lane and jammed into the back of the 580. Realizing he was now on an old forest service road coated in powdery snow, Chase drove as fast as conditions allowed, but couldn't break away from the powerful Chevy.

What would Wen do? he asked himself.

Before an answer came, the road opened onto an edgy canyon. He knew it wasn't safe to be traveling more than twenty-miles per hour on something with a drop that treacherous. Glancing down, he saw the speedometer was clicking in at fifty-four, just as a sharp curve raced up at him through the fog.

Chase pulled the wheel, but it wasn't enough. The Mercedes soared over the cliff. All fifty-seven hundred pounds of steel, plastic, and leather dropped straight down. Chase, still buckled in, braced for the crash.

The driver of the Suburban also failed to make the turn, but the two-seconds of warning Chase had given him let him jump out just as the three-ton monster went off the edge.

Believing he was about to die, Chase had a sudden reprieve when the front end lowered, and below—

Big, beautiful, and hopefully deep water, he thought, pulling out his favorite weapon, a custom multitool.

A fast few moments later, the Mercedes smashed into the lake. In less than a tenth of a second, both front airbags deployed. The force of their impact slammed Chase back against the seat. Almost instantly, the windowless SUV began sinking. Chase punctured the driver's airbag with the multitool's blade, then slashed the seatbelt. As the Mercedes sank, he fought through the shifting, tangled body of his "passenger" to squeeze himself out through the open windshield.

The water, remarkably clear and incredibly cold, was also deep. The Mercedes appeared to be driving off into the depths without him. The Suburban came past him as if intent on continuing the car chase. He couldn't tell if anyone was left inside, and he looked around wildly, expecting a new attack.

Bullets filled the water like dozens of deadly microtorpedoes.

Chapter Three

GUANGZHOU, CHINA

Lights from passing cars reflected off the painted cinderblock walls of a back alley, behind almost a mile of warehouses, in the old section of town. Chun had been waiting for ten minutes, surprised that Jin wasn't already there.

He's never been late before...

He looked at the clock on the dashboard. Jin was seven minutes behind schedule.

Seven minutes could be lost anywhere. No sense to panic yet.

Still, panic wouldn't necessarily be an overreaction. Jin could be dead, and if he was, Chun would also be dead soon. *Very* soon.

When Jin finally arrived, Chun noticed his disheveled hair and patchy stubble. "Please forgive my being late," Jin said in Mandarin, looking over his shoulder.

"Are you all right?" Chun replied in the same language, nervous himself. This was the riskiest operation they had ever undertaken.

Jin swallowed hard and nodded. "Yes, just tired." He kept looking around quickly, his eyes darting like prey.

Chun thought back to a time in his life when something like this would've been unimaginable, back when he was still married and his son was still alive. Chun, like most citizens of the People's Republic of China, considered risk a four letter word. He, along with all of his neighbors, coworkers, and the people he passed on the streets during his daily commute, followed the party line. It wasn't because he was afraid, but because everything seemed fine, as it should be. However, that illusion had come crashing down once his son had become involved in an antigovernment demonstration.

"Were you followed?" Chun asked, squinting his eyes, ready to take a blow, a habit fostered by too much bad news in his life.

"Of course not," Jin responded as if insulted, but Chun noticed how he kept checking behind him.

Chun didn't like to think about what had happened to his son, but something in Jin's mood and the eerie dark of the night brought the awful memories flooding back. He couldn't recall now if his son's demonstration had been about Hong Kong, or Taiwan, the Chinese President taking unlimited powers, or something else. But there had been a crackdown. His son had been sent off to prison for what was supposed to have been a two-year sentence.

Then, during his first few months of incarceration, he'd died.

"Do you have it?" Jin asked after apologizing again for being late.

"Yes," Chun replied, raking long, boney fingers through his thinning, spiked hair, thinking the question unnecessary. This was everything, the very thing he'd been working toward since they'd taken his son. More than likely he'd been murdered in prison by the Communists, but there would never be a trial, no way to prove any of it.

Unable to deal with the grief, Chun had left his wife soon after. Then, almost accidentally, Chun had met some people who knew things that he didn't, things that his son must have suspected or heard about. For the last six years, Chun had been a member of the underground, trying to bring down the communist oppression and corruption.

"And?" Jin asked. "How does it look?"

"It's pretty bad. The advances they've made are considerable."

"It's only been eight months since our last intercept," Jin said. "How far could it have gone?"

"I think the last round of data must've been older than we thought. Maybe the dates were calibrated wrong. *Something* was off, because it's hard to imagine they could've moved this far ahead in so short a time." Chun looked down the street as a car passed the opening to the alley. Both men tensed, as it seemed unusual for a vehicle to be there at that hour.

"It kept going," Jin said, relieved.

"You'd better get this down the line," Chun continued, not wanting to explain the disturbing information contained in the reports. More than the danger, it was a difficult topic.

Jin nodded. "With any luck, I will have this delivered by morning."

They had learned that the government monitored all communications, that even encryptions could not be trusted. Thus they moved data at night, and in person.

Chun recalled the images of the school children wearing headsets. The Chinese government had claimed it was a small program—simple monitoring, nothing else. *Lies!* Chun thought angrily, squinting again, breath shallow. Love for his son and pain for his loss intertwined in his gut in a numb, vicious knot.

But now they had evidence.

Jin turned to go before stopping and turning back to face Chun. "Is it the proof?" he asked hesitantly.

"Yes," Chun whispered, his passion getting the better of him. "The Mind Project has expanded. It now includes millions of children and factory workers."

"Then they *are* doing it?"

He nodded. "The government is building a database."

Jin's face was terrified, both from fear of getting caught with such sensitive secrets, and for the horror of what the Mind Project meant. "Exponential growth and machine learning . . . *that* is why it is accelerating at an astonishing rate."

"Yes. The Mind Project has developed a device that can accurately predict the thoughts of people." Chun paused, looked up the alley, then in a more urgent, but still hushed tone, added, "And they are planning to use it to take over the world."

Chapter Four

The driver of the Suburban had jumped out just as his vehicle followed the Mercedes over the cliff into the lake. Banged up and a bit woozy, he finally got to his feet and looked over the edge. Only the back end of the Mercedes was visible, while the Suburban was sinking twenty feet away. After seeing no sign of life, he fired almost a full magazine down into the water, then waited another couple of minutes. He snapped a few photos with his phone, then jogged back up the road, planning to help his comrades with the woman.

She had made it into the woods with five of them still on her. The Suburban driver expected her to already be in custody, until he stumbled upon the body of one of his team, almost cut in half by machine gunfire. Twenty yards later, he found another, neck snapped. And then Marcus, his close friend, leaning against a tree . . . at least he *thought* it was Marcus. It was difficult to be sure since his face had been shot. The mess that remained made him sick. Two hundred yards beyond that nightmare, maimed and draped over a dead log, was Drake, unclear how he died. Suburban shook his head in disgust and kept moving.

Finally, he saw the woman fighting with Pyle. Based on everything he'd just seen, he assumed Pyle had only seconds left to live. Fortunately, in the midst of their hand-to-hand combat, she hadn't heard his approach.

"Freeze!" Suburban yelled, firing a couple warning shots. "I'd like nothing more than to avenge my buddies and kill you."

Wen turned slowly to face him, furious she'd lost her gun in the last fight. "Why don't you then?"

"Don't tempt me."

"You're telling me that after all this, you weren't sent to kill me?" she asked, trying to buy time, concerned about Chase, figuring it was just these two men left, and knowing she could take them.

Just keep the conversation going . . .

A blow to her side knocked Wen off her feet. The man she'd been fighting stood over her, holding the heavy, four-foot-long log he'd used to club her. Before she could react, he hit her again in her leg. "Just in case you were planning to kick me."

Suburban used his boot to shove Wen's face into the cold, snowy dirt, while the other man duct taped her ankles together, then taped her wrists painfully behind her back.

"By the way, your boyfriend's dead," Suburban said. "I left him at the bottom of a frigid lake."

She writhed against her bonds, trying to gain contact with either one of them. "I could kill you with my bare hands if I were free!"

The man clubbed her in the gut. She had a high pain threshold, but he hit something that almost made her pass out.

"Where to?" he asked Suburban, dragging Wen by her feet. She struggled to turn her head to keep her face out of the snow and dirt.

"We need to find a ride."

"Where's the Suburban?"

"Bottom of the same lake."

"What about back at the house?"

"It's burning. Someone hit a propane tank or something," Suburban said, checking his GPS. "Rich dude had four cars in the garage, and they're all on fire."

"Not easy to find a ride with this cargo," he said as Wen's battered body bounced over the rough terrain.

"This way," Suburban said, looking up from the GPS. "We may get lucky."

"*Lucky*," Wen growled. "The only luck you can hope for is that I'll kill you quickly instead of slowly."

Suburban kicked her already tender ribs and stuffed a bandana in her mouth.

I will kill you, she thought, thinking of Chase, desperate to believe they were lying to her, that he had escaped or someone else had him. *Either way, you two are going to die.*

Chapter Five

Bull stared at the screen, checking the data a third time. Her eyes disagreed with her brain, as the visuals seemed almost unreal. A familiar feeling crept in, as if she were looking inside somebody's private drawer or jewelry case; a place where secrets were kept, the most important ones, the ones people didn't want anyone else to see. That sense was the main reason she loved hacking. That voyeuristic thrill.

However, this was *much* more than that.

As she reviewed the open document on her screen, Bull realized that it wasn't just secret or important, it was more along the lines of *world-altering* and dangerous . . . *extremely* dangerous.

She had stumbled upon it while working on a hack for The Cause, an underground movement also known as "WOLF" by its members. The group had originally been started by a few radicals, intellectuals, and activists intent on bringing about income equality throughout the world, but had quickly evolved into a full-fledged revolutionary movement seeking to take down the current world order and the elites.

Bull missed her freelance hacking days, when one could wander and search for trouble and treasures on her own, like a surfer riding a perfect wave or a snowboarder getting the right day of powder. This find reminded her of earlier times, which rekindled that lost elation because she wasn't *supposed* to have discovered it.

Nothing close to this kind of hit was in her routine anymore. Bull's days were filled with important work now, making a difference instead of just stealing and flinging hazards, as she used to say. But she believed in what The Cause was doing. It stirred her rebel spirit as well as being a lot safer than her old freelance work or the stuff she did for Chase and Wen.

It had been that work that had cost her the use of her legs. That had scared her. She'd handled it with her typical sarcastic grace, telling friends, "Well, it's not like I was a downhill skier or marathon runner. I just sit behind computer screens all day. Wasn't using my legs too much to begin with." Her buzzed, bleached white hair and heavily lined azure eyes accentuated this twenty-something brave-sounding digital whiz, a martyr to the internet realm.

And there had been another silver lining—she'd fallen in love.

Bull had met Chase's partner Dez a few times before her shooting, but she hadn't really *known* him. Dez had lost a leg while helping Chase, and ever since, he'd been working to advance solutions for amputees, paraplegics, and quadriplegics.

After her own tragedy, she turned to Dez. To the surprise of them both, sparks flew. It turned out they had more in common than just their leg injuries. With their intense affection for computers, common belief in The Cause, and true closeness with Chase and Wen, they seemed to be in constant conversation.

That they also saw the world in the same way stirred a burning passion that neither had fully experienced before. Bull soon moved in with Dez, and the two had explored that mutual passion ever since.

While Dez spent his days primarily working on secret AI projects that he and Chase had created, Bull pursued WOLF initiatives round-the-clock. She was in constant touch with members of The Cause, including more than twenty other hackers she'd personally recruited. Turns out hackers shared a common thread for anti-authority beliefs and revolution.

The screen mesmerized her, and just that fact made it even more intense, because Bull had spent *years* staring into screens. "I look into the digital matrix more then I observe our three-dimensional reality," she often said, especially when trying to illustrate and legitimize something she had found that others couldn't see or wouldn't believe. While she stared into the glowing pixels as morning's first light penetrated the edges of the floor-to-ceiling drapes of Dez's penthouse overlooking San Francisco, she felt both excitement and dread; elated at digging up such a rare and valuable treasure, and fearful of what it meant, a position she'd been in many times.

Dez will be awake in an hour, she thought, navigating the whisper-quiet ultra-advanced wheelchair into the bedroom, her strong, lean arms easily sliding her lithe body out of the seat and into the bed next to him. She gently kissed his face and softly touched his chest. Dez stirred.

"Mmmm, tired." His sleepy voice was playful, yet serious.

Bull was somewhat irresistible. He didn't realize she had *very* bad news. She let him have another moment of sleepy bliss before wrenching him into the reality of the day, one she was about to ruin.

Chapter Six

Suburban and Pyle left Wen tied to a tree and entered an RV campground. The area would have been packed in the summer, but its ninety-six spots were currently filled with no more than four diehards. Suburban entered the first RV they came to, a vintage fifth wheel that looked about fifteen years old, but the pickup truck it was attached to seemed to be a recent model. He roughed up the terrified senior citizen couple he found inside, bound and gagged them, then left them in a neighboring trailer whose owners must have driven into town.

"I'll get in trouble for not killing you," he told them before he left, "so don't do anything stupid. I don't want to regret leaving witnesses, but I don't enjoy killing grandparents."

Suburban started up the pickup truck just as Pyle returned with Wen.

He threw her in the back of the fifth wheel RV, tied her to a handrail, and was about to slam the door when barking erupted from three little yappers in big white plastic carriers. A cat lounged on a pillow on top of the crates as if they were her prisoners.

"Shut the dogs up!" a big green bird said. "Damn dogs, *rawk*, damn dogs!"

He shook his head, shut the door, and climbed in the passenger side of the pickup. "I think we just hijacked Dr. Doolittle's RV," he said as Suburban pulled out.

Chase surfaced near the base of the cliff, gasping. The angle of the outcropping he'd driven off made it impossible for the man to see him. Freezing, he clung to a rock, sucking in air after holding his breath for longer than he'd thought possible. After waiting four agonizing minutes to make sure the killer was gone, he made the difficult climb, followed the trail of dead bodies, and eventually wound up at the campground. Seeing two RV trailers without vehicles attached, Chase kept walking until he came across one with a truck. It was a handmade job, more of a wooden shack built atop the pickup's bed, complete with shake shingles and a metal smoke stack. It looked like something out of a kid's book, like it might sprout wings and fly off to a faraway kingdom to rescue a princess.

Just what I need, he thought.

"This your rig?" Chase asked the long haired bearded hippy who answered his knock at the carved backdoor, etched with peace signs, a rising sun, and flowers.

The guy laughed. "Yeah. You a census taker or something?" he asked with a bushy raised brow, skeptical of Chase's wet clothes. "Man, what happened to you?" He looked up at the sky as if he might have missed some major weather event.

"Listen, some men just kidnapped my wife, and I—"

"*What?*"

"I need your truck."

"No. I wish I could help, but this is all I got."

"You drive then. We need to go. Here." Chase struggled to get his wallet out of his wet jeans. "Three hundred bucks, just drive me into town."

"I don't know, man . . . I don't want trouble."

"*Please*, they have my wife. I'm a wealthy man, I can pay you more, but we need to go *now*."

The man looked hard at the shivering billionaire, and must have believed him, because he grabbed a blanket and tossed it to Chase. "Okay, let's go."

"Thanks," Chase said, climbing into the passenger seat.

"I'm Lefty, by the way."

"Chase Malone."

At the entrance of the campground, Lefty asked which way. Chase had no idea, but suggested whatever way led to the closest town and prayed he was right.

"Lefty, I need you to speed."

"Man, roads are a little dicey," he said. "But I'll push it."

The snow had eased up a little, and was now really just heavy flurries, but the wind was making it seem worse.

"You got any heat in this thing?" Chase asked, hugging the blanket tighter around himself.

Fifteen minutes later they finally spotted the RV way up ahead.

"That's got to be them," Chase said.

"How do you know?"

"They needed and obviously got a ride the same place I did."

"Right on," Lefty said, for some reason amused by the logic. "Hey man . . . is that your wife on the roof?"

Chapter Seven

Chun noticed the car following him long before he reached his home, and assumed they knew where he lived. *They must already have Jin,* he thought, *or they wouldn't just be following me.*

They have the data...

Chun made the seemingly crazy choice to go straight home for two reasons: he knew it was his best chance to escape, and he needed something from his apartment.

He left his car double parked in front of the sixty-year-old residential building as if he was going to be right back out, but Chun knew he'd never see his vehicle again. Running up the stairs to his apartment, knowing it was faster than the slow elevator, Chun wondered if they would already be up there waiting for him. Once at his floor, he left the stairwell cautiously, moved quickly down the musty hallway, unlocked the apartment door, took a deep breath, and entered.

It looked just like it had when he'd left it. No one else was there.

He grabbed two stamped, addressed envelopes and

without even a final glance at the apartment, pulled the door shut and locked it behind him, hoping that detail would delay anybody who decided not to wait for him to return to his vehicle. Chun ran back into the stairwell and listened carefully before descending.

This is my last chance to do good and make my life count for something, to make my son's life count for something, he thought as he reached the ground floor. He slowly opened the back door, searching for threats. The weight of his shattered family, coupled with all the disillusionment and loss, slowed his movements. His chest tightened and breathing became more difficult. He moved into the shadows of a small alley and attempted to calm himself.

How ironic, he thought, having gotten the idea of using mailers as insurance, from an American movie, *such a simple technique.* While continuing down the sidewalk, Chun worried that it wouldn't work, even though he thought it clever.

Why didn't I take the mailers with me when I met Jin? he chided himself. *Because if I'd been caught with them and the original, there would be no hope. I did it right.* Both envelopes contained duplicates of the evidence he had given to Jin. *Poor Jin . . . no doubt he is already dead.*

A block away from his building, Chun ducked inside a doorway. The lights from an approaching vehicle spooked him, but it seemed unconnected. Two blocks later, Chun reached the first green China Post letter box. He looked around, careful to keep his face concealed in the darkness, then dropped one of the envelopes in. Walking casually away, he tried to look natural and wondered if he would make it the six blocks in the other direction to the next green letter box.

Each passing car turned his stomach. He glanced at

every darkened window, tensing his reflexes, bracing for a bullet. *Maybe I've seen too many of those American films*, he thought, his only enjoyable reprieve in his otherwise miserable life. Then he recalled how much his son had loved Hollywood action movies . . .

Halfway to the final box, Chun saw the first police car.

Chase, wishing he could drive Lefty's rig instead of relying on an amateur to get him close, shouted commands. "Keep with them! Keep your speed steady!"

"Not sure I can do both at the same time."

"Get closer!"

"They're bigger, what if they push me?"

"*Push back!*"

"Man, I didn't sign up for—"

"Get me close enough to jump and you can be done with this!" Chase yelled, already leaning out the window.

Suburban checked his sideview mirror and couldn't believe his eyes. "Chase Malone, back from the dead," he said.

The other man automatically checked his mirror and caught a glimpse of Wen on the edge of the RV's roof, coming toward them. "Pull over!"

"What?"

"The woman is out!"

"*Out?*"

"She's on the roof!"

"Damn it, I thought you secured her," he snapped,

easing off the gas pedal. "I can't stop. Get out there and shoot her."

The other man climbed out the window, into the bed of the pickup, and quickly scaled the front of the fifth wheel, his gun aimed at Wen.

After some surprisingly skillful driving, Lefty got Chase right where he wanted. Chase launched himself into the pickup drivers' window. Suburban, trying to keep the truck on the road, reacted too late, and was unable to get a shot off. Chase pulled him down onto the seats, punching his face repeatedly, the now driverless vehicle swerving out of control.

Chapter Eight

Chun saw a second police car approaching from another direction. He quickly turned around and retraced his steps, turning into a side street. It would take him out of his way, but there was no other choice.

They must be looking for me now, he thought as a delivery truck passed him.

Another police car forced him to take his third unplanned turn. Then he got lucky. Just across the street, the round silhouette of a China Post letter box gave him hope. It wasn't the one he'd chosen weeks ago when he'd rehearsed this escape, but it would have to do.

A little breathless when he reached it, Chun gulped in the brisk night air, said a quick prayer to his son, and slipped the final envelope in.

That was the easy part, he thought, quickly walking away, knowing there were cameras, but needing to get as far from it as possible.

Twenty minutes later, he wasn't even in the same section of the city anymore. He stopped for the first time since the post box and caught his breath, then sat on a nearby bench, wondering what to do next. By now, they would have ransacked his car and apartment, dissecting his mundane life—a life that was now over, at least in the way he had known it.

Yet he was somehow still alive.

What if they catch me and torture me? Will I talk? Could I endure their methods? The pain? Will I tell them everything I know?

Maybe I should just end my life now. How would I do that? Jump off a bridge? Walk in front of a bus?

The thought made him shiver.

Chun looked all around, waiting for the assassin to find him. But there was nobody.

Maybe there is a chance. He had one other contact besides Jin. *Maybe he can help me escape.*

With nothing left to lose, he started walking again. *They are going to kill me anyway. I can try anything. All I am risking is what is already lost.*

The thought liberated him. Chun's new plan was completely dependent on the hope that his other friend was still alive.

But if they discovered Jin and me, they must also have him.

He suddenly remembered his phone. He knew from the movies he had to get rid of it.

But then how will I call my friend? Maybe I could borrow somebody's. If I make it through the rest of the night, maybe I can get to a coffee shop in the morning. I could easily convince somebody I've lost my phone, and there is an emergency.

If I can just get through the night.

He wondered if he should get even further away from the last post box before he ditched his phone. There were risks either way. The dilemma was maddening.

Just as he decided to throw his phone away, it rang. For

an instant he felt as if he'd been shot, like an invasion into his mind.

They know! They know I'm thinking about my phone! They know where I am!

Chase got an elbow into Suburban's nose. His foot came off the accelerator as the pickup climbed a steep grade. His hands released the steering wheel, sending the out-of-control vehicle onto the rough shoulder. As the pavement made a wide turn, the truck did not. In the confusion, Chase managed to get Suburban's gun, put two bullets into him, and several more into the seats and dashboard.

Then the truck bounced completely off the road. The four-foot drop-off jolted and shocked the connection between the fifth wheel and the pickup. The joints severed. The RV broke free and catapulted off into the ravine in a wild, horrendous lurch.

Chapter Nine

"What is it?" Dez asked after realizing he didn't have the energy to resist the purring kitten Bull had briefly become.

She nipped his ear. "I found something."

"You're *always* finding something. Is this about The Cause?" he said, rolling over, tired of the time she spent on the revolutionary movement. He didn't think anything *they* were doing could be worth waking him when he considered sleep so precious.

"No, but I was working on it *for* The Cause when I found this document. But, you know, everything ultimately affects The Cause." She seductively slid a spaghetti strap back up on her untanned shoulder.

"I dreamed of a parallel universe and The Cause was *still* there," he said, pulling the strap back off.

"Build me a portal," she said, giving him another kiss. "And take me there." She slid it back up.

"Working on it, baby." He pulled it back off.

She giggled.

"Well, want to tell me what you found, or do I have to wait until breakfast?"

"You need to see it," she said, her expression falling at the memory of it.

He groaned in defeat. "All right."

After getting his prosthesis on, Dez followed her to the computer room. Bull said nothing, just pointed to the screen.

He studied it for several minutes in total silence.

"Wow . . . this . . . this *was* worth waking me for."

She nodded. "Never a doubt."

"Have you gone any deeper?"

"Yeah."

"And there's *more*?"

"Yeah."

"How much?" he asked, turning to give her a concerned look.

"I don't know," she said, mirroring his dread. "I'm afraid to go too far in case it unravels."

"But you can hold the thread?"

"I'm not worried about that," Bull said, motioning at the monitor. "I'm worried about this." She scrolled down and then clicked an active link. Another screen of similar information surfaced. She pointed to a small icon that appeared to be a police badge.

"What is that?"

"It's an alphanumeric line of code."

"Really? That looks like an icon? Some kind of logo or emblem . . . maybe a security shield?"

"Exactly. It's code *and* a signature that looks like a security shield."

"Have you clicked it?"

"Of course not. It's a trap."

"How do you know?"

She looked at him like that was the most ridiculous question she'd ever been asked. She wanted to say, *It's what I do*, but then decided it didn't even deserve a response.

"So what's it *mean*?" he asked impatiently.

"It means it could unravel."

"And *that* means?"

"It means we've got to stop or they'll know we've been here."

"Who?"

"Them." She pointed to the top lines on the document. The pace at which she rifled through pages always impressed Dez. He'd been around computers his whole life, and he was fast, and he knew engineers that operated with blazing speed, but he'd never seen anyone like Bull, with the ability to cycle through twenty monitors while working three keyboards, touch-pads, and mice.

She brought up another page. "This is the icon magnified. See the alpha numeric symbol? If you take out the components and arrange them in a code sequence, you can see what happens—and it's *not* good."

"How do you know which order to put them in?" Dez asked, not out of curiosity, but wanting to know what method she'd used.

"I didn't," she responded, smiling at his interest. "I just rearranged them in every possible combination."

He looked at her as if she were a freak.

"I didn't do it manually, silly. I wrote a program."

Dez was a coder who knew how to create programs as well, and had worked with Chase, one of the best. He knew it wasn't as simple as it sounded to create. "How long did it take you?"

"I don't know, thirty or forty minutes? It doesn't matter. The point is, do you see what that means?"

He studied it more carefully. "Oh my god."

"Can that be possible?" she asked.

He thought about Chase, the things they had created together, and nodded slowly.

She looked at him in disbelief. "I was afraid so."

He continued to nod slowly, as if fading off into a trance.

"Are you okay?" she asked, catching his unshaved cheeks in her hands.

"Yeah," he said unconvincingly, in a voice that sounded like a combination of a groan and a whisper. "It's just . . . " He took her hands in his.

"What?"

"I don't really feel too well."

"Because of this?"

"Of course because of this," he said. "I've got to get some coffee."

She knew that what he really meant was he needed to get into the kitchen and make something. Cooking was what he did when stressed, or pretty much any time. Lucky for her, he was a gourmet chef, another reason to fall for him. Bull couldn't cook a can of beans, and even her toast was rarely successful.

"Okay, but we need to tell Chase and Wen."

"Why? I doubt even *they* can stop this."

Chapter Ten

By the time the pickup truck came to a stop on a snowy slope covered with dried-out weeds, Chase had total control of his prisoner. Using the roll of duct tape he'd found on the floor of the cab, Chase secured Suburban face down across the front seats, then ran to help Wen.

Wen, who wore a small, jeweled ring that opened into a concealed razor, had cut herself free. She'd been on her way to attack the men in the pickup's cab when Chase had appeared. After Pyle crested the roof of the RV, she dove toward him. His first shots went wide, and he never got another chance. Wen repaid his earlier assault on her, kicking his face with one foot and his gun with the other. She landed flat on the edge of the roof just as the truck went off the road. Pyle managed to hold on in spite of the blow and violent movements.

During the uncontrolled vehicle separation, Wen clung

33

to the corner wall. While the fifth wheel careened sideways, rolling, twisting, and folding, Pyle lost his grip, and Wen was thrown off as the heavy mobile home crushed her assailant. She slid down the slick ravine, staggering to her feet as the RV shell rattled past, narrowly missing her.

Stunned and disorientated, Wen instinctively reached for weapons, then remembered Chase. Beginning to claw her way back up the slope, she heard him calling her name.

"I'm here," she yelled, gripping her stomach where she'd been kicked repeatedly.

Chase's face appeared at the top of the slope, frowning when he saw her holding back the pain. "Are you okay?"

"Alive. What about you?"

"Cold and wet, but I'll live." He looked at her, and she knew he knew.

"Good. Help me get in the RV."

Chase glanced down at the tangled wreckage and hoped she didn't expect anyone to be alive in there. "Why?"

"There are pets inside."

Chase wondered if they had the time, if more shadow people were coming for them, but knew Wen was not going to let animals suffer if she could help it. A few minutes later, they had pulled the three plastic crates out, plus the cat, while the bird sat on his shoulder. Miraculously, they were all uninjured.

"Damn dogs, *rawk*! Wrecked the house, *rawk*!"

Chun wanted to throw his phone as hard as he could to make it and all his problems go far away, to wake from the never ending nightmare. Instead, he calmed himself down, and looked at the number.

New panic filled him when he recognized it as Jin's.

Maybe Jin got away . . . maybe he has a plan. Perhaps things aren't all that bad.

He answered the phone. "Hello?"

"Chun, where are you?"

Chun looked around, not even sure. He wasn't certain he should say, anyway. "Were you followed?"

"Yes, but I lost them"

"Me too."

"It's not safe to go to our homes. We should get together. Figure this out."

"Okay."

"Do you have additional copies that you gave to someone else? Someone we should warn?"

"No," he lied, deciding there was no reason to tell Jin about the mailers.

"Good. I can pick you up."

"Is your car safe?"

"I've already switched it with a friend from work," Jin assured him. "Tell me where you are. I'll come right now."

"Okay." Chun gave him the location and asked for a description of Jin's borrowed car.

Jin told him the make, model, and color, then said, "I'll see you in twenty minutes."

As soon as the call ended, Chun dumped his phone as planned and walked ten minutes to where he said he'd be.

During that same ten minutes, the people holding Jin turned him over to the MSS for further interrogation, which would eventually be followed by prison and probable execution.

Chun didn't know that then, because he'd never seen that movie.

However, Chun *did* know enough to wait and watch

carefully until he saw the car. Chun couldn't see into the front of the car very well since it was still dark, but there were definitely two people in the front seat.

"Poor Jin," he whispered to himself, knowing it had been a trap. He took one last glance at the car and receded back into the shadows. All he had to do was get to the other side of the building and disappear through a large park.

I wonder what they'll do to Jin, he pondered as he reached the back of the building. *I guess I'll never see him again . . .*

Two men grabbed him. His last thought before a cloth bag was yanked over his head was that he might be about to see Jin again after all.

Chapter Eleven

Wen reached the pickup truck first, as Chase was having an argument with the bird about the dogs. She reached in and dragged Suburban out by his feet. His shoulder took most of the impact, but his face still hit the hard, snowy ground. He grunted, absorbing the blow.

"I should kill you," she said through gritted teeth.

"But you won't." His words were labored. Blood from his leg turned the snow red.

She pulled his head backwards. "No, not yet anyway." She let his head go. "Where were you taking us?"

"I don't really know anything," he said, spitting snow and leaves. "Someone is meeting us."

"Where?"

"Not far from here."

"Tell me *exactly*."

He told her as Chase arrived.

"I'd like to dump him in the lake," Chase said, setting the dog crates next to him. As soon as the two he'd been

37

carrying saw the one Wen had brought, they began yapping again.

"Damn dogs, *rawk*, damn dogs!"

They laid their hostage in the badly damaged truck bed and put the animals in the back of the cab. The bird wasn't happy, and used a surprising vocabulary of curse words to make sure they knew.

Wen retrieved the large phone they'd taken from her earlier and checked to see that it still functioned, that its encryption protections remained. It had been custom built so she would have no doubts.

Once they reached the main road, they found Lefty pulled over on the shoulder.

"I didn't know what to do," he said, seeing Chase get out of the truck.

"No problem," Chase said, seeing how distressed Lefty was. "Thanks for waiting."

"I just wasn't sure," he said again, pulling on his scraggly beard.

"Really, it's cool. You saved us."

"I did?"

"You did. Thank you."

He nodded, apparently still unsure.

"Hey, could you do me one more favor?"

"Uh . . . " Lefty said hesitantly.

"Don't worry. This one is easier. Would you mind taking these pets back to the campground? I'm sure their owners are pretty worried about them."

"Yeah, sure, I can do that."

"Thanks. And please give the owners of the RV this card. Tell them if they call that number, someone will make sure they get a new fifth wheel." He handed Lefty a card along with a few more hundred dollar bills.

He looked at Chase suspiciously, but agreed. "Thanks man."

As they pulled away, Chase told Wen that he felt a little guilty saddling Lefty with the angry bird.

"No other choice," Wen said. "*Damn dogs, damn dogs!*"

Bull looked over. "Don't you think we should call Chase immediately?"

"We're gonna have to call him," Dez said. "But let's go a little deeper first."

"That could be dangerous," she said. "The people behind this aren't the friendly type."

"Are you saying we don't need to lose any more limbs?"

"I should say not," she said with an ironic laugh. "My point is, we've been in over our heads before, and it didn't go so well."

"Are you kidding? We're *living* over our heads. Chase and Wen, The Cause—we're caught up in the end times, the battle to save the world, some sort of crazy tech *apocalypse*. Do you think this is going to *surprise* Chase?"

She shook her head, pushing the button to steer the wheelchair, knowing it was best to get him into the kitchen. He followed her down the hall, past a line of abstract paintings he'd collected from a famous California artist.

"Well, I'm not surprised," Dez said. "Greedy people are always going to screw things up for the rest of us."

"Lucky I came across it."

Dez got around her and kneeled in front of the wheelchair. "Lucky? You think this is *lucky*? This is either the way we're going to die, or it's how humanity slips into a dystopian future where none of us are going to *want* to live."

"I know. That's why it's lucky I found it."

"You've been hanging around Chase too long."

"Because we can *stop* it," she said seriously. "Now get out of my way, gimp."

He laughed. "Yeah, you also *sound* like Chase. But there's not enough of us, and what if we don't stop it?"

"We can. There's always a way."

"Now you sound like Wen."

"Thank you."

He laughed again as he got to his feet. "To stop it, we'll *have* to go deeper, and if we go deeper, they *will* find us."

"I know."

Dez didn't talk again until they were in the kitchen. He began to crack eggs. "I don't think we have a choice," he said reluctantly.

"There's a chance that the code is only there to trap us."

"How did you find that?" he asked. "Tell me *exactly* how you stumbled into this, and how protected it is."

"It was part of a dark web locked stream. From nine months ago."

"Nine months?" he echoed, astounded.

"It's left over."

"You mean someone forgot it?"

"Not exactly. If the person setting up the initial files for the stream didn't know precisely what they were doing, it can leave a ghost image . . . sort of like an imprint on the matrix."

"So they *think* it's gone?"

"Yeah. The icon was part of the stream. It's imprinted there to protect the stream, to make sure nothing goes outside its given parameters."

"But they really don't know?" He pointed to the eggs and then to her. She nodded.

"I'm starving." He loved it when she admitted to hunger, rare for his waif of a girlfriend. "No, I can see the rake indicators," she continued.

Dez had been with Bull long enough to know the hacking term, which meant they had pulled up all remnants of the stream to make sure the tracks were covered. "Then this is just . . . here?"

"I was doing a boxed run. The Cause. Looking for something connected."

"Then maybe we *were* lucky."

Chapter Twelve

Ennis Cavanaugh walked purposefully into the back entrance of the Gold Building, the tallest structure on K Street in Washington, DC, as if he owned it—because he did. The billionaire also held deeds to other large sections of the most important city in the world. He often debated with people from other countries whether Washington still held that title, recognizing other points of view (America's declining influence, the financial capitals of New York, London, Beijing, Dubai, whatever), but he believed as long as the United States military was the most powerful on earth, and control of the Pentagon lay in Washington, it would retain its crown.

Ironically, though, he was working to change that, and he believed he had the keys to the kingdom.

Ennis was also head of the consortium, a group consisting of several major banks secretly acquiring telecommunications companies and other tech related firms. One of the consortium's attorneys was already waiting for him.

The two men exchanged pleasantries before the lawyer launched into his concerns. "You're leading a worldwide effort to rollout the next generation technology standard for broadband cellular networks."

Ennis, crossing lean suited arms across a narrow chest, looked at his counselor, waiting to hear something he didn't already know.

"You *can't* launch it secretly."

"It's not entirely secret."

"But 5EX is not *just* a successor to the prior networks," the lawyer said.

"No," Ennis said, smiling. "5EX is incredibly advanced, with instant streaming and download capabilities."

"The exposure . . . you *know* what I'm talking about."

"I'm late for a meeting," Ennis said impatiently. "Don't worry."

"You pay me to worry."

"5EX doesn't just give us access to power, it gives us access to *everything*. It *is* the power."

The strange glint in his otherwise dull eyes always made his assistant nervous.

Wen heard the noise first, and leaned out the window. "Choppers!"

"Where?"

"Just landing, other side of those trees." She pointed at what must have been three quarters of a mile away.

"Two?" Chase asked, thinking of the shadow people. "They must have been expecting to pick up all of them."

"And us," Wen added. "Pull over up there."

"You think we're going to take them with two guns and

almost no ammo? Unless you have a multi-tool you're not telling me about—"

"We need to find Grimes."

Mumford Grimes was a key shadow person who had been pursuing them for years. After previously capturing and releasing his closest associate, they believed they could turn him, that he could be convinced to help Chase and Wen find out who was sending the armies after them.

"I ran over two shadow people before I went in the lake. I didn't get a chance to see their faces before, and after it would have been kind of hard to tell . . . maybe Grimes was one of them."

"Grimes wouldn't have been so easy to kill." Wen had checked everyone she'd taken out, hoping she hadn't removed their only chance to hunt their hunters.

By the time Chase and Wen got close enough to see, the two pilots were standing outside the helicopters. Three other shadow people were about sixty feet away from the choppers, two smoking cigarettes. The third looked angry, like he'd just gotten out of a prison fight, his submachine gun visible, his eyes scanning the area.

Wen took out the first one, and was on to another before any of them reacted. Chase came from behind a tree and fired. Three of his last seventeen bullets found flesh as the third man went down.

The pilots charged with pistols, but Wen had anticipated the move and dropped the first easily. Chase, out of ammo, tackled the second one, who fired wildly. Fortunately, he wasn't a good shot.

Just as they were about to question the two injured survivors, four gun-wielding men emerged from the back of one of the helicopters.

Wen cursed in Mandarin, knowing she'd blown the

reconnaissance. Yet even in fight mode, she searched their faces for any sign of Grimes.

"Get in!" she yelled at Chase.

There was only one 'in' she could have meant. He ran to the other chopper. Wen used the final rounds of her last magazine to spray cover fire and reached the chopper an instant after Chase.

"Gun!" she yelled, pointing to three guns inside the craft. He started shooting while Wen opened the throttle completely. As the rotor speed increased, she pulled up on the collective and depressed the left foot pedal.

"Hurry, they're getting closer!" Chase yelled, but she couldn't hear him above the noise from the engine and rotors.

Finally, the chopper achieved lift. Five feet above the ground, a man jumped on one of the skids. The helicopter immediately pitched.

"Get him off!" Wen shouted.

Chase didn't hear her, but was already leaning out the opening. He hadn't been expecting the man to shoot, but he did. Bullets pierced the airframe and grazed Chase's jacket.

Before Chase recovered and tried to return fire, the man had climbed up into the chopper. Suddenly face-to-face with the guy, Chase realized he had the advantage. The man's gun hung slack around his shoulder, as he'd required both arms to pull himself inside. Chase pulled the trigger, but at the same instant the man made a martial arts move and knocked Chase backwards.

Wen, flying the helicopter, now nearing an altitude of five hundred feet and climbing, could not help him.

Chase managed to keep his gun, but the man was now in control, and raised his weapon to shoot point blank. In the time of a breath, Chase shot, and then shoved the man, who fell backwards, partially hanging out the opening until he plunged to the ground.

"Adios James Bond!" Chase said as he slid down on the floor, exhausted.

His break was short-lived, as suddenly he saw the other helicopter flying next to them.

Chapter Thirteen

Chase pulled on a headset. "Do you see them?" he barked into the microphone.

Wen's response came back through the headset. "Yes."

"What do you want me to do?"

"Shoot them, please." He was always amazed at her quick comebacks and coy smile, both of which gave him confidence, and deepened the affection he felt for the lethal woman.

Chase thought it sounded like a good idea, but Wen's flying made it immediately clear that he could not get a steady shot. "You know how it is when *I* drive and *you* try to shoot?"

"Deal with it." Wen put the chopper in a dive, attempting to get some distance between them. "They'll be back on us in a second—*get a shot lined up.*"

Chase knew there would be no excuses as she blazed straight and smooth twenty-feet above a wide, shallow river. He took off his headset and braced against the opening, aiming. "Ready," he said, although he knew she could no longer hear him.

The pursuing chopper appeared as if out of nowhere, descending into the space above the river, coming from a far less steep incline than Wen had feared, the pilot pushing the bird fast.

A passenger fired at the same time Chase let loose, forcing him to abandon his position after the initial volley.

Bullets ripped across the airframe. Wen reacted by taking another impossible angle. Chase believed she might actually try a sideways roll as the helicopter tipped, throwing him against the opposite opening and nearly sending him out into the water.

Before Chase could get a firm grip on anything, he was tossed back against the rear deck as Wen pulled the stick, forcing the chopper into a crazy steep climb. "Are you *trying* to achieve zero gravity?" he yelled.

Wen didn't answer since she couldn't hear him, but responded by taking them into a full inversion.

"I was kidding! I was *kidding*!" Chase yelled as he rolled onto the ceiling before slamming back against the floor. The vomit-inducing maneuver would have impressed him if he hadn't lost his gun and sliced his arm open on some unknown jagged hazard during his acrobatics.

Grabbing the weapon before it slid out of the opening, he knew what was expected of him as she brought the bird level again directly behind their pursuers. Still dizzy and disorientated, he somehow lined up and fired. Wen brought them dangerously close to the other helicopter, allowing Chase more opportunities to shoot. He didn't waste her effort. Dozens of rounds ripped across the enemy chopper.

"Something's on fire!" Chase yelled, watching a trail of black smoke pour from their target. "They're going down!"

Chasing Mind

But they didn't. In an amazing bit of flying, and some incredible stroke of luck, the shadow people's helicopter peeled off into a blind.

Chase pulled his headset back on. "Where are they?" he yelled.

Wen knew she should fly in the opposite direction of the injured craft. *Get away*, her training dictated. Yet Wen could not. There were shadow people down there to ID, to question.

"We need answers," she said, barely audible.

"What?"

"We're going to find out."

"Now we're the pursuers," Chase muttered, readying his gun, searching the ground and air ahead, desperate for a glimpse of them.

Out of a nearly invisible void, the shadow copter rose in a cloud of smoke, obscuring the canyon beyond. Shooters hung out each side of the craft and commenced firing the moment Wen's mind registered their presence.

"Damn it!" Chase yelled as he blasted away.

Wen knew he'd never be able to get them both. She also knew that if the shadow people landed one bullet in the wrong place, it was over. She pushed the helicopter forward.

"What are you *doing*?" Chase shouted.

"I believe you call it 'chicken'."

If he didn't know her so well, Chase might have tried to talk her out of it. He might have closed his eyes if he wasn't trying to hit something. He might have jumped to end it sooner if he didn't have complete faith in Wen's strategies.

Instead, he continued unloading the contents of the magazine into the opposing forces.

At the last second, some frightening fraction of time Chase never knew existed before, Wen pulled up, the skids of their helicopter clipping the blades of the shadow people's chopper.

Horrible scraping, grinding, and metallic screeching fought with the *thwap-thwap*ping of the rotors as bullets penetrated metal and glass across both birds.

In the smoky turmoil, the shadow people's pilot lost the battle. Their chopper spun and slammed into the high canyon wall, sending it into a freefall against the limestone cliff.

"How did you know?" Chase yelled as they banked into the canyon.

"I didn't," she admitted. "When you're dead either way, fear flees fast." She batted her eyelashes.

"Hell yeah!" Chase whooped, trying to sound braver than he felt at the moment. "Let's go get some lunch."

Wen checked the navigation system for the closest town. "Sounds like a plan. We're not too far."

Eight minutes later, Wen broke his meditation. "We might have a problem."

"I hope you're going to tell me they don't have a decent fish 'n' chips place down there," Chase said, pointing to the town just ahead.

"We're out of fuel," Wen said.

"Of *course* we are."

"Don't worry, I can still land it."

"Of course you can."

She set it down at the edge of a shopping center's parking lot.

"Nice flying," Chase said.

"Thank you."

"What now?"

"We walk to the car rental place," she said, getting out. "It's just down the street. I saw it while I was landing."

"Of course you did."

Chapter Fourteen

Ennis fingered the domino in his pocket, pushing his thumb into the single black dimple, then slid his thumb across the smooth white surface until he reached the three dots on the other end. The domino symbolized the situation they were facing, one that he knew well, where they were playing the odds, the numbers for and against. His finger found the smooth black back of the piece. It added something; a calmness opposed to the numbers.

Ennis closed his eyes, picturing the dominoes falling.

There was a single knock on the door before it opened.

"O-tis," he said, as if he were singing the name.

"Hey Dad," said his thirty-three year-old son.

"Just about to set it off," Ennis told him, flashing an excited smile not often unleashed from the emotionless man.

Otis walked over to the other side of the large space. His father's office occupied the entire top floor of the Gold Building. A huge portion of that area was covered with dominos. Both father and son spent hours creating the chains. They had reveled in setting them off for as long as the young man could remember.

"It's fantastic!" Otis said after surveying the entire field.

"Thirty-two thousand dominos," Ennis said. "I've been waiting for you to do the spin."

"Me?" Otis looked at his father, feeling like a little boy whose dad just said he could take the wheel of the car.

"Do it."

Unlike his father, the young entrepreneur sported fitted, open-necked collar shirts without a tie. He clicked his heels and raised a saluted hand as a comic gesture, then spun a coin. They watched as it picked up speed and seemed to transform into a silver ball. It spun around the open surface for a few moments, seemingly missing the lead domino, but slowly worked its way over.

"I think it's going to make it," Ennis said. He dug his hands deep into the pockets of his pleated tweed slacks.

The coin started slowing, its momentum failing, then it twisted one last time and went down, sliding just a fraction, as if planned, perfectly hitting the lead domino. It teetered, faltered, and finally toppled, setting off the reaction the two men were looking for.

"Do you have the cameras on?" Otis asked, crouching slightly, anticipating the win.

His dad gave him a look, then said, "This isn't my first day on the job."

"This is *magnificent*," Otis breathed as the dominoes crossed a narrow bridge, split into three chains, one jumping into a tank of water, causing it to overflow and send a new line tumbling. The pieces moved up ramps, around corners, into tunnels, displaying colorful patterns, until the final domino dropped from a ledge above their heads.

Ennis caught the domino, a red one, in his fist. "It was good. *Very* good."

"Can we top it?" Otis asked, repeating the question he had asked after every previous domino series they had done since he was seven years old.

His father thought back on more than a quarter of a century of set ups, and smiled. "Don't we always?" He tossed Otis a caramel cream, something they had always celebrated with.

"This time I was thinking of a water theme," Otis said, catching the treat.

Ennis looked at him quizzically.

"You know what I mean. Boats, waterfalls, floating dominos, bridges."

"Yes, something extravagant," Ennis said. "I love it. And maybe we could do some sort of submarine. Even something shooting missiles. Could be very cool."

"And what about mermaids?" Otis asked.

Ennis laughed again. "You and mermaids. Never grew out of that, did you?"

"Still hoping to find one," Otis said, laughing. "But we really are late for the meeting."

"They've got plenty to talk about without us. And I wanted to chat with you first."

"What's up?"

"I know you're not a hundred percent behind the 5EX."

Otis shrugged. "Yeah, but I told you. Whatever you think, I'm onboard with you."

"I know, and I appreciate that. But that's mostly because you're my son. I want you to share the vision because you *see* it. It makes sense to you."

"It does appear there's parts of it that I get. But I guess

my biggest issue is the potential health problems. Some of the studies suggest it can be catastrophic."

"Listen, I told you, there are protected areas, we won't put the towers near where we live. Anyway, plenty of our researchers don't see the same results as the worst of those trials. And we have more studies underway."

"Studies versus reality . . . you know . . . "

"Even on the overall rollout, if the health consequences *do* turn out to be as serious as you fear, we'll adjust. But we'll have time to get there. We'll be in the lead. We *have* to be in the lead, you know that."

"I know, but how many people are going to suffer along the way?"

"It's like candy. People eat candy because they want to enjoy the treat. But if they eat too much, they'll suffer the health consequences, right? Diabetes, obesity, and all those things lead to cancer, cardiovascular disease, whatever. Yet people still eat candy. They still drink soda, alcohol. They still smoke cigarettes. They do all these things that will kill them because they want the pleasure of it. Do you see what I'm saying?"

Otis re-wrapped the caramel and held it up to his dad. "This is different."

"They're going to use this technology because everything is instantaneous. They want everything *now*. It's got to be faster, quicker . . . *now*."

Otis frowned. "Maybe so, but when this thing rolls out and blankets the world, we could lose millions of people—*tens* of millions—before there's time to adjust."

Chapter Fifteen

Bull looked at the screen again. After manipulating the icon in the code strings multiple ways, she realized it was more than a single line of code, it was the key. As she worked through the shifting data streams, she found a maze, each turn and twist dependent on moving a different character in the code strain.

"*Of course* it's not sequential," she muttered after moving the second positions to follow the first pattern she'd used.

"Could be leading you into a dark hole," Dez said, chewing on a chunk of a perfectly golden, cranberry chocolate scone, a signature recipe of his.

"I don't think so."

"A minute ago you thought it was a trap."

"If it is, I can get out of it. Do you know how many traps I've navigated like this?"

"This is *massively* complex, though."

"It was *before* I found this key." She continued tapping characters and rearranging. "Boom, boom. Look at that."

Dez saw characters come into view again. It started to make even more sense. "It's a screen name."

"Yes," Bull said. "MarathonManCatamaran."

"Is he the one who wrote the document that led us here?"

She nodded.

"Then he may have done it on purpose?"

"I'm certain of it. Nothing else makes sense. This ghost image *shouldn't* be here. It should have been pulled up by the rakes. And for five other cross securities . . . He *wanted* us to find it."

"Us as in you?"

"Us as in somebody who would recognize it. Somebody like The Cause."

"But isn't he taking a risk that somebody within his organization would find it?"

"Maybe, but they wouldn't really be looking."

Dez nodded.

"Once they thought they cleaned the trail and removed all traces, a quick sweep would confirm that," Bull explained. "The ghost image isn't just sitting there, remember? First I had to find the way into the other document."

"What did he want us to do with it?"

She kept keying away. "MarathonManCatamaran, MarathonManCatamaran, MarathonManCatamaran."

"Are you trying to conjure him into existence?"

"I think he wanted us to find it so we would try to stop it . . ."

"Why didn't *he* stop it?"

She exhaled heavily. "Because he's just the coder. He has no way to stop it."

"Yeah, well, I'm just a coder, and you're just a hacker. Too big for us." Dez thought back on how he and Chase

57

had sold their RAI invention, and then couldn't prevent the people who bought it from using it for nefarious purposes. He had warned that they were too small, their enemy too large, but Chase had insisted. So they fought, and Chase and Dez had won.

He held up another scone, rotating it. Bull glanced at him for a moment, loving that intense passion for beauty in him, and taste. He broke off a piece and plopped it in her open mouth, like a little bird.

"We are so much more than just a hacker and a coder," Bull said. "We are Chase and Wen, we are The Astronaut, we are you and me. The Cause. We are thousands of people in opposition. We can stop them, we will stop them, and MarathonManCatamaran knew we would."

Dez nodded again. He could not deny the facts and force of her statement. "Then I guess we need to bring Chase and Wen in."

"Yeah," Bull agreed. "And the first thing they need to do is go to Mexico."

"Why?"

"Because MarathonManCatamaran is hiding there."

"Hiding?"

"He left breadcrumbs—the evidence, the documents, all of it—and then he ran.

He knew *they* would come after him. That he might not survive."

Dez raised his eyebrows. "So how do you know he's in Mexico."

"That says read the numbers." She pointed to another icon that appeared to be a polar bear. "It's the beginning of an IP address. And if you look here and here and down here, and then I restart the coding sequence material, you'll see the rest of it there and there."

"Okay," he said, impressed.

"I just searched. That IP address is near Lo De Marcos, a fishing village an hour or so north of Puerto Vallarta, in the Mexican state of Nayarit, on the Pacific side."

"Why do Chase and Wen need to see him?"

"Because he knows a lot more than just what's on these pages. And because they need to save his life."

Chapter Sixteen

Ennis caught the caramel his son threw back at him, insulted and rejected. If it had been anyone else, he might have raised his voice, but Otis was the most important person in the world. "No, it's not going to be anything like that. We have the control."

"Mind control," Otis said. "It's scary stuff."

"It's coming whether we do it or not. We're just lucky that the consortium is winning the race. Wouldn't you rather it be us in charge of this than . . . well, *anyone* else?"

"Of course, but . . . it's not just that," he began, knowing he wasn't going to win this argument with his father. "What about the whole 'privacy' thing?"

"I know that's the big issue for you, but privacy is not necessarily a *good* thing."

Otis blinked owlishly back at his father. "What?"

"Sure, a couple hundred years ago in Philadelphia, some guys in powdered wigs and stockings thought privacy was the most important thing in the world. And maybe back then when we had a king ruling with an iron fist and invading people's homes, maybe it was something that we needed to protect. But now . . . privacy is sort of the opposite. The only people concerned about privacy are criminals, terrorists, drug dealers—people doing things they *shouldn't* be doing."

"Right, crooked politicians, power-hungry bankers, *wealthy business people*," Otis added with theatrics that disarmed his father before he could react in anger.

"Yeah, something like that." His perfectly cropped grey hair suddenly looked white, framing a now old face.

"So now privacy is the hindrance to a sharing and open society?"

"That's my point."

"Good for all?"

"Right."

"Then I can make the argument that you should release all this information to the public about the 5EX plan," Otis countered. "*Everything* you're doing, and which areas of the country, specifically neighborhoods where the *wealthy* live, that will be protected from the 5EX."

"My, my, my, you are speaking your mind today, aren't you?" Ennis sat down, fatigued.

"You know I get a little braver on drop days," he said, referring to the times when they set off the domino series. "Kind of invigorates me, know what I mean?"

"Oh yeah, I know what you mean. That's what I did before the meeting. But I still think you're looking at the privacy thing all wrong. Certain things . . . eventually the public *will* know what's going on, but they don't need to know this moment."

"The public would probably think that same thing about their own thoughts, that the consortium doesn't need to know right away."

"Stop looking at it from that standpoint. I've told you before, imagine if we knew the thoughts of a terrorist, a child molester, a wife beater, a thief, a vandal, a gang member . . . What if we could *see* children and teenagers start to head down the wrong path, their thoughts turning bad? What if we could intervene so we could *save* them?" Invigorated, Ennis rose and stood opposite his son. "Don't you *see*? You give up a little privacy for the people that don't need it. In exchange, you get all the benefits to society."

"I know that. I know you're trying to do the right thing. Make society better." Otis' steady eyes countered his father, not in defiance, but rather confidence. "And make *yourself* richer."

"Hey, people deserve to gain from their hard work, their vision. It's always been that way. That's where big innovation comes from—the incentive to improve one's life." Ennis sheepishly looked at his son, the single person who could put his ego in its place, if only for a moment. "In my case, in the case of our partners, we're doing a lot more than that."

He'll never understand, Otis thought regretfully. "I told you, I'm behind you."

Fight me damn it! Ennis thought as he pushed his anger back. "I want you *next* to me."

"Not yet, but maybe it will come eventually, Dad. I really might get there. Let's see how the meeting goes, and let's see how the first rollout goes. We'll have a lot more answers then."

Ennis had to admit, he was proud of his son. Exercising both loyalty to his father, to their firm, and also maintaining the integrity of his own judgment and opinions. Keeping an open mind while not becoming a yes-man. It was a fine line to walk.

Ennis reached out for his hand, and they shook warmly. He put his hand firmly on Otis's shoulder. "You've been well-raised."

"Yes, sir, I sure was."

The two men left the office, entering a small foyer that led to a private elevator which took them down three floors to the waiting members of the consortium, and a meeting which would change the world.

Chapter Seventeen

Chase and Wen managed to get a quick lunch, Chase not even minding that it wasn't fish 'n' chips, but rather cheap sushi. He loved to see Wen devour food in a refined, proper way, amazed she could pack so much away in her small frame. The only thing she insisted on was not wasting, and asked for a to-go container.

"I like it, it's just the nori. I chew and chew, and it's sort of like gum. You have to swallow at some undetermined point," he said while discreetly taping the large bandage on his leg under the table.

With their leftovers secure in Wen's hand, he hugged her waist tightly, opened the door to their rental car for her, and then took the driver's seat. Before she could speak, an encrypted message came across Wen's phone. "It's The Astronaut," she said.

The Astronaut was one of a handful of people close to them, but he had nothing to do with space travel. The moniker had been coined by someone in the CIA to describe the small number of highly intelligent savants who had been identified by the intelligence agencies around the world. These men and women were highly sought after for their complex and diversified skills, but, in some cases, they became targets for assassination, as they often took contracts for opposing sides.

Out of necessity, The Astronauts had become experts at evasive tactics such as disappearing and hiding. Chase and Wen's astronaut, Nash Graham, was one of the most brilliant, and worked almost exclusively for WOLF. WOLF had helped Wen escape the Communist MSS in China, and Chase had (reluctantly, at first) learned to appreciate and support their mission to break up the elite's hold on society.

The Astronaut's voice came through the speaker. No video was available. "Where are you?"

"Somewhere in northern Arizona," Wen replied. "About to head into Nevada."

"I was afraid you might say that . . . You've got company."

"We just shook a mini shadow army," Wen said. "You're telling us there's *more*?"

"Yes, and this exceeds the threat posed by the shadow people."

"MSS?" Wen asked, dreading his response. After Wen had defected from China and her MSS past, they had enjoyed more than a year of anonymity by erasing her identity from all Chinese databases. But one mission too many, tangling with her former employers, had unraveled their double lives. Now the most vicious intelligence agency in the world was hunting them.

"I'm sorry to say yes. I've tracked them through Ghost Dragon," The Astronaut said, referring to the ultra-secret and incredibly secure MSS cyber network. The Astronaut had managed to regularly break into it while in a long cat and mouse game with the Chinese administrators to block him. What they *didn't* know was he had managed to create what he called a 'wormhole' that allowed him near constant invisible access, while causing the administrators to believe they had thwarted his efforts and blocked his attacks.

"How close are they?" Wen asked as she checked the side view mirror. Chase, who was driving, continually glanced in the rearview.

"I'm just getting your location now," he responded. "I will have to do the synch and overlay. It should take just a few seconds for the projections to come back."

"Looks like a car coming up behind us," Chase said, pushing the accelerator.

"That's not them," The Astronaut said. "They're another twenty minutes behind you."

"Well, that's good news," Chase said.

"Regretfully, that is the last good news I have," The Astronaut said. "The communications I've intercepted from Ghost Dragon are very clear: kill Chase, and capture the boy."

Tu, the eight year old Chase and Wen had rescued from an extreme experimental genetic manipulation program secretly run by the Communist Chinese, was now being raised by Wen's grandmother, who they had smuggled out of China at the same time.

"It goes on to say that if capture is impossible, then Tu is to be terminated. They have actually sent two separate teams of assassins, along with the units pursuing you, specifically to eliminate Tu."

"Why would they go to all the trouble to kill Tu when we've kept him secret and not shared any of the data about him?" Chase asked.

"Because they don't know that we'll *continue* to remain

silent," Wen replied. "The MSS worries that any day we could expose him and their secrets."

"We should go," Chase said.

"You mean to Tu and Zǔ mǔ?" Wen asked, then continued without waiting for his answer. "No. We would lead the MSS right to him. They found us, we can't let them know where Tu is."

"I'll make the arrangements to get him and Zǔ mǔ to the next safe house," The Astronaut said, referring to one of the many contingency plans they had in place for just such a situation. For quite a while, Tu and Zǔ mǔ had been able to live a somewhat normal life with new identities, but they were always ready to move quickly.

"All right," Chase said reluctantly. He had become extremely attached to the young, highly sensitive, intelligent little boy. He felt like an older brother, best friend, and father all rolled into one. And after losing his own father, the relationship had taken on an even more special quality. He had to fight his instincts not to go and protect Tu against the evilest of monsters.

"Have you checked Heaven?" Wen asked.

Heaven, the equivalent of Ghost Dragon for the US intelligence agencies, got its name because it was said you had to die to get in there, and nobody was really sure it even existed.

The Astronaut knew Wen wanted to know if the Americans had detected the presence of the Chinese teams inside the United States. It would mean more trouble and complications for them, as well as Tu. "I've checked. No indication yet. However, as usual, there are several completely dark operations, and there are actually several *more* than I would typically see."

"Meaning there could be a counter action already underway," Wen said.

"These MSS agents pursuing us," Chase began, "any idea how they found us?"

"Nothing yet," The Astronaut said. "But we're working on it."

"Thanks, and I guess the more important question is, how is the attack coming?"

"It appears to be a vehicle—a cream colored SUV—and a helicopter."

"You're kidding me . . . *another* helicopter? Haven't we had enough of those for one day?"

Chapter Eighteen

Wen watched the screen on her special phone. A dot gave her the approximate GPS location of the cream colored SUV and helicopter. "Pull off here," she said to Chase.

"Truck stop," he said approvingly, already guessing at her plan.

"Hello," Wen said to a skinny, gray-haired trucker just about to climb into his cab. "Could you do us a favor?"

The man's face wrinkled as if to punctuate his response. "*No.*"

"We need a ride to Vegas."

"Good luck."

"Five hundred cash," Chase said.

The man stepped down and studied them both carefully. "Cops after you?"

"No. Our car broke down and we're late for an important meeting in Vegas."

"Luggage?"

Wen shook her head, a pleading look on her face.

"No luggage, look like you slept in a gutter last night . . . I think you're full of—"

"*Please*," Wen said. "We're desperate."

"*Eight* hundred," Chase insisted.

Wen checked the dot. It was close, maybe less than three minutes away.

"No cops?" the man asked again skeptically.

"No," Chase repeated.

"But *someone's* after you?"

"Yeah," Wen said before Chase could deny it.

"Someone dangerous?"

"My ex-husband. He's only dangerous to me. Only beats up women."

The man stared at her, trying to decide if she was lying. When his eyes softened a bit, she knew they had him.

"A thousand," the man said.

Chase nodded.

"Cash. Right now."

Chase paid the man.

Back on Interstate 15 South, doing a steady sixty-five miles per hour, Wen watched from the truck's cab as the dot got farther away, confident that, at least for the moment, the MSS and the shadow people had no idea where they were.

After they waved goodbye to the trucker, Wen and Chase checked into an off-the-strip hotel, found a place to get some new clothes, then started returning calls.

"Bull left a couple of pretty urgent sounding messages," Wen said.

"I hope she's not going to say an army of a thousand purple mutant minions is after us."

"Today, that wouldn't surprise me," Wen said, pressing Bull's number.

"Did you get the files?" Bull asked.

"I see them coming in now."

"Read them. Call me back right away."

Fifteen minutes later, they were talking again.

"I was having a bad enough day *before* you dropped this mess on us," Chase began. "Wen's still reviewing them."

"It's insane, and I don't even understand the difference between our current cell networks and this 5EX stuff."

"They don't want anyone to know," Chase said. "5EX is divided into smaller geographical areas. We call those areas cells. All the devices in each cell are connected via radio waves through a local antenna in the cell."

"Connected to the internet, or the phone network?"

"Both," he replied. "But the difference with 5EX is that the bandwidth is *massive*. We're talking download speeds of up to twenty gigabits per second."

"Wow."

"Yeah, that means laptops and other computers will share the same space."

"Including IoT," she said, referring to the Internet of Things. "All kinds of things. Machine-to-machine, smart home features, refrigerators, security systems, cars—"

"*Everything*," Chase said. "And they do it by accessing higher-frequency radio waves."

"Why didn't they do it before?"

"Tech just caught up, but one issue is higher-frequency radio waves have a shorter useful physical range, so 5EX will have to utilize networks with three different types of cells, each with unique antenna designs."

"Maybe they've overcome that."

"It's possible," he said. "They're obviously a lot smarter than I am."

"No way," Bull said. "Now *that's* impossible."

"There has to be something more to it," Chase said.

"It sounds impressive enough to me."

"Not the 5EX itself, but how they're taking it into surveillance."

"That's why you need to talk to MarathonManCatamaran right away."

"I guess we're heading to Mexico."

Margot, the leader of The Cause, had, over the course of seven years, pulled together a large and diverse collection of intellectuals, revolutionaries, dissidents, artists, scientists, writers, and many others who saw the state of the world as far less than what it could be. The general mission of WOLF was to bring about income equality, stop the exploitation of the planet, end poverty and hunger, and improve the lives of all people. However, the short definition of their purpose, according to Margot, was to confiscate the wealth from the corrupt elites, redistribute it to the rest of the world, and criminally charge those who had unfairly benefited.

An even shorter answer, which she only uttered in private to a few close confidents, was to start a revolution to change the world.

Chase and Wen had a complicated relationship with the leader of one of the most secretive and dangerous organizations in the world. While they backed WOLF's lofty ideas to improve lives, they didn't always agree with Margot's methods. Still, they shared many common goals. It had been The

Cause that had been most instrumental in helping Wen escape China, and the group still had an enormous network of operatives inside the communist nation. Since Chase saw the Chinese government as the greatest threat against using technology to universally and peacefully better life for the world's population, WOLF was a critically important tool in his fight.

Chapter Nineteen

After talking to Bull and reviewing the 5EX data, they knew their next call was to Margot.

"We have been monitoring China's mind project for more than a year. It's primarily run by the massive tech company Baidax," Margot said. "It's not easy information to obtain, but they have recently made some breakthroughs that are very concerning."

"Which are?" Chase asked.

"I've just sent you the latest." Her usually sharp, raspy voice softened for an instant. "Read it with the knowledge that six of our members paid for it with their lives."

"I'm sorry," Wen told her.

"We just received your data," Chase said. Margot had sent the encrypted report to one of their secure drop sites on the darknet. They reviewed it as the conversation continued. "So it's true. You've verified inside China the same information Bull referred to, and that was *true*."

"Yes." Margot was a woman of few words and long pauses. She was all about minimalism.

Chase and Wen shared a glance. It was far worse than they'd initially thought.

"According to the last report we received, they can read minds at levels that, in some cases, are conversational or first-person apparent."

"What does that mean?" Wen asked hesitantly.

"It means that they receive the same amount of information as if they were having a conversation with the subject."

"Same as if the subject were there with them?" Chase asked.

"As if you were reading my mind right now," Margot said. "You would be getting the information just as I am telling it to you, and additionally some extra background."

"That's . . . frightening."

"Yes, and there's more. Apparently they've had success in manipulating and directing the thoughts of the subjects."

"Does that mean they can tell a person what to think?" Wen asked.

"The way I understand it, the method is not as direct as that. It works best, as you might imagine, in people whose thoughts are leaning one way to begin with. Say, for instance, a subject wants to trust the government, but they're unsure for some reason. The mind control can push them over the edge, so to speak. Lock them into, well, whatever they want."

"So they could do the same thing for a political candidate?" Chase asked. "For example, if a person is considering supporting somebody, the mind control could actually make them support another candidate?"

"Yes, but, as you know, China doesn't have elections like you do in the West."

"Right, but I wasn't thinking about China. I'm imagining what would happen if they used this in western countries. Like the United States."

"That is certainly a possibility," Margot agreed. "The question is, how would they get the people to take part in the experiments, and therefore deliver the mind control?"

Chase did not want to share the additional information he had. It wasn't that he *didn't* trust Margot, it was just that he didn't *need* to. Wen had taught him that in the kinds of situations they played in, it was smarter not to trust someone more than necessary.

Wen looked at him as if wondering if he had made the decision to tell Margot about 5EX. She shook her head, indicating her agreement not to share that information at this time.

"Will you be getting any more information?" Chase asked.

"It may be a while. Unfortunately, our two best sources have been compromised."

"Compromised?" Wen asked.

"One of them is dead, the other is missing."

"Then the MSS knows they got this information out," Wen said, already calculating the odds that based on her and Chase's history, and her defection, the MSS might be concerned that the information would get to them.

"They may not know. Our contacts failed to deliver."

"Then how did *you* know?" Chase asked.

"The one who disappeared managed to mail us the information."

"Incredible," Wen breathed.

"I'm sorry, an urgent matter just came up. I'll have to sign off," Margot said abruptly.

"You'll let us know if you get more information?" Wen asked.

"Of course."

After the call, Chase looked at Wen and said the same thing she was thinking. "Chinese technology is used by the consortium. Do you realize what they can do?"

"Finally mass mind control of the population," Wen said, the statement sounding so surreal and dangerous that she shivered.

"Or the Chinese have *already* stolen the consortium's technology..." Chase said.

"That would be even worse," Wen said. "In fact, I can't imagine *anything* worse."

"Unless they *both* join forces."

They were quiet for several moments.

"Where do we go first?" Chase asked. "We can't go back to China."

"We have to start with the consortium, it's our best lead." She raised the leftover container of sushi.

"Mexico it is."

"We've got to be extra careful on this one," Wen said, popping a piece of sushi in her mouth.

"Why?" Chase asked. "What if they get inside our minds?"

Chapter Twenty

Rob Carpenter stared at a bank of security monitors. He was addicted to watching them. Nine of them showed every possible movement outside of his 1978 Dodge camper van parked inside El Pequeño Paraiso RV Park.

He dug into a fresh avocado, smearing it on a warm tortilla, sprinkled a touch of salt and freshly minced garlic across the green creaminess, spooned on salsa Mexicana—onions, peppers, tomatoes, cilantro—squeezed on just enough lime, dropped on a few soft beans, rolled it all up into a tight doobie, and savored his first bite as he continued watching the monitors. A couple and their son walked by on their way to the beach. They had no idea they were under constant observation. His camera's 180° view saw them until they disappeared through the gate leading to the sand and water.

"I could live on these," he said to himself as he chomped further into the tortilla, and he mostly did. Five tortillas later, he prepared what he called "Mexican baklava," again starting with a warm tortilla, spreading on a thin layer of fresh almond butter, covering that with honey, and finally folding it twice. "Yummy," he said, checking the cameras. This time a cute little dog scratched himself under the frame of the camper across from his. The dog, "Bruno," belonged to the people who ran the "resort." The place was mostly filled with snowbirds from Canada—Montréal, Vancouver, Ontario—senior citizens just relaxing and living cheap in the warm, humid air. Occasionally a younger couple or small family would stay in one of the rentable rooms for a few nights, but it was mostly silver haired folks in RVs.

In between walks on the beach, playing canasta, watching movies, and a range of other similar group activities, Carpenter would check his email, and then the Internet. He made sure to hop through various servers, but ultimately he wound up at a very specific place. It was a routine he did several times a day—*every* day—since he'd dropped out and disappeared into Mexico's expat underbelly, lost in a seam where no one could find him, not even the people looking for him.

Rob scrolled down to a certain point, found an icon, tapped it, and then entered a memorized eighteen digit code into the drop-down window. He clicked his mouse and glanced away as the results came up, because in the more than three hundred times he had done this sequence, he'd always gotten the same blank screen in response.

But this time was different.

Carpenter gasped as an IP address pinged back.

"San Francisco California," he whispered, staring at his screen in total disbelief, trying to suppress the fear welling inside him. He checked the monitors again, almost certain gunmen would be out there. "And so it begins," he said quietly, looking to see if the cheap lock on his flimsy door was secure. "The beginning of the end."

Sitting in a private lounge at the Las Vegas Airport, Wen and Chase had remained sequestered with her special phone and their new laptops.

"Can this really be real?" Wen asked. "Can they truly read minds?"

"Tech is moving so fast," Chase replied. "AI is merging with multiple highly advanced technologies. I know it sounds crazy-sci-fi, but yes, I think if all the components are in place, the right minds can make it happen." He doused lemon juice on a succulent piece of fried fish while stuffing a few fries into his mouth.

Wen looked at the files Margot had sent from The Cause and checked them with everything Bull had forwarded to them. "I'm looking for patterns, anything that would connect the two, any weaknesses that would give them away."

"Aren't patterns The Astronaut's department?" Chase asked. The Astronaut had a special gift for patterns. He could see details in data that even computers missed. He always said, *'The more patterns, the better, because a pattern of patterns leaves its own pattern that most will never see.'*

"He's already working on a way into the programs, but I want to find some means to stop the consortium and Baidax from implementing 5EX at all. Am I the only one who sees this? What are they really getting at?" She wrote the letters *S E X* on a piece of paper.

"Just a bunch of uptight frat boys with one thing on

their mind. Mm-mm, that was good." Chase licked his fingers. "Not as good as Hungry Clam, but it hit the spot."

"Look at this." She shared the screen so he could see photos of factory workers and schoolchildren wearing mind controlling headsets. They both stared at the children, some the same age as Tu.

"We saved him," Chase said softly, knowing Wen was thinking about their precious little boy as well, hopefully running carefree and making Zǔ mǔ happily crazy.

"Can we save them all?" Wen asked, sounding sad. Chase wondered how the communist government could be so cruel as to subject its own children to gene-altering, mind reading, and other experimentation.

"I asked The Astronaut to put through an encrypted call to Zǔ mǔ and Tu," Chase said.

"Good. Do you think we should tell him about this?"

"That was our deal."

Although Tu was a child, his engineered mind exceeded the intelligence of most adult's. He knew how important their work was, and had asked them to always tell him what they were involved with so he could help. They had agreed, and many times since, Tu had offered great insights into the complex things they were working on. His mind, like The Astronaut's, was quite unique and extraordinary, but his was even more special because it had been precisely designed by scientists to produce the highest levels of human intelligence.

Chapter Twenty-One

"Chase Bank," Tu began, using one of his favorite nicknames, "Zǔ mǔ says we might have to go. I don't want to move. I like it here."

"Yes," Chase said across the video call. "Unfortunately, that is the case. We have to keep moving around, so help her get ready just to be sure."

Tu's eyes watered. He had still not gotten over the events in China. They had almost been killed several times, and had witnessed too much violence and death.

"This will not be like that," Wen told him, knowing where his thoughts had gone. "It's different."

"Why is it different, Wen?"

"Because we are in America now, and we have lots of people looking after you."

"All the security people?"

"Them, and many more who watch you through other ways from the sky, on the computers. Bull, The Astronaut, the whole world of WOLF, and us, my little angel."

"The Cause is very big, aren't they?" Tu asked. "Very, *very* big."

"Yes," Wen said. "So *many* people are keeping you safe. We will never let anyone get you." She looked at him for a long moment before he spoke again.

"Okay. Where do you have to go?"

"We're going to Mexico," Chase said. "China and a group in this country are trying to control people's minds."

"You can't let them do that."

"No, we can't," Chase said softly, smiling.

They explained everything they knew about the Baidax, the Chinese mind program, and the consortium's plans. It didn't take Tu long to reach the same conclusions they had; if the Chinese and the consortium got together, this would be a *much* more dangerous problem. However, Tu made the point that even without that eventuality, the consortium obviously had some capabilities along the lines of the Chinese, and the Chinese were most definitely seeking some similar technology that the consortium possessed.

"I will work on this problem," Tu said. "We had a girl at Jang House who had the ability to read minds. Not as powerful as what you describe here, but she could look at your face and tell you your thoughts. She was my sister, but sometimes it was spooky, when she would look at me and tell me what I was thinking. She was always right."

Jang House had been where the Chinese secretly kept all the children, none of whom were related, in spite of Tu calling all the girls his sisters. He had been the eldest of the kids, and the only boy. It had been difficult for him to leave behind the only family he'd ever known. Ever since the day Chase and Wen had rescued him, he worried about what had happened to them.

"But this process is more serious," Tu continued. "The

Chinese are reading minds. Engineers at China Electronics Corporation and Tianjin University created the 'Brain Talker' chip. This can read brainwave activity. They claim it is for a human mind to control a computer."

"BCI," Chase said.

"Yes, 'brain-computer interface.' They have manufactured a working BCI device. It processes transmitted neural signals from background noise."

"A real Brain-Computer Codec Chip . . . "

"Correct," Tu said. "With an ability to isolate minor neural electrical signals and decode information with maximum efficiency—okay, like this?"

"They're way ahead of us." Chase frowned, squinting at the screen. "What are you doing?"

"Zu-ey is teaching me how to make gomasio. If I grind it clockwise, it is more yin. If counter-clockwise, more yang. I love it, and eat a lot of it, so she says I have to make it. So, okay, also at Ningbo University, funded by Communist government, Neuro Caps is a big brain surveillance project. They put it in factories and schools, making subjects wear built-in sensors in hats. They are collecting a lot of data, using it to make the programs read minds better. Some believe computers can make images, or 'mind movies', of the thoughts."

"You know a lot about this."

"This worries me," Tu admitted. "But I would like to see one of those videos of inside a person's thoughts, especially somebody important, like a president. I don't think the Chinese and these big companies want to do all the good things. They want to do the things that can make them more money and more power. Zu-ey says I make gomasio perfect."

"Dangerous," Wen murmured to herself.

"It would be good to use this technology on the Chinese leaders to see clearly their intentions," Tu added.

"I think that would be an excellent idea," Chase said, smiling. His whole life now revolved around trying to do just what Tu had suggested. *The technology is coming whether we were ready or not,* he thought. *Faster and faster, more and more powerful, able to do things we couldn't even imagine. And there will always be those wanting to use it to take more than their share, to gain leverage above everyone else. It's happening every day. It's why the billionaires get wealthier and everyone else falls farther behind.*

Chase didn't think there was anything wrong with making money, but he did recognize the responsibility of the wealthy to make sure the playing field was level, that each person had the same chance with the massive technological advances, so they could be used to improve the lives of everyone.

"The Astronaut will keep you up-to-date," Wen said. "Even if we can't call in sometimes, just like always, he will get word to you."

"And I will get word to him when I find a way to help you two beat the bad guys," Tu replied solemnly. "And you know what it will be?"

"What?" Chase and Wen asked at the same time.

"It will be what it always is. The way to stop them will be with the very thing they are using to try to win. Then, even if we can't read their minds to show what they've done and what they think, it will be something with their own methods that will beat them."

Chapter Twenty-Two

The Central Intelligence Agency is an old and powerful organization. People believe they have a sense of the famous CIA, but few have any idea of its true depth. There are many secret divisions within the mighty agency. The Corporate Intelligence Security Section, or "CISS," perhaps the most secret of them all, had been formed as a joint operation of the CIA, NSA, and FBI; its mandate: to prevent war between corporations.

Inside the CISS Headquarters building in Vienna, Virginia, Linda Moore knocked on Tess Federgreen's office door. Tess's assistant had already cleared the way for Linda to go in, but she always knocked anyway. After the third time, and still with no answer, Linda opened the door.

At her desk, Tess was staring into a monitor, lost in total concentration. Linda, Tess's right hand, cleared her throat. "Tess? Should I come back?"

"What? No, we don't have time. We'll have to do it now."

"Any sign?" Linda asked, catching the fire in Tess's green eyes. Tess ran CISS, and wielded power unequalled in Washington. It was a tough job, and Tess was a tough lady. She generally kept close tabs on Chase Malone. However, in recent weeks, he had, once again, given them the slip.

"No, unless you count the normal bogus sightings," she said bitterly, kicking her cowboy boots against the side of her wooden desk. Chase utilized an elaborate system simply named "Decoying" to thwart Tess and his numerous enemies. CISS monitored facial recognition surveillance cameras around the world, border crossings, airline flight itineraries, and a vast array of information on a constant basis, yet on any average day, Chase Malone could be reported appearing in up to thirty to forty different locations. Tess knew it was a ruse. Chase had a dedicated team whose only job was to prevent her, and the others who were pursuing Wen and him, from being successful in locating the couple. The frustrating practice was quite effective, and kept her constantly angry.

CISS likewise had several operatives who spent the better part of their days following up on the phony leads. Chase's people created new traps as fast as her people could run them down. Still, the world was not as big as some would think, and with significant tools at her disposal, she usually had a fairly good idea of where he was, or at least where he *might* be.

"It's been *six days*," Tess said, with the tone a parent might use when talking about a troubled runaway teen.

Linda was well aware of how long it had been. "He was in Petersburg under an alias, Owen Silvious, visiting his friend, Mars, in federal prison."

Tess knew it had been him. She also knew Chase knew she would know he knew, because Tess monitored and watched *everyone* who came to visit Mars. From there, he and Wen had checked into a hotel in Charlottesville, Virginia, then promptly disappeared. She'd immediately had local FBI agents asking questions at the hotel to follow-up.

"FBI get anything?" Linda asked.

"No. It's as though they went into the Hotel California."

Linda looked blank, not sure of the reference.

Tess stared at her as if she was from another planet. "You know? 'You can check out any time you like, but you can never leave.'"

"But you knew he wasn't in the hotel anymore . . . "

"No," Tess said, exasperated. "He's somehow beat me once again."

Linda silently recalled their history in her head. Tess and Chase had worked together a surprisingly large number of times. She had saved him, he had helped her, and yet it seemed he despised her. Linda believed Tess would never admit it, but his feelings toward her broke her heart, since Tess had grown very fond of Chase and Wen. However, Tess was Tess, and if need be, if they interfered with her mission, she would not let her personal feelings get in the way.

It's the paradox of her relationship with him, Linda thought. Chase Malone was the only thing she had ever seen make Tess torn. He distracted her often.

"There's a crisis in China," Linda said, finally getting to her real reason for being there.

"Another one?" Tess groaned, pulling her long hair back in a ponytail. This month it was auburn. "They do grow more frequent, don't they?"

"So it seems," Linda replied, handing her the folder and

pointing to her screen. Tess still preferred to have some reports in writing, even though Linda had already sent it to her computer. This time, however, Tess ignored the folder and clicked open the window on another screen.

"No surprise, it involves artificial intelligence." The tech wars between the US and China occupied much of her bandwidth. "Why is Baidax partnering with the consortium?"

"It is dramatically out of place, isn't it?"

"This can't be good . . . They're obviously looking to circumvent the others—in this case, the US' position. China wants to go on its own standard while the US leads the rest of the world."

"But 5EX is too important. We can't let China take over," Linda said.

"You know that during the negotiations these past eighteen months, China has been claiming—or lying—that they were willing to unify under one standard."

"Obviously they've been working towards something else behind-the-scenes."

"Obviously, but now we know. Looks like the consortium and Baidax have decided to bypass US negotiators."

"What are we going to do?" Linda asked.

Tess thought for a moment. "Set up an appointment for me with Ennis Cavanaugh."

"Will he listen?"

She shook her head. "If I can't convince him, I'll have to kill him."

Chapter Twenty-Three

Chase and Wen were about to board a private jet to Mexico when they received an urgent message from The Astronaut. They maintained a sophisticated networking system for leasing jets through shell companies and aliases. However, the shadow people and others who tracked them monitored charters and private planes, making it challenging. FAA requirements to file flight plans and other regulations sometimes also left them exposed, and many times they had to send decoy planes to alternative destinations.

"There's a cell of shadow people nearby," The Astronaut reported.

"Can we line up another plane?" Wen asked.

"Too risky. I've booked first class seats under assumed names."

"We're going *commercial*?" Chase said, astonished. They owned a stack of the finest false passports, often traveling as a Canadian couple from Vancouver, but there were other concerns when entering a country with throngs of tourists.

"Safest way to travel."

"What about our weapons?" Wen asked.

"You'll have to get the groceries delivered. I've already placed an order."

Having "groceries delivered" was their code for buying weapons, gear, etcetera. The expensive service, run by former CIA and MI6 agents, provided what they needed in most countries around the world.

"Having no weapons initially is a challenge," Chase said.

"I don't like it," Wen agreed.

"No choice," The Astronaut said. "There'll be a cache of weapons within six hours, dropped at a tiny tortilla factory in Lo De Marcos."

After they cleared customs at the Puerto Vallarta airport, an Uber driver named Jacinto picked them up. Chase tried not to be annoyed by the tiny, pale green Hyundai, but the orange and green interior bothered him.

"Nice car," Wen said, knowing it would make Chase laugh. She called him a car snob, but did wish he was driving instead of Jacinto, in case trouble followed them. She checked the road behind them, wishing she had a weapon.

"Yes, much thank you," Jacinto replied in broken English. The next fifteen minutes were filled by him explaining that he'd spent a few years working as a cook with his brother in Chicago, but eventually the lure of the Mexican Riviera had brought him back home. He seemed a cheerful man.

As soon as he discovered that Wen spoke Spanish, he grew even happier. From the backseat, she asked about his family, how he liked being an Uber driver. He told her proudly about his fourteen-year-old boy, and ten-year-old daughter.

"Both speak very good English that they learned in school," he told her in Spanish. "Uber is okay. I make good money, especially December through February when Americans and Canadians come. It's better then. The crowd are very big."

Occasionally Wen interrupted to tell Chase an interesting place that Jacinto had pointed out as they were passing—the names of certain areas, new construction projects, expensive condominiums, whatever. Otherwise, Wen and the driver babbled in Spanish, small talk about local culture and history.

Later on, as they drew closer to Sayulita, Wen noticed Jacinto became noticeably agitated. She asked him if something was wrong, but he said no.

As was her habit, she had been continually checking the road behind them to be certain they were not being followed. Although they felt it unlikely anyone knew where they were, shadow people always seemed to show up when they were feeling at their most secure.

Wen tapped Chase's leg, a signal to be alert. She studied the curving road behind them—one lane of constant traffic moving in either direction, with no real areas to pass. A few vehicles back, what looked to be a local car caught her attention. It didn't look like a vehicle the shadow people would normally use, but Jacinto was now splitting his vision equally between the rearview mirror and the road in front of them.

Wen knew something was wrong.

"Are they following us, Jacinto?" she asked in Spanish.

"Who?" he replied.

In that instant, Wen knew they were. "That bright blue Nissan," she said in a stern voice.

"No, I think they are just on the same road," he said.

"Then why are you nervous?"

"I am not nervous," he said. "I am happy."

Wen had seen this man happy. In the short time they'd known each other, she'd seen him laugh, filled with pride, speaking humorously about his children's exploits. She knew now he was anything *but* happy.

"I don't believe you," she said. "The Nissan is following us, and you know they are."

Chase immediately assumed that the driver had somehow been hired by the shadow people. He figured that any moment they would come under machine gunfire and began looking for a way to escape. However, Wen knew that something more complicated was going on.

"I want you to pull over," she said, as if issuing an order.

"It's too dangerous to pull over on this road right now, Señorita."

"Up there," Wen demanded. "Pull into that stand selling coconuts."

"It's not a good idea," he insisted in a shaking voice as they sped on past the coconut stand.

"You're lying, Jacinto," Wen said. "If you don't tell me the truth, I'm going to have to take control of this vehicle." She climbed over the seat and dropped into the passenger seat next to him.

Jacinto looked at her, startled. "What are you doing?"

Wen saw fear in his eyes, quickly deciding that it wasn't *her* he feared, but someone else. "Are these people making you abduct us?" she asked slowly in Spanish.

"No, no, no, no, nothing like that."

"Then why are they following us?"

"I . . . I do not know."

"If you don't know, how do you know it's nothing like that?"

"They . . . they just want something . . . do not worry."

"I *am* worried," she said, gripping his shoulder in a horrible squeeze that made him release his hand from the steering wheel as he cried out in pain.

"Stop, please! You're hurting me very much!"

"I told you, I'm going to take control of this vehicle if you don't tell me in the next ten seconds *who* those people are, and *what* is going on."

"They'll kill me and my family!"

Chapter Twenty-Four

The consortium partners were waiting in a large conference room, most in deep conversation. Small groups huddled around the windows looking down on K Street, watching the bustling activities of the nation's capital below.

As Ennis and Otis entered, the murmuring drone silenced, and everyone moved toward the table.

There were fifteen of them in all, counting Otis. And as a full voting member, he *did* count. He'd been involved in the program since the beginning six years earlier, not long after he'd gotten out of college. Otis told his father that, in a way, 5EX had been his life's work. Yet he'd spent much of that time trying to dissuade his father in private, while publicly supporting him.

Otis had not always remained silent. During key meetings and important times for 5EX, he would raise concerns to test the waters, always on the lookout for allies, anyone else who shared his apprehensions or had doubts of their own. He was always diplomatic about it, and his father allowed it because his son was good at finding flaws and correcting them. Ennis wanted them all corrected in time.

However, this was different. This was the final meeting before the first implementation.

Everything was about to change.

An hour earlier, Ennis had spoken with Steve Sykes, his top specialist for INSIGHT and the man he'd put in charge of the secretive side of the Mexico tests. All the initial "in-lab" results were exceeding expectations. "We are recording private thoughts of the subjects in incredible detail."

"Wirelessly?"

"Yes."

"Will it scale?"

After round-the-clock work in several Mexican cities, Sykes had assured him that INSIGHT, riding on the 5EX rollout, was going to be "mind blowing." Ennis took that confidence into the meeting.

The board room was quiet as Ennis opened the proceedings by thanking them for their patience. "I had several urgent matters to attend to," he said. "And I knew you had much to discuss without me."

There were a few stifled laughs.

"However, I think you'll agree that what I have to share with you today is well worth the wait." He surveyed the room, savoring the suspense. "You are all certainly aware of the Chinese tech giant, Baidax . . . "

Most of them nodded.

"The Baidax Board has agreed to utilize our format, 5EX, as their standard."

The murmurs around the room were loud and contentious.

One man with short silver hair scoffed. "Why is this *good* news?"

"Because we've just included more than one-fifth of the world's population," Ennis shot back. "The billion and a half we were missing."

"But the Chinese regime is not on the same page as us," the man countered.

"They cannot be trusted," a woman in a navy blue business suit and red framed glasses added.

"We can handle that. The ruling communist party is only as stable as their population is happy," Ennis said slowly.

The man looked confused for a moment, then smiled.

"Are you going to try to play chess with the Chinese president?" asked a man with a shiny bald head and necktie knotted so tight it looked like it might strangle him. "That seems to be a fool's errand."

"They don't know about INSIGHT," Ennis said, referring to the consortium's most guarded secret, the aspect of their implementation that would make 5EX world changing.

"I should hope not," the man said, aghast. "But how long do you think it will take them to discover it?"

"INSIGHT is completely protected. Not only will they be unable to find it, we will collect all that data, *and* be able to use it to strengthen our position with the Chinese . . . even *weaken* them," he said, emphasizing his last three words.

"Sounds dangerous," the woman in red eyeglasses said. "The Chinese are going to insist on a backdoor."

"Of course they will," Ennis agreed. "And we'll give it to them."

"Sounds even *more* dangerous," the same woman said.

"They will have access to a *special* back door."

"I'm no tech wizard, but the Chinese are some of the best in the world at this stuff. I think it's too risky trying to double-deal them, and to simply hope they won't notice—"

"It's an entirely different framework," Ennis said, "built on a separate chassis, if you will. They won't even have access to our side of the data, and won't be looking. They want 5EX access for different reasons. They can't even imagine INSIGHT." Pacing closely behind each member, he stopped, rested his dry hands on the fat shoulders of the man with the tight tie, patted them in a fatherly manner, then moved on and stopped beside his son.

"But one day, it becomes public. And then what?"

Ennis glanced at Otis as he answered. "By then, it'll be too late."

Chapter Twenty-Five

Ennis tipped a domino on his desk, setting off a small line of thirty-six dominos, as he took the call he had no interest in.

"Is this a secure line?" Ennis asked, setting up the dominos again.

"I only deal on secure lines," Tess said tersely. "Why don't you tell me what the hell the consortium is doing with the Chinese." She was uncharacteristically eating an apple into the mouthpiece of the phone.

"Why, is there a law against it?"

"As a matter of fact, there are *many*. The Bureau of Industry and Security, a division of the Commerce Department, has a list of items under export control. As you well know, certain electronic components, finished products, telecommunications equipment, and information security, need specific Export Control Classification Numbers for anything planned for export."

He tipped the lead domino again. "I'm aware of what we are prohibited from selling."

"*Or* sharing."

"Maybe you should talk to our lawyers," Ennis said as the last one fell. He started to set them up again. "I can transfer you to our legal department."

"I don't know who you think you're dealing with," Tess said. She stopped chewing. "I can have your company shut down within forty-eight hours, and you could be in custody within ninety minutes after I hang up on you."

"Really? Is that your job? To threaten American citizens?" Ennis wasn't exactly bluffing. The consortium had many high-level contacts, lots of favors owed, many assets with which to leverage. Yet it was a delicate time, and he wasn't interested in entanglements or going to war with Tess's specific department of the CIA.

Just prior to the call, Tess had ordered full surveillance on Ennis Cavanaugh, his son, and anyone identified as being involved with the consortium. She'd told her assistant, "I want to know every time one of these people sneezes. Give me a full profile on them, on everybody they talk to. Get the NSA to give us everything, and don't be surprised if one or more trails lead to the White House—and I want that, too."

Tess knew the consortium was pushing something beyond 5EX. She just didn't know what yet.

Wen ordered the driver to turn into the next town, San Francisco, also known as San Pancho, an authentic Mexican beach town carved out of the emerald jungle.

Jacinto slowed his Hyundai as congestion turned traffic on San Pancho's main drag into a crawl. Wen's eyes darted in every direction, searching for escape, an advantage, some place to make a stand . . .

"Let us off here!" Wen yelled.

"I'm sorry," Jacinto called again as they jumped out and jogged toward the center of town.

Half a block later, Chase stopped. "What about here?"

Wen glanced into a large open brick building filled with rows of books and a giant tree sculpted from recycled metals. There was a comfortable sitting area, breezy and creative looking.

"It's some sort of community art center," Wen said, already deciding there weren't enough escape routes. "No, we need more crowds."

They continued running into the thick of the tourist section, where heavy set, sunburned gringos outnumbered the locals. Chase followed as Wen dashed down narrow cobblestone streets, looking for anywhere to hide. The Nissan had only been six or seven cars behind.

"They'll be on us any second," Wen hissed.

They found themselves in a busy flea/farmers market—booths filled with colorful clothes for sale, souvenirs, handmade wares. Wafts of fragrant Mexican food and fresh baked goods competed with tacky trinkets for attention from the many tourists and locals, happily mixing.

"What's the plan?" Chased asked as they passed a stall with a man selling handmade pottery in an array of dazzling colors.

"We need to know who they are," Wen said, stating the obvious. "But we can't lose sight of the mission. We have to get to Lo de Marcos, and these people are trying to prevent that."

They moved rapidly through the market, dodging gringos and everyone else who was enjoying the leisurely mode of Mexico. "Shadow people? Or trying to stop us from finding out more about 5EX?" Chase asked.

"Based on Utah, I'd say shadow people. But the coincidence of *where* we are makes me think it's connected to 5EX."

Chase failed to avoid crashing into a man selling silver jewelry. Necklaces, pendants, and rings hit the ground as the man stumbled over a table where a woman was selling incredible looking cinnamon buns and other pastries.

"Lo siento!" Wen apologized.

Chase tossed a five hundred peso bill at them as he and Wen kept going, still walking far too fast in the tight, crowded aisles.

"There they are!" Wen said. "This way!" She turned a corner.

Chase stole a glance back as he followed, seeing two men crashing through the crowds. "They're right behind us."

"We're going to have to split up," Wen said.

"That rarely works out well!"

"Remember Entreamigos? That cool recycled art place with all the books?"

"Yeah," Chase said, already knowing he had lost the argument.

"Meet there after."

"After *what*?" he asked breathlessly.

"After you kill the one that follows you."

Chase had killed more people than he cared to think about in the last couple years. Each one haunted him, taking a bit of his soul each time he ended a life. He'd learned to do it out of necessity, self-preservation, protecting Wen and Tu . . . but this was a difficult one. They were running through a crowded coastal village in Mexico with no weapons, no plan, and no idea who was after them.

"Any ideas on how I should do that?"

"Use your multitool," Wen said. "You go that way, I'm going this way."

Chase wished he'd *had* his multitool, but since they'd flown commercial, he hadn't been able to bring it. He felt naked without it. Wen made fun of him, calling it his security blanket, always reminding him it didn't count as a weapon, even though it had gotten him out of quite a few jams.

"You know I don't have it!" he yelled as he ran in the opposite direction.

"Improvise!"

Chapter Twenty-Six

Tess checked a screen on her desk as the first report came up on Ennis Cavanaugh, the dapper gentleman whose couth and engineered responses expertly evaded the toughest questions.

"Our agreements and partnerships with the Chinese pose no security risks," Ennis said coolly, not knowing she was reading about his every move as they spoke.

"Apparently you don't understand that it's not up to *you* to decide if what you're doing causes security risks or violates any rules," Tess said, tightening her auburn ponytail.

"We have priority."

"Priority with what or whom?" Tess asked.

"We've already received clearance for this."

"You tell me who signed off on it because *I* sure didn't, and in this realm *I* am the authority." Tess was waiting to see if he mentioned Holt Gatewood or HITE. Because of the nature of the technology, she believed it was possible that HITE was involved.

Holt Gatewood was the only one who could circumvent her. Even the US presidents who came and went for short little stints of time, all political and naïve, didn't have the credentials to do so. The American people liked to believe that their commander-in-chief had the ultimate say in all matters of national security, but that wasn't even close to true. Ennis Cavanaugh had learned that long ago. He didn't need Tess to teach him the way the real world worked.

"Tess, you're going to do what you have to do, but do me a favor?" He smiled smugly. "Keep your ego under control, because the timing has to be *just right*."

"I assure you, Ennis, that my ego plays no part. But I will not allow the Chinese to get past us on this, and maybe you don't understand how they work. You let them in, they're going to take *everything* from you, and you'll never even see it happen." Tess knew that the technology Cavanaugh and his group were playing with could alter the balance of power in the telecommunications industry, mobile, Internet of Things, and the web itself. She had no doubt he knew it as well.

"We've got partnerships," Ennis said. "Maybe *you're* out of the loop, but that doesn't mean we've done anything wrong, or that we're going to slow down our plans."

"You *cannot* deploy this," Tess said. "This is a time bomb."

"Oh, so you want to wait 'till the Chinese deploy it?"

"I thought you were working *with* the Chinese."

"Today, but not everything is as it appears," Ennis said. "You should know that better than anyone else."

"I've got thousands of trained people who know how to deal with the Chinese, and even for them, maneuvering through something of *this* magnitude would be incredibly difficult. I think you're way out of your league." She started pacing, moving an item on her desk a few inches over, and then an inch back.

"Likewise."

"You're greatly underestimating your adversaries if you think you can just sit in your penthouse office and outsmart the entire Chinese government."

"You're wrong about that."

"You've just proven my point."

"Which is?"

"That you're making a dangerous situation far more dangerous than it already is, and you are *not* equipped to handle it," Tess snapped.

"Or maybe it's *your* thousand people who aren't equipped to deal with it." He knew he was twisting the knife in the wound.

"Don't push me, Ennis! *My* thousand people are only the tip of the missile that's gonna destroy your world."

Ennis ended the call without responding. *Tess Federgreen is not going to stop us*, he thought as he tossed a domino, accidentally setting off seven hundred dominos before he could stop them. *She may have to have an accident.*

He picked up the phone again to call the person who could make that happen.

In fleeting glimpses, Wen had already assessed the two men chasing them. Both wore long khaki pants. One had on a gray t-shirt, the other a blue one. Each had pistols in slide-holsters. She hoped the one in the gray shirt would go after Chase, since he was the weaker. Wen made sure they saw her as she ducked into a deserted side street with few vendors. Running full speed while formulating a plan, Wen spotted a sign pointing to baños. "The bathroom is a perfect place for him to die." she whispered.

She came around the backside of an unused mosaic fountain and waited until she saw the man in the blue t-shirt jogging down the street.

"You've got the easy one, Chase," she whispered, hoping he'd be all right.

The man looked in all directions.

"Good," she said to herself, having already guessed he'd stop and survey her whereabouts. "Now check the baños."

Wen smiled as he did just that, entering the restrooms, apparently figuring she must have hidden inside. She sprang onto a low roof. Seconds later, he came back out, scouring all directions again.

Your only hope is that I'm hiding behind the building, she thought.

As he walked cautiously around the building, Wen pounced. She came down hard, deciding there was no time for questioning him, not with Chase still exposed. In a swift, silent, practiced motion, she snapped the man's neck. Before allowing him to slide to the ground, she grabbed his pistol, passport, and phone, shoving the weapon in the waistband of her shorts under her shirt, and stuffing the other items into her pocket. She did a fast search for any tattoos, a clue to indicate shadow people. Nothing.

After quickly leaning him against the dirty back wall of the little baños building, she fled in search of gray shirt and Chase.

Chapter Twenty-Seven

Chun scanned frantically around the facility and immediately knew he was at one of the mind control centers located in a secure section of the University. He had read about them in the secret reports.

I wonder if Jin is also here? Or maybe Jin is already dead . . .

He imagined for a moment technicians were going to hook up some sort of suction machine and pull out all of his thoughts and memories, taking the last bits of his son and happy family life from him in the process. Then these same cold, drone-people would drop him into a large drainage pipe filled with some acidic concoction of chemicals that would delete the rest of his body, which would finalize and erase the last evidence that he had ever lived.

But his concerns quickly shifted as he looked around the sterile room.

Chun fought against the restraints securing his arms and legs to a reclining examination chair. His eyes darted from computer screens, to a two-way mirror, to racks of various electrodes and surgical instruments.

They are definitely going to experiment . . . to extract whatever information I have.

In a way, he was happy the MSS had advanced beyond the need for torture to obtain the answers they sought. Still, he wondered if there was any way to prevent them from learning that he had mailed the envelopes.

The mailers should have arrived by now. I stayed on the run long enough.

Can they read my thoughts at this moment?

He tried to stop thinking, but the panic and pressure were too strong.

Everything could be compromised. What if the entire organization has already come down?

He knew the only way they could have caught him was through interrogating another member.

Only two others knew I had gone out . . .

A pretty woman entered the room, followed by a young man. For an eerie moment, he suffered the realization that the young man reminded him of his son, and was probably around the same age as his son would've been now. The woman, although much prettier than his wife, had a similar profile.

They are doing this on purpose. They have intentionally chosen them to stir my emotions, to help invade my memories.

He stared at them in a kind of horrified disgust, yet was also desperate to go back to how things had been before.

Perhaps it is just a coincidence . . .

The woman introduced herself as Doctor Pān. She smiled, trying to put him at ease.

"I am Doctor Lei," the man said, and quietly explained the procedure as if Chun was there voluntarily. "It will be quite simple. No pain."

"We will ask easy questions," Doctor Pān added. "All the

time, we will be monitoring your brain activity. The electrodes are very advanced."

"Will I remain conscious?" Chun asked, trying to gauge more about the outcome than the process. He also believed that if he was conscious, there might be a way to block his thoughts, to keep the mailers secret.

They assured him he would be awake the whole time. What they didn't tell him, because they themselves didn't know, was that this would be the last day of his life.

Chase was sure he'd gotten the fast one, the skinnier of the two. The man with the gray shirt, who looked to be about his age, was only ten feet behind him. Definitely American, because when he got close enough, Chase heard him yell profanities in perfect English at the people he was knocking out of his way.

Chase raced into an alley, thinking it would bring him onto the main street. "Damn!" he snapped, realizing he'd trapped himself in a dead end.

Without looking behind to see how close Gray shirt was, Chase threw himself onto the painted brick façade of the building, using honed climbing skills to find a way up the wall. The decades old bricks provided just enough contour for his hands to grip. He expected a bullet to bring him down any second, but ignored the fear and kept climbing.

Still not looking down, he could hear Gray shirt's labored breaths just below him. Chase looked up and calculated it was a two story building, but a third floor was partially constructed, meaning he'd reach the top and have a ten foot drop to the lower roof.

Seconds later, he was there.

The man's hand clapped around Chase's leg, trying to pull him back. Chase pushed his arms down the other side of the wall to give himself maximum leverage, knowing once they were on the roof, he would be an unarmed man against one with a gun.

Chase kicked his legs. Gray shirt fought, pulling, punching, and clawing his calves, but Chase had the high ground and the strength. While Gray shirt used up valuable energy yelling and cussing, Chase managed to get his right leg free and bring it back with full force, his foot connecting hard with Gray shirt's face. The blow snapped his head back and caused his grip to release, sending him backwards, smashing onto the cobblestone street at the end of the alley below, dead.

Chapter Twenty-Eight

While fixing the lines of dominos he'd wiped out, Ennis held a brief conversation with one of the members of the consortium. A loyalist from the beginning, the man was in international banking and had contacts with money launderers, major drug cartels, and other crime families. Ennis gave him Tess Federgreen's name.

"Do you want it done?" the man asked.

"I'd like it ready to go, just in case," Ennis replied. "I'll let you know for sure tomorrow."

"Fine. I'll make the arrangements."

Next, Ennis called another valuable contact, someone close to the president of the United States, who knew of the consortium's 5EX plans—at least the public part.

After they'd exchanged pleasantries, Ennis got right into it. "Call off your dog,"

"What do you mean?" the official asked.

"Do something about Tess Federgreen. We're all playing on the same side, but she's not subtle enough to navigate this. She thinks everything is a battle, especially with the Chinese."

"We'll talk to her," the official replied, his stomach already in knots at the thought of crossing Tess.

"I'm just trying to get through, you know? The president told me himself that 5EX is a priority for the administration."

"It is," the man assured Cavanaugh. "We'll handle this." Although, he wasn't at all sure they could actually stop Ironwoman, as they non-affectionately referred to Tess.

Another call was waiting for Ennis when he hung up. This one was from the Consortium's security chief. "Ever hear of Chase Malone?" the man asked Ennis.

"Young AI wizard, made a billion selling his tech, then checked out."

"Right."

"Why should I care?"

"Because he just became your biggest nightmare."

Tess, sitting in Mission Control, continued to review the information CISS was receiving on the consortium and Ennis Cavanaugh.

She looked up at her deputy, Linda. "Did you see this?"

Linda nodded, pursing her thin, painted lips. "Just."

"Cavanaugh's playing CIA. He thinks he can beat the Chinese at the double-cross game. He's a fool."

"Oh . . . I thought you were talking about this," Linda said, pointing to her screen.

"He's going to have me *killed*?" she said, sounding more amused than scared. "Well, I guess I did the same thing by putting a COD on standby."

A COD, or CISS of Death, was a last resort Tess used to eliminate an otherwise unsolvable problem.

"Yes, but *your* order is sanctioned by the government," Linda said.

"Maybe his is, too," Tess said, now sounding a little more worried. "Dispatch an IT-Squad to pursue Ennis Cavanaugh. I want another on the consortium. Something more is going on here than just 5EX."

Linda sent an immediate message to the IT-Squad operational leader. The elite CISS teams were made up of special ops highly trained in computers and related technologies, along with military weapons and tactics. IT-Squads were the best, and always on stand-by.

An analyst interrupted them. "Tess, we're getting blocked."

"How?" she asked. "Do a work around."

"We can't."

"Really?" she said, frowning back at them. "The consortium must be protecting something big . . . Okay, get the NSA involved."

"That's just it," the analyst said. "It's the *NSA* that's blocking us."

While climbing down the other side of the building, Chase gripped a connecting timber that split apart in his hand, plunging him fifteen feet to the ground. He braced for a hard impact, but landed in water instead.

"This is a *private* swimming pool!" someone yelled at him in English as Chase surfaced.

"Sorry," Chase said, swimming to the edge and pulling himself out. "Didn't realize."

"Hey, where did you come from, anyway?"

"Wish I knew," Chase said, opening a gate in the fence around the pool and slipping away.

Dripping wet, he jogged toward the art center where he and Wen had agreed to meet. A block later, he ran into her.

"Are you clear?" she asked.

"Yeah, he's dead. I couldn't get to his body to check for tattoos or ID, but he wasn't Grimes, and he was American."

"Why do you always come back soaking wet?" she asked, looking him over.

"Long story."

"Tell me later?"

"Over a Negra Modelo," he said. "Or four."

She scanned the area as they walked. "See anyone else?"

"No. You?"

"Just blue shirt. I got his gun. No tattoos, but he did have ID and a phone."

"That'll help."

"Hope so. Also an American."

"Where to now?"

"They left the Nissan on the street. Let's go see if there's anything useful in it."

A few minutes later, they reached the vehicle where the men had left it, partially blocking the flow of traffic. Two local police officers were checking it over.

"They can have it," Wen said. "Let's get out to the main road. We can catch a bus to Lo De Marcos."

"Assuming there aren't any more of these guys out there."

"There's *always* more of these guys," Wen said.

"Hold on," Chase said, ducking into a shop while Wen, annoyed at his lapse, kept an eye on the streets.

Chase returned a few minutes later with a Mexicolate.

He knew the fresh blended chocolate drink, made from hand roasted cacao beans, would transform Wen.

"What's that?" she asked, still bothered that he'd done something frivolous after they had just killed two men.

"Life is short," he said, handing her the cup. "We have to live."

Chapter Twenty-Nine

Chase and Wen reached the highway just after one of the local Compostela buses passed.

"I think it's twenty minutes until the next one, but Mexico time is different, so it could be longer," Wen said, finishing her chocolate. "I'm not anxious to hang around here waiting for the local officials to find those two dead Americans back there."

"We'd better stay out of sight," Chase said. "Shadow people, Federales, or San Pancho Policia, the odds aren't in our favor."

Before they could withdraw too far, a pale green Hyundai pulled up next to them. "Jacinto?" Wen said, ducking to look in the window.

"Should we kill him?" Chase asked, only half joking.

"Please," he said, rolling to a stop on the broken pavement and gravel. "Let me take you to Lo De Marcos."

"We don't trust you," Chase said.

"I know, but I make it up to you. I've been circling around, waiting, hoping . . . "

Wen leaned in the window and studied his face. "I believe him," she told Chase before turning back to Jacinto. "I have a gun now. If any little thing makes me nervous, you'll be the first to know. Understand?"

"Yes. I'm very sorry. Very happy you let me have another chance."

Chase and Wen both agreed taking their chances with Jacinto was better than standing along the highway for another twenty or thirty minutes, waiting for trouble to arrive.

During the drive, Jacinto explained how he had been approached only an hour before he'd picked up Chase and Wen in Puerto Vallarta.

"They knew everything about me," he said. "They would kill me and my family if I didn't do what they said."

"Which was?" Wen asked.

"I was to drive down a road just past San Pancho. They would follow us and take you. I'm sorry, I didn't know what else to do. Will they hurt my family?"

"They won't hurt anyone now."

Jacinto dropped them off at the private house Bull had arranged for them to rent, just a block away from the beach. Chase had wanted something right on the beach, but nothing was available.

"We won't be in town long anyway," Wen said. "We go meet MarathonManCatamaran, find out what else he knows, get a good night's sleep, and return to PV in the morning for a flight back to the States."

"You don't really think it's going to be that easy, do you?"

"A girl can dream, can't she?"

Chase shrugged as his phone pinged. "Bad news," he said, reading a text. "No groceries today. Some problem with the Federales. They'll try again tomorrow."

"No weapons," Wen said, in a way that made it sound like 'no oxygen.'

"We've got the pistol you took from the guy in San Pancho."

"Not enough ammo."

"We aren't expecting any trouble."

Wen looked grim. "That's when it comes."

"Every time we get near a file or operation called 'INSIGHT', the NSA shuts us down," the analyst told Tess.

"Something else is going on here," Tess said.

"What is the consortium hiding?" Linda asked.

"And how are they getting the NSA to cover them?" the analyst added.

Tess looked at them both, then whispered, "What the hell *is* INSIGHT?"

She put the entirety of Mission Control on the consortium, 5EX, Ennis Cavanaugh, Chase Malone, and INSIGHT.

"Take it as a challenge, people. Don't let the NSA beat us," she said, believing her best were better than their cohorts at the National Security Agency.

It didn't take long for them to uncover consortium members with connections to the NSA.

"Get me the director," Tess said, intimately familiar with turf wars and not afraid to battle the most powerful people in the country.

"It's higher than that," an analyst said. "We've got direct links to the White House."

"Fine," she said. "I'll talk to the most important one first. Get me the NSA director, and as soon as I finish with him, I'll talk to the president."

"What about this?" Linda asked, showing Tess the latest surveillance reports on the man Ennis had spoken with about terminating her. "He's engaged a mechanic."

Tess understood the term, and had to grapple with the fact that it would be too dangerous for her to leave CISS headquarters until this matter was resolved. "Have an IT Squad pick up the mechanic."

"And Townsend?" she asked, referring to the consortium member who'd arranged it.

"Not yet."

Linda nodded. "What about the Ennis Cavanaugh COD?" she asked quietly, recalling their earlier discussion about a Ciss of Death.

"I need a little more venom from that snake before we cut its head off."

Chapter Thirty

Lo De Marcos' streets alternated between cobblestone, dirt, cracked pavement, and thin gravel. Chase and Wen walked down the paved road that ran parallel to the beach. A row of patched together Airbnb's and RV "resorts" were on their right, vacant lots, some improved gringo homes, and a small bird sanctuary filled with dozens of sunning turtles and a variety of mostly white marine birds populated the other side.

"Lots of golf carts," Chase observed as another group of seniors from Canada and the US cruised by at about twice the speed they were walking.

"Kind of strange with no golf course around."

They suddenly heard a loud speaker announcing "Gas, Global Gas" in a dramatic, drawn-out speech, followed by the honking diesel horns. Soon the source of the commotion came into view—a truck filled with propane tanks.

"Interesting form of advertising," Chase said as the truck grew closer.

Wen saw it as a risk. The distraction of the noise made

hearing anything else around them impossible, and when she imagined the explosive power of the truck's cargo . . .

"There it is," Chase said when the vehicle had finally passed. "El Pequeño Paraiso."

Wen swiveled from watching the truck get farther away to the colorful sign for their destination, surrounded by pretty flowers. The wall across from the entrance was completely draped in floral vines.

Chase stepped around the corner. Two or three dozen RVs were packed into the space among small trees and other plants. A series of two narrow four-story buildings completely surrounded the "trailer park", and somehow it all seemed charming in the tropical breeze and humid air.

"A good place to hide," Chase said. "It's almost invisible from the little road out there."

Wen, scoping out the high points, corners, and all the other places threats could be, didn't answer.

"So this guy bought a little used RV, drove it into Mexico, parked at an obscure RV park on the ocean in a tiny little fishing village, and just disappeared?" Chase said as they wandered farther in, trying to find him.

"His name is Rob Carpenter," Wen said, although Chase already knew this. "Bull said he'll have US plates, and since almost all of these are Canadian . . . it shouldn't be too hard."

"Hey, we're looking for our buddy from the States," Chase said to a passing woman wearing a yellow sun dress. "Do you know where Rob is?"

"Oh, he's in the little Toyota, just down that row. Fourth one in, I think."

"Thanks!" Chase told her cheerily.

Wen shot him a quick smile. "Impressive use of your charm."

"We look like tourists," he said. They were both wearing shorts and linen shirts. Wen had the gun she'd taken from the man in San Pancho in her backpack.

"What are the odds he used his real name?" Wen asked.

"Maybe he's using a different last name."

"This must be it," she said, unaware that Rob had already seen them coming.

Chase knocked on the door. Surprisingly, Rob answered.

"Hola," the man greeted with a goofy smile, straightening his dark rimmed glasses then folding his muscled arms over his chest and leaning against the doorway of his kingdom.

"Hi," Chase said. "Rob?"

"Last time I checked." He had an easy smile, sort of innocent.

Chase gave an obligatory half-laugh. "I'm Chase, and this is Wen. We were hoping to talk to you about MarathonManCatamaran."

Rob maintained his smile, but Wen detected the fear that flashed through his eyes.

"What?"

"MarathonManCatamaran," Chase repeated.

"Oh, yeah, I think that's a place on the beach that rents boats."

Wen knew he was lying, but they had to be careful.

"We know you used to work for the consortium," Chase said calmly.

"What's the consortium?" Rob asked, looking genuinely puzzled. "You got me mixed up."

Chase smiled. "Look, we know about 5EX, the documents you sent, the secret sites on the internet."

"Man, I don't know *what* you're talking about. Do I *look* like a tech guy?" He pointed his fingers up and down his body, indicating his baggy shorts, stretched and faded t-shirt, and week old beard.

"Don't worry, we're not with the consortium," Wen said softly.

"Neither am I," he said. "Now please believe me, I'm *not* this Catamaran guy you're talking about."

"I know," Chase said. "But they're going to launch 5EX in less than forty-eight hours, and that will be catastrophic. And *you* can help prevent it."

Rob stared at them, his smile fading for the first time. He said nothing.

"You left breadcrumbs for the Cause. We found them. We came. There isn't much time."

Rob shook his head slowly, but still said nothing.

"We can *help*."

He looked beyond them, as if searching for killers. "What exactly did you find?"

Chase sighed, tapped a few buttons on his phone, then held it up so Rob could see.

Bull's face filled the screen. "Oh, hey, Rob. They found you."

"Who are you?"

"I'm the hacker with WOLF that found your clues, and then found you."

"How did you do that?"

Bull quickly explained the signature icon, and all the other steps she had used.

Rob nodded absently. "You're good."

"Thanks. That means a lot coming from Marathon-ManCatamaran. I can't believe the stuff you laid."

He smiled. "But how did you find me *here*?"

Bull shrugged. "I hacked into all the consortium companies, primaries and subs, and searched for recent resignations and terminations, then did a whole lot of weeding out, access, age, other relevant demo. Eventually came up with a name, crossed that with the IP in LDM, and got lucky with customs."

"You *hacked* ICE?"

"Yeah. It wasn't the first time."

Rob blew out a breath. "Okay, I hope I'm worth all the trouble."

"Thanks, Bull," Chase said, "talk to you later." He ended the call and looked back at Rob. "So, can we talk now?"

"Sure . . . Let's go for a walk on the beach."

"Is it safe?"

"First lesson about the consortium," Rob said. "*Nowhere* is safe."

Chapter Thirty-One

Rob explained that he was an engineer on the 5EX project for a subcontractor and had seen some files he wasn't supposed to. "I quit my job the next day citing health reasons, said I'd been diagnosed with an aggressive form of esophageal cancer, and took off. It's been almost a year, I've been watching them ever since."

"How?" Chase asked.

"Some back doors, I kept."

"We can get in?" Chase asked excited.

"Nah," he said, a queasy look on his face. "Two days ago, all my access slammed shut. They found my holes."

"Do they know where you are?"

"I don't think so . . . I hope not . . . they shouldn't be able to . . . "

"Why *here*?" Wen asked, trying to get him away from his fear. "I mean, it's beautiful, but . . . "

"A few years ago, a friend told me about spending three weeks here. Said something I always remembered: 'LDM is the perfect place to disappear.'"

"Are they looking for you?"

"I don't think so."

"Then you were pretty brave to leave the breadcrumbs."

"Brave or stupid, it's a fine line."

"I know what you mean," Chase said, eyeing the group of funky restaurants at the edge of the water, tables filled with people drinking cervezas, glass bottle Cokes, eating from platters of fries and fish. It smelled *wonderful*.

"So you're all with the Cause," Rob continued. "I only know a little about them, from the same friend."

"We do help WOLF, but we also manage to get in trouble by ourselves. I'm Chase Malone."

Rob looked at him with wide eyes. "*That* Chase Malone?"

"Yeah."

"Didn't I read somewhere that you were dead?"

"It's not true."

"Apparently." Rob shook his head. "Did you lose your fortune?"

"Not really."

"Then you're the stupid one. No offense, but you've got a billion dollars in the bank, a beautiful woman," he said, pointing to Wen. She smiled as he continued. "You're both *young*. What are you thinking? Shouldn't you be living it up on a private island somewhere?"

"Wish I could, but I have one major flaw," Chase said, taking Wen's hand. "I don't like bad people."

"Admirable that you think you can fix the world, but you're a bit outnumbered by the bad people."

"No," Wen said, before Chase could answer. "There are seven and a half billion good people. The bad ones only number in the thousands. *They* are the ones outnumbered."

Rob nodded and said, "No, gracias," to a woman

trudging up the beach with an armful of blankets for sale. "Well, I wish I could say I was the same kind of heroes as you two, but I came down here because I wanted to be as far away from the effects of 5EX as possible."

"You're being modest," Chase said. "You left a trail. You took files. Can we see them?"

Rob shook his head. "I didn't want anything to do with that stuff. That's the kind of information that gets a person killed."

Chase was disappointed. "Can you tell us about it?"

"That I can do."

"What made you run?"

"Here's the thing," Rob said. "If this were *just* about 5EX, in the sense that it's going to flip all kinds of biological switches . . . There's talk about the flood of high band frequencies causing cancer, major neurological issues, a whole gambit of things impacting health. I'm not sure about those claims, but I do think we need honest, non-biased studies."

They stopped while Chase bought a bag of an interesting assortment of sweets from a man pushing a heavy cart packed with colorful candies through the sand.

"My problem," Rob continued, "was with INSIGHT."

Chase and Wen exchanged a glance.

"The consortium is going all in," Rob said. "At first it had been neuroscience-backed pedagogy for children. Maybe you've seen photos of children attending classes, where they all have probes attached to their heads?"

"Yes," Wen said.

Chase nodded as they stood and watched the sun setting.

"The technology shows a teacher testing children's brain activity in real time. They can tell if the kids are paying attention, if they're retaining the lesson, etcetera. But INSIGHT is way beyond that."

A couple teenagers carrying surfboards walked by, and Rob waited until they had passed before continuing.

"It's like with the students, but on a massive scale. It's all linked to MRI brain imaging scanners and EEG, ERP, and full implementation of neurofeedback technology that shoots decades ahead of available scientific capabilities."

"You're talking about systems that record a brain's electrical activity," Chase said.

"Yeah, but on *entire populations*, and not just blips and readings. They can know what you're thinking and *change* your mind."

"How?" Chase asked. "Clinical recordings of brain electrical activity are usually taken at sixty-four scalp locations. Researchers can take that up to two or three hundred. That's going to allow identification of only general features of activity in limited areas of the brain, meaning there's a serious limitation to the amount of data that can be collected."

"You're thinking of it like the way things are," Rob said as they turned and headed back down the beach. "The consortium has gone way beyond the now, like in the future. I'm telling you they can read minds."

"How do they achieve that scale?" Wen asked.

"They use 5EX."

"They're going to use the cellular networks to read people's minds?" Chase asked.

"Yes," Rob said. "Think of the probes attached to the kids' heads like an ethernet cable that brings you internet. Now imagine if they could get those same results without hooking you up, like getting internet from WIFI. *That's* what INSIGHT does. If a person is near a connected device, the consortium can read their minds *and* control their thoughts."

"A cell phone is a connected device," Wen said. "That means—"

"Exactly. Cell phone, tablet, laptop, internet of things—all of them just tools to control us," Rob said. "Everyone can be read and manipulated."

Chapter Thirty-Two

Chase stared at Rob as if he'd just said aliens had landed, and in a way, he had. The implications of what the consortium was about to do were stunning.

"We need to know how they're doing it," Chase said, hardly believing someone in this century could figure out the technology to read and manipulate people's thoughts.

"I actually might have a few files you may be interested in," Rob said as they walked through the beach gate back to his RV park.

"Really?" Chase asked, excited.

"Yeah, but they didn't come from me."

"We haven't even seen you."

Rob nodded and winked at Chase.

They looked at Rob, waiting for him to go get the files. Finally, after an uncomfortable silence, he said, "Oh, they aren't *here*. I told you, I'm not interested in dying. Keeping that stuff around . . . well, that would be a sure death sentence."

"Where is it, then?" Wen asked.

"I can take you there in the morning."

"Not this evening, tonight?" Chase insisted.

"Mañana," he said, waving over his shoulder and heading back to his RV.

Chase and Wen carried their shoes as they walked barefoot up the beach. The few people there had mostly congregated on the south end, among a cluster of three small surf-side food joints. A handful of tourists wandered along the waves as the sky turned from pink to purple.

Wen's special phone vibrated. She saw the number and clicked on the extra encryption mode. "It's Margot," she said, pushing speaker and turning up the volume, knowing it would be hard to hear above the breaking waves.

"It is much more serious than we thought, and bigger," Margot said. Chase and Wen looked at each other, both thinking she had discovered the consortium's connection. "We're losing a disproportionate number of members in China."

Chase knew WOLF had been a target of the MSS even before they helped Wen escape. But after he and Wen had rescued Tu and seemingly exposed China's Communist government's genetic engineering program, The Cause had been under increasing pressure there.

"We've lost seven of our operatives inside China in the last twenty-four hours. That's the most we've lost in a single day other than when you were in the country getting the boy out." Margot had been against them taking Tu, having known it would bring considerable extra attention on WOLF.

"Still, the MSS could just be—"

"We discovered a disturbing pattern. All seven had one thing in common," Margot said impatiently. "They were each working on the mind project."

"Then that's how the MSS is finding us," Wen said. "The leak is WOLF."

"Then they know what we have," Chase said.

"Maybe," Margot said. "But they also have somehow targeted exactly the right people, and they've done it very quickly . . . I know these people. I don't believe they would've talked so easily."

"They must be using mind reading on them." Wen said.

"It's the only explanation," Margot responded. "Using information from the ones they capture to go deeper, and find more."

"That means they're much farther along than we were assuming . . . more than we even thought possible," Chase said.

"It explains a lot," Wen agreed. "Must be how they're locating us. There could even be a connection to the shadow people."

The idea that the MSS and shadow people might be working together terrified Chase.

"And you think it's *all* coming from WOLF?" Margot asked, sounding almost offended.

"Those are the minds they've gotten into," Wen said. "We need to do a review of who has access to what."

"We've also got to get word to Sepio," Chase added, referring to the elite security company protecting Tu. "The MSS may already know exactly where he is."

"I don't know if we're going to be any more help to you with the mind project," Margot said. "Our network has been completely decimated. We are going to have to play defense because the MSS will use the advantage they've gained from our operatives to further infiltrate our organization inside *and* outside China."

"The MSS smells blood," Wen agreed. "They're going for the kill now."

Chapter Thirty-Three

The following morning, Chase and Wen knocked on Rob's RV at first light. They had been worried he might have fled in the night, or worse, been killed, but he answered the door with a yawn. "Whose dumb idea was it to get up at this hour?"

"Yours, I think," Chase said.

"All right, let's go, but give me a minute." He turned back inside, humming a familiar tune, and came back out unchanged except for the addition of a mug of coffee in one hand, a sun hat in the other.

They headed up the sandy shore. Fifteen minutes later, they reached an old dirt road off the beach.

"Look at that lagoon," Wen said, pointing up ahead to a picturesque body of water separated from the ocean by a very narrow strip of sand. The sunrise, red, orange, and pink, reflected in still water filled with egrets, cranes, pelicans, ducks, and other waterfowl. It was a breathtaking masterpiece.

"It's beautiful!" Chase said, marveling at the lagoon, the

beach, and the churning Pacific all in one amazing view. "like a postcard."

Wen gazed at the far end of the lagoon as it touched the base of a massive cliff that rose above to a peak overlooking Lo De Marcos and the surrounding coast. "It's so peaceful," she said, wondering how long it would remain that way.

"Ready to see the plan?" Rob asked.

"Sure," Chase said, already too exhausted to go up the mountain in the warm tropical air.

"We're gonna go where we can shine," Rob said, smiling. "Work and a view. Plus we'll be saving the world, so . . ."

Sometimes I get tired of saving the world, Chase thought. *How many times can I die?*

Wen, looking at him, could see his fading energy. "Remember, it's worth it. And you love it."

"I love *you*," he said, always touched when she read him.

A train of working animals and strong men came up the street. The burros were loaded to capacity with bags of concrete and water.

"I don't really like horses," Chase said, as if this was news.

"It's not as bad if people aren't shooting at you," Wen assured him.

"Yeah, well, can you guarantee me that?"

She smiled. "We'll be all right."

"Wait until you see the view from up there," Rob said. "It's an incredibly beautiful spot. You can see up and down the coast for miles."

"Is there another way?" Chase asked on his second

attempt to mount his horse. It wasn't that he didn't know how to, or that he couldn't do it, he just *really* didn't want to get on it. He thought back to when he was pursued through a Nevada snowstorm on horseback, still unsure how they had survived that—or many of their other adventures, for that matter. He recalled another time in Mexico when they had been followed by too many men to count, on horseback, into the jungle. The results of *that* ride had been horribly brutal.

He looked at the horse.

"Go on, he won't bite," Rob said. "His name is Fábrica de Pegamento."

Wen started laughing.

"What's so funny?" Chase asked, backing away from the horse.

Rob, failing to keep a straight face, said, "It is a gentle horse."

Wen, from atop her horse, explained, "The horse's name translates in English to 'glue factory.'"

Chase couldn't help but smile. He pulled himself up into the saddle as if he'd done it a hundred times. "Just like Clint Eastwood," he said.

"Your job is easy," Rob said, steering the horse up the trail. "You just ride. The horse has gotta do all the climbing. And the burros . . . look at those loads."

"Ever wonder what these animals had planned for today before we decided what they should do?"

"Probably something like relaxing in the shade," Rob said, smiling.

Wen scanned the area one last time before they left. Everything seemed clear, but she felt the pull in her intuition that something wasn't quite right. "Keep your eyes open," she said to Chase as she rode past him.

He wanted to ask her what they were going to do without weapons. Although Wen had the Beretta from the San Pancho guy, Chase didn't even have his multitool. But he knew what she would say, the same thing she always did: *"Everything is a weapon. Whenever you find yourself in trouble, use whatever is available as a weapon to defend yourself, to get away."*

As the group readied to depart, Doug Black sat behind the pond, not moving. He'd done this too many times, and knew moving was always a mistake. Instead, he waited, and listened.

Chapter Thirty-Four

They followed the "road" along the river, making small talk until they came to a concrete bridge.

"This bridge is fairly recent," Rob explained. "They used to have to ford the river back there where it's shallow, but certain times of year, the water would be too high even for that."

"Is that why they built the bridge?" Chase asked.

"Not really. One of the wealthy land owners, Miguel Medina, had it constructed for his daughter's Quinceañera."

"What's that?"

"Throughout Mexico, the fiesta de quince años is to celebrate a girl's fifteenth birthday. Medina put on an extraordinary event to honor his eldest. He needed the bridge so his many guests could attend more easily."

They continued on the other side of the bridge, walking toward the jungle.

"Hey, nice multitool," Chase said, noticing the familiar object in Rob's hand.

"Thanks."

Wen rolled her eyes.

"Want to sell it?"

"You need one?"

"Always," Chase said.

"Here," Rob said, tossing it to Chase. "It's yours."

"Thank you!" Chase said. "You got more?"

"I collect them."

"You just made a friend for life," Wen told Rob.

Tess stormed out of Secure and into Mission Control where Linda was waiting. "No luck?" her deputy asked.

"I got nowhere with the NSA. They're stonewalling on this one!"

"And the White House?"

"The president isn't available. Do you remember the last time the president didn't accept my call?"

"Never."

"That's because it hasn't *happened*. Three presidents, and they've *all* taken my calls, no matter the time, no matter the reason. So tell me why."

"One word," Linda said. "INSIGHT."

"Do we know what it is yet?"

"Yes, and it's big. Scary big." She proceeded to explain to Tess everything they had learned thus far.

"My god," Tess breathed. "What are they thinking?"

"Exactly," Linda said with a nervous laugh.

"This isn't funny," Tess snapped. "It all makes sense now. But how did I not see this coming . . . how did we not *know* about this?"

"They had us all so worried about 5EX that we missed the real threat."

"Sleight of hand," Tess said. "Ennis Cavanaugh is a real magician."

"Activate the COD on Ennis?"

Tess nodded. "Yes. I'd like to do it myself."

Linda knew Tess was a crack shot, and still went to the shooting range almost every night. "Then that's a-go?"

"Not yet. We need to know how deep the Chinese are in on this. Get me everything we have on the mind project, and have the analyst on the third floor match it with every last microchip that has anything to do with 5EX."

"Got it."

"And, Linda, keep that CISS of Death ready."

Doug Black watched Chase, Wen, and Rob from a safe distance; a spot up on the ridge where two trees had fallen in just the right place so he could easily walk up the trunk and wind up twenty feet off the ground. If it weren't for the mosquitoes, he could happily stay all day.

He reported the activity into his radio. After they crossed the bridge, he had a suspicion he knew just where they were heading. "Should I move?" he asked.

"Negative. Continue observing."

Black didn't like the idea of observing. He checked his gun, took a sip of water from his canteen, and watched Wen in particular. "You sure are an interesting one," he said to her, as if she could hear him. "I've never seen anyone look so relaxed while being that vigilant. What are you afraid of, sweetheart? Certainly not me."

He laughed. His graying sandy hair, pulled back into a low ponytail, framed a rugged face. Warm eyes darted nervously, but not out of nervousness—more like looking for opportunity yet reluctant to act on it. He thought himself a good catch, and smooth talked the ladies, not caring about having a different one each week. He actually would have been a good catch if his work wasn't so dangerous, illegal, and often wrong.

"But hey," he'd say, throwing his hands up, "one day I'll settle down and build custom tiny houses . . . *if* I live that long."

Once she ascertained the nature of the INSIGHT project, Tess initiated the encrypted video call with two experts who would be able to bring her up to speed. One was an astronaut—not Nash Graham, but a man almost as good, Claude Lemon. The other was a scientist who worked on such brain wave projects for the CIA. She only had one question.

"Is it possible?"

"To read minds through a cellular network?" Lemon asked. "Absolutely."

"Technically, yes," the CIA scientist replied. "However, on the scale you've described—"

"My in-house expert says it can't be done," Tess added.

"Get a new expert," Lemon said. "It *is* real. It *is* happening."

"That's a bit of a stretch," the scientist said. "With brainwaves and electrodes . . . I mean with synapses—"

"The Chinese are years ahead of that photo of school children," Lemon said.

"Yes, but that's connected," the scientist insisted.

"There are others doing it wirelessly."

"Who?" Tess asked.

"Perhaps the most advanced on this track is a domestic agency."

"Which one?" the scientist asked.

"I can't say, but, Tess, I'm certain you can find that out. The point is that all the technology is there. It's spread out among different industries, nations, agencies—secrets and coded patterns. Let us not forget that with AI now, these diverse, seemingly random attributes can easily be brought together, new discoveries manufactured from what before might have just been confusion."

Tess knew he must be referring to HITE, an agency few even knew existed. She also knew the situation was far more dangerous than she thought.

Chapter Thirty-Five

Chase stopped in front of a fairly opulent estate that seemed out of place among the smaller, older, more primitive, and sometimes dilapidated residences. Rob explained that the home belonged to the head of the Medina family.

"The one with the daughter?" Chase asked.

"The same," Rob said. "They use that long green lawn to land ultralights."

"Nothing like a private runway in paradise. That's quite a lush lawn, too. They must have a herd of sheep, or goats—"

"No, they cut it."

"Wow . . . must take a week."

"Have you ever seen other kinds of aircraft land there?" Wen interrupted, gathering her hair in a ponytail. "Like small planes?"

Chase smiled, knowing she was always gathering intelligence for potential needs.

"I've never seen any," Rob said. "But it sure is flat enough, and looks long enough."

"So where did Medina make all his money?" Chase asked.

"Everyone in Mexico makes their money from hard work," Rob said, flipping one peso coins onto the dirt road. "And I don't ask too many questions from someone who's helping me."

"What's he helping you do?" Wen asked.

"Destroy 5EX."

"What?" Chase said. "I thought you were just down here hiding?"

"Yeah, well, it's a good place to hide in case I can't achieve the impossible."

"A hero after all," Wen said, smiling. She pointed to the coins on the road.

"Only if it works." He lifted a shoulder. "Kids find 'em. It's a game I like to play."

"What exactly *is* your *game*?" Chase asked.

"I'll explain once we get there."

"And this wealthy local man is helping you? Why?"

"He likes engineering projects."

"Lucky for us," Chase said, deciding to accept the empty answer for now.

They continued walking as the jungle encroached, narrowing the dirt road. A pair of iguanas sunning on one of the trees seemed to be watching them.

"What's that?" Wen asked, pointing to a small, old, industrial-looking building.

"The Sanctuary at Lo de Marcos," Rob said. "They take care of stray dogs and cats, even some chickens and geese. I think they might also have a donkey or two. It used to be a pig farm. Now, in the kennels, volunteers nurse the animals back to health."

"I noticed a lot of dogs in the town," Wen said.

"Not as many as there used to be. They've really stepped up, and now they spay or neuter a lot of dogs."

Chase welcomed the shade as they entered a section of larger trees a bit further along the trail. The day was already getting hot.

"Wow, I love that tree," Wen said, pointing. "It looks ancient, like it's been there for a thousand years."

"That's one of my favorites," Rob agreed. "It's also an important one. See that old arched gate? That's where I hide the key."

"The key?"

"Yeah. For the office building."

They followed him over to the gate. Rob began removing the tightly held bricks a little at a time. Wen continually checked to make sure nobody was following them.

"Why don't you just keep the key at your place?" Chase asked.

"Because even if they get me, they still won't get the key," he said, glancing at Wen, knowing she would understand. She did. Finally, he extracted the key. "Even with this, they can't get in. It opens all the padlocks, but it's also fitted with a failsafe twenty-one digit keypad. Only I know the code."

With the key in his pocket, he carefully put the black bricks back in place. Around the next corner, they came to a configuration of five large metal shipping containers resting on concrete foundations, stacked two high.

"The office building?" Chase asked.

"Yep."

"Pretty big footprint you got there. Don't people wonder what this is?"

"People don't ask too many questions. It's on Medina

family land. They assume it's just his storage. But being out here, at the edge of the jungle, far from prying eyes, has its advantages."

Rob unlocked the heavy padlocks, looked around again, and pulled the doors open, revealing an inner door with a keypad. Taking one last glance, he entered the digits. Chase got the first five and three in the middle, but that was it.

A blast of stifling heat hit them. It was dark inside.

"Taking us into a furnace?" Chase asked.

"Don't worry, it has ventilation and fans. I just need to power it up."

The three of them were so focused on the interior that none of them noticed Doug Black, now much closer, watching them from behind some low, bushy palms a few hundred feet away.

Rob shut the door behind them. "It's got an interior lock," he said, latching it.

"And lights, I hope," Chase said.

"Yeah, hold on," Rob said, feeling around.

"That's *not* the switch," Wen said sternly.

"Oh, sorry," he said with a nervous laugh. "Here we go."

Fluorescent bulbs flickered to life, illuminating a startling array of equipment and controls.

"What *is* all this?" Chase asked.

"The resistance," Rob said.

"I don't understand," Wen said. "How did you pull this off?"

"The Medina family," Rob explained. "They're going to help me disrupt the Telmex experiment that the consortium has set up. That is, if we can get that antenna to broadcast a broken signal."

"It will break the 5EX circuit?" Chase asked, impressed.

"You can really make it so 5EX won't be able to work?" Wen added.

"5EX relies on a networked technology," Chase explained. "Think of it as an electrical circuit. It must be complete for the energy to move."

"Right," Rob agreed. "If we can get towers up all over the place, we'll break the chain. Problem is, they're doing their first test rollout the day after tomorrow, at dawn. I'd almost given up hope we could stop them."

"Pirated towers? Steal the signal?" Wen guessed.

Rob nodded. "Correct."

"But even if we could wreck the rollout, doesn't that just buy a little time?" Chase asked.

"Yeah," Rob said, a heaviness in his voice. "But when you're trying to beat the devil, there's nothing more valuable than time."

Chapter Thirty-Six

Chase studied the equipment, trying to understand the elaborate set up. "It's already getting pretty stuffy in here," Chase said.

"Oh, yeah." Rob opened a series of slits in the roof just big enough to vent the air, then hit another switch that turned on a circulatory fan.

"Quite sophisticated," Chase said. "I didn't see any power coming in."

"It's underground. Comes from the house back there."

"What's the next step?" Wen asked impatiently.

"There's a battered tower up on the ridge, we need to rebuild it," Rob said. "Concrete, welding and boom we're back in business."

"Then what?"

"We have a guy, Juan, who works for Telmex, he's a member of the Medina family."

"So he's our expert?"

"Yeah. He got us all kinds of Telmex manuals, operating procedures, schematics, and data issues . . . but most of this is beyond my educational level, know what I mean?" His boyish looks caught the seasoned, rakish billionaire off guard, and Chase realized he had hardened from the hell he'd been dealing with in the world; the greed, the violence, the sadness. He looked at Rob and saw himself for a moment—that chance of relaxation, of carefree brilliance, light joy, the ability to let it go over a beer and lazy lifestyle.

Why can't I have that? he thought. *Not in this lifetime . . .* Then Wen took his attention. *I love her. It's us, not just me alone against it all. Still . . . life on the beach . . .*

"Show me what you got," Chase told Rob.

"How many men does Medina have?" Wen asked.

"As many as we need," Rob replied.

"And weapons?"

"Not sure on that one, but I think he's well-armed."

"What's this microwave antenna for?" Chase asked.

"Gets us to the tower on the ridge."

"For controls?"

"Exactly." Rob went on to explain the broad aspects of his plan. "What do you think?"

Wen looked at him. "It will either work, or get us all killed."

Doug Black took several photos of the storage containers and tagged them with GPS. He radioed in a status update. Convinced he knew the contents of the giant metal boxes, his speculation went wild with what the three of them could be doing inside for so long.

I've got to get inside to see if I'm right about what they have.

He would need tools. There was no doubt his superiors were going to have him destroy everything.

And them? he wondered. *How much time do they have left?*

"So you knew we would find you?" Wen asked, returning to the unfinished conversation from their first meeting, while Rob worked on some kind of receiver.

"Not *you*, exactly," Rob said. "But I knew The Cause existed. That they might be monitoring and would get my message."

"Why didn't you just contact WOLF directly?" she asked.

"For one thing, I had no idea how to find them. Even if I did, it would've been too risky."

"Riskier than leaving a message on the dark web?"

"Yeah." He chuckled. "It was likely only going to be found by The Cause. The consortium wasn't going to get it."

"What does the consortium know about The Cause?"

"The consortium has a task force that targets WOLF. I mean The Cause is completely against 5EX, as well as a lot of other things the consortium is trying to do. All these fringe groups are like PAE organizations that seem to pop up in every town."

"PAE?" Chase echoed questioningly.

"People Against Everything," Rob said. "When something like this happens, or a new technology is introduced, those groups, or individuals, have zero chance. Nothing they can do and no amount of pressure they put on their local politicians can stop the consortium. However, WOLF is organized, wealthy, powerful, and the only worldwide movement."

"And, ironically, most people don't know it exists."

"Not the average citizen, but the consortium sure knows. And the people in the true positions of power around the world know."

"WOLF is more powerful than ever," Wen assured him.

"Good," he said, wanting desperately to believe her, looking at her a little too long. "Because the consortium is coming. And you have no idea what they can do."

"We have some idea," she said, squinting her eyes and turning away from him.

"Maybe you think you did. Maybe you even *did*. But once they get 5EX up, you won't know anything anymore."

Both Chase and Wen looked at him.

"If the consortium gets the rollout done successfully, then it's all over," Rob said. "This is the only chance to stop them."

Chapter Thirty-Seven

Chun knew they were reading his mind, and he was powerless to stop it.

Maybe the people who will interpret my thoughts will learn how horrible this is. Perhaps my son's death and, potentially, my death, will show them that the government has gone too far.

What upset Chun the most was that those in charge of the mind project would have the power to change the minds of the participants.

It isn't just one way monitoring. He turned his thoughts as if speaking directly to the researchers. *The government will use your work to maintain absolute power over the population. These tools are a two-way manipulation.*

He recalled the examples he'd seen, the benign applications of making a child want to study more, "helping" a child remember math equations, historical dates, how to spell words, making them more agreeable in class. "Assisting" a teacher, a factory worker, any employee of one of China's many large companies, in concentrating on their job. "Guiding" them in not making mistakes, learning skills quicker . . .

What comes next? Party loyalty, eradicating anti-social behavior, essentially turning any segment of the population they choose into drones.

Doctor Pān and Doctor Lei looked at each other nervously.

Chun continued thinking. *The latest round of research showed that even after the headsets were removed from the subjects, the planted thoughts still remained.*

"He's talking to us with his mind," Pān said as they monitored the results.

"I know, I know," Lei said. "Things we are not supposed to think about."

Her expression seemed drenched in the irony of his statement. Doctor Pān's thoughts filled with fear. *Now we may be in danger.*

Chase continued rummaging through the equipment in the container.

"You think what you read in the docs I posted is scary?" Rob said, pulling up his baggy shorts and fiddling for something in his pocket. "It's far more terrifying than that." He popped a piece of gum in his mouth.

"Is it just theory?" Chase asked. "Or can they already read your thoughts?"

"Any connected device. Imagine trying to organize against that. And that's just the beginning." He blew a bubble and popped it loudly.

"There *must* be a way to avoid their probes."

"Sure," Rob said. He squatted and stared at the floor.

"Just stop using computers. Give up smart phones and tablets, go back to the way the world used to be, form an underground resistance."

"Well, as crazy as that sounds . . . "

"It would hardly have a chance to work, even in the best of situations," Rob said, his voice edged with the tone of a horror movie narrator. "It's got no chance in a 5EX world because we're talking first generation here. And this stuff is being built with AI machine learning." He looked up. "Chase, you know what I'm talking about. It's going to keep improving, getting better and better. Soon they won't need connected devices to get you. It'll just be picked in the air." He stood up, adjusting a piece of equipment.

"We'll never escape the thought police," Wen said, "and the dystopian state."

"They'll be able to know everything, and right now it's just intentions and emotions. But what they've already got on the table is everything." Rob told Wen to hold a cable while he reached around a tall rack of blinking lights. "The algorithms will be able to interpret it," he continued, "to know precisely what you're thinking."

"The surveillance state's Holy Grail," Chase said, seeing what Rob was after and handing him a long coil of braided com wire.

"Can you imagine?" Rob asked. "They'll know every thought. Like, hey, I want to have pizza for dinner, ice cream for dessert, and then I want to sleep with that waitress over there. And then what comes next is pictures in your thoughts. They'll be able to watch *videos* of it, man. I'm telling you, I've seen all this in their plans. If we don't stop it, we'll be living in the worst possible version of Orwell's novel *1984*."

"It may already be too late to stop," Chase said, looking

around at the piles of expensive items, having a hard time imagining it was enough to figure out a way to destroy the consortium's massive network.

"Oh, and the funny thing?" Rob said, reaching for a screwdriver. "At least half of us are going to get cancer and die from 5EX. It just *keeps* coming. The human body can't handle those waves, and they know it."

"They've done studies?"

"Lots of them, covered up," Rob said. "But they don't care how many die. May even prefer to cut the population down."

"They keep making more," Chase said.

"Especially when they know your thoughts," Wen said.

"Yeah, and once they know them, they can control and manipulate your thoughts, so they can have you do what they want."

"So do you have an idea, one that might really work?" Chase asked, handing him another sized precision screwdriver. "Or did you bring us here just to scare us?"

"It's big, man. And like anything big, a little bit of pressure in the right place, and it cracks."

"All of this," Chase said, waving his arm around the interior of the container, "can give us a way in?"

"I think so." Rob smiled. "When we get back to town, you should meet with Juan, the TelMex guy, and put your heads together."

"Okay, I guess with inside help we might have a chance."

"Only if we bring 5EX down during the rollout." He looked at the time on his phone. "We've got just under thirty-nine hours to build the tower, set up the equipment, test it, and make the intercept."

Chase looked at Wen, raising his eyebrows. "A slim chance."

"But still a chance," she said.

Chapter Thirty-Eight

Black watched as they mounted their horses and started up the hill. As soon as they were safely out of sight, he grabbed his two-way radio and called in the report. "White rock, moving above the line," he said, calling the code name assigned to them.

"Follow," was the immediate response.

He crept out of the brush, staying close to the path's edge, worried that at any moment they could double back and find him. He was particularly concerned about the woman, having noted she was always vigilant, obviously highly trained. "She's a high-value asset," he'd reported.

He tried to keep them in sight while staying as far back as possible, but at times he would simply rely on the sound of their voices.

They aren't being particularly quiet, he thought to himself.

However, as the climb grew steeper, their talking lessened, and the woman didn't look back as much. It gave him the freedom to take a few more chances.

Careful . . . he warned himself. The woman is thorough. She's not going to let her guard down.

Black had watched her long enough that he started being able to predict when she would turn around. He played a game with himself, trying to guess her moves. A few times he nailed it.

I'm impressed, he thought, *since her only pattern is that she's careful enough not to work in any pattern.*

Black didn't know that Wen had been trained by the MSS to specifically avoid revealing anything that could be used against her. She prided herself on not being readable, and gave no indication when she was about to shoot, attack, run, or whatever. She refused to give any advantage to an adversary. Instead, her training taught her techniques that would allow her to show a different type of sign, and soon he figured out that she was actually projecting false tells.

Damn, who is she? And who trained her? he wondered as a fresh wave of panic hit.

Wen looked back down the trail as her horse brought up the rear. Always on edge, she only relaxed a bit as they got higher, doubting anyone would have known their destination, and confident no one was following. Yet she couldn't shake the feeling that someone was out there. Experience had refined her instincts to filter out the normal paranoia that came with being constantly pursued.

She looked up into the trees. "This seems like a place where howler monkeys should be," she said to herself, knowing they were not in this part of the world. The sounds of the jungle, the hoofbeats and murmurs of conversations between Chase, Rob, and the Mexicans who were accompanying them created the background noise from which she listened for any isolated sounds that would alert her to danger.

As they passed a large ornamental gate to a mountain mansion, Chase dropped back so his horse was just in front of hers. "Don't you love Mexico?"

"Yes," she said. "I'd like to come back sometime when we don't have to kill anyone."

Chase nodded.

After the gate, the trail grew even steeper, and as they rounded another turn, the jungle encroached further.

"That's a road out to the highway," Rob said, pointing to a wider trail branching off to their right.

"You call that a road?" Chase asked.

"It will be one day," Rob said. "Maybe. It's what they tell the people when they sell lots, to convince them they'll be able to get building supplies in."

Grimes continued switching windows on his laptop, digging deeper into the data someone had died to compile, the Belize sun warming the inner coldness he felt only the tropics could thaw.

"It must be pretty big," Shelby said, doing her best to sound uninterested and not upset by his secretiveness.

"It is."

Shelby smiled at his frustratingly difficult way of communicating. "Where are they?"

"You mean Chase and Wen?"

"Yeah. We're supposed to be on our way."

"Utah was a typical disaster. The team Belfort sent

wasn't big enough, wasn't good enough, wasn't anything enough. They totally underestimated them."

"Like we do?"

"That's different," he said, winking at her, "and you know it."

She did know, but decided not to say. The wink helped.

"Then they went to Mexico. Two men. I mean, they had more, but they only sent two men to take them out. *Two men.*"

"Two men against Chase and Wen," Shelby said, as if telling a joke. "I know how that turned out."

"Yeah. They ended up in San Pancho, small coastal town."

"Who?"

"Chase, Wen, the two operatives—"

"I love San Pancho."

"Well, they should have sent you then, because—"

"The two operatives. They're dead, of course."

"Of course."

"Did we know them?"

"Janssen was one."

"Oh, too bad. He was all right."

"Yeah, not a bad guy."

"Where are they now?" she asked. "Chase and Wen, I mean."

"Looks like they headed north, Lo de Marcos. But that's not official."

She raised her sunglasses and looked at him.

As if sensing her stare, Grimes turned and met her eyes, knowing she'd be surprised. "I've got some side contacts."

"Uh-huh." She squeezed suntan lotion onto her thighs. "So Belfort doesn't know where they are?"

"If he does, he hasn't told us yet."

"But he wants us in Mexico, so at the very least he must know they're still there."

"Yeah. How can he not know exactly where they are?"

"So why aren't we going?" Shelby asked, rubbing the lotion in such a seductive way, Grimes couldn't help but stop thinking, only for a moment.

"I don't know enough yet."

"You know we're working for Belfort."

"Yeah," he replied, turning away to look back at the screen. "But it's a mess. It's a damned freakin' mess."

Chapter Thirty-Nine

As they reached the top, one final short section of jungle remained before the first view opened up. The locals were already unloading supplies.

"The concrete will have to be hand-carried to the tower site," Rob said. "The jungle has reclaimed the high ground."

Chase looked up and could see the tower laying over palms and other trees. The twisted, rusted metal looked like it had endured a war. "Hard to imagine how we're going to reach the tower," Chase said. "Let alone put it back together."

"Hard work," one of the locals said, smiling, as if talking about relaxing.

Chase nodded, smiling back. "I'll bet."

"What brought that tower down?" Wen asked.

"No one's really sure," Rob said with a shrug. "It's been a long time . . . the trees, storms, vandals, poor construction or lack of maintenance, I don't know. I'm just glad it's here."

"You really think you can fix it?"

"Not me, but they can." He pointed to the Mexicans, hard at work with their machetes, hacking a wider trail. Others were hauling the bags and tools.

"I don't doubt that," Chase said, swatting a mosquito.

"Go check out the view," Rob said, pointing.

As they approached the edge, even with all their traveling, the scene wowed them. Unspoiled mountain ranges crisscrossed up the coast for as far as they could see, ribboned all the way with sandy beaches.

"The beauty of Mexico," Chase said.

"I had no idea," Wen breathed.

"I hope it lasts forever." He put his arm around her as they absorbed the stunning panorama. "You heard Rob on the way up. There's already plans for multibillion-dollar developments from the Saudi's, Dubai businesses, others . . . It's a shame. But look, we're already standing on the grounds for a future villa. They've divided the whole ridge into buildable lots."

"An ancient petroglyph," Wen said, pointing past a large boulder.

They walked over and took a look.

"Amazing . . . must have been up here for centuries."

"And now," Wen said, waving her arm at the surveying lines crisscrossing and dividing the mountaintop into dozens of parcels for future homes. "Look how much of the jungle they've cut away. And the bulldozing for the roads all the way up. Sad to see all the scarred land exposed."

"And all for millionaires and billionaires who might show up for a few weeks a year to what will be their third or fourth or even fifth home."

She raised an eyebrow. "Billionaires like you?"

"Not like me!"

"I know," she said. "I was teasing."

What they didn't see was Doug Black. He had also reached the peak and found he could relax in the lower vegetation, knowing there was nowhere left for them to go. He wondered what exactly they were doing up there with all the supplies and local help. He'd inquire later with his contacts around the small village, but his guess was they were restructuring the old radio tower for signaling boats on the ocean and perhaps other towns.

But why?

Chun collapsed in the reclining lab chair. The electrodes covering his body stung, maybe from sweat collecting around them, as if trying to wash the foreign objects off, but the adhesives and restraints would not yield. A headache like he had never experienced shut down a part of him. The light was blinding. Even the tick of the clock reverberated through him as if guns were being fired in the room. His thoughts were melting at least that's how it felt. But his two interrogators, doctors Pān and Lei, also had headaches. Theirs's were caused by something different though, something far more dangerous.

"I don't know what we should do," Doctor Lei whispered, the stress of what they'd just learned from Chun already eating at his entire sense of security.

"We must report it," Doctor Pān said quietly, looking around for the monitoring and recording devices she knew must be present.

"That is not the safest course," he said. "We could wind up like him."

"What else is there to do?" She was silent for several long moments while her bright mind calculated the possible scenarios that could lead to various unpleasant ends. "Run?" Her voice was so quiet, she wasn't sure he'd heard her.

"Yes. It is our only choice."

She switched to writing on a pad. *How far could we be expected to get? They will come after us. Look what happened to this guy!*

He looked at her, the terror of that realization already hitting him. *We know what he knows.*

She nodded, looking at Chun. *We call his contacts. We get to The Cause.*

Chapter Forty

The fragrant air, thick with humidity and tropical flora below, floated by in a cool breeze at the top of the peak, a welcome change from the heavy air of the jungle. It gave Chase a chance to think, to reflect on the odds against what they were doing.

"What is it?" Wen asked as they walked along the edge of the green cliff.

Chase stopped and stared out to the horizon. "What if this doesn't work?" he asked. "I mean, we've got a bunch of local guys up here with bags of concrete, pry bars, donkeys . . . *donkeys*."

Wen laughed.

"And we're going to try to send a signal out to a shrimp boat somewhere. That's assuming they even get that rickety tower standing again. We're going to need every inch of that fifty feet. It's just . . . it's hard to imagine."

"It's not like you to be so pessimistic," she said, taking his hand. "We're the optimists, remember?"

"I wish we had a better plan."

"At least we *have* a plan."

"We're talking about a really crazy dystopian world if we fail, and I don't even think the general population will notice it happening."

"I don't know," Wen said. "Even in China, people notice the great freedom. Under the heaviest oppression in the world, they still look for ways to bring change."

"But that's just a few of them. It's not the general population, because, in a way, the general population *welcomes* the oppression. The security, the familiarity, the consistency, the *knowing*. They let it go." He ducked low to avoid a branch filled with hundreds of seed pods shaped like sharp spikes. "You're talking about the few who understand what's *really* happening."

"And those are the people we have to reach. It doesn't take a million people to change the world." She patted him on the shoulder. "It just takes one."

"Or, in this case, two," he said, smiling, grateful for Wen's reassurance. He kissed her. "It's just crazy enough that it might actually work."

"It'll work, because it *has* to work."

"A wing and a prayer," he said as the joyful voices of the workers reached them through the trees.

"All it's really doing is buying us time," Wen said. "Until we can come up with a better idea"

"But if this test brings down the 5EX network in Mexico, we can replicate it around the world. One guerilla strike after another. Like pirates taking on the Imperial Navy."

She nodded. "We can do it."

Chase and Wen had worked their way back around and stood high on a makeshift metal platform, which got them above the foliage in order to see Lo De Marcos spread out below.

Chase and Wen's elevated position allowed Doug Black to get a good look at them for the first time in nearly half an hour. He watched everything.

Wish I could read lips or had equipment to eavesdrop on their conversation, he thought, needing to know what they were saying. Instead, he made notes on a tiny paper tablet kept in his pocket. Every recorded time and movement would contribute to his payday. *Information is money.*

He carefully noted the time, even which direction they were looking in as part of his last entry. By the time they got back around to the others, the first ten foot section of the radio tower stood solid in fresh concrete.

Are they really going to rebuild that old thing . . . and use it? Black kept out of sight, but close enough to hear.

"It's real," Rob said, seeing Chase and Wen return. "It's going to happen!" He popped a large pink bubble and chewed furiously, as if the motion would make it all happen sooner, but Black knew they would be unable to finish today. The concrete had to set before they could stack additional weight on it.

So they'll be back tomorrow . . .

"The guys will untangle, straighten, and weld the remaining section before they leave. They'll come back up at first light to attach it," Rob explained, spitting his gum into the drying concrete and pressing it in with his foot.

"Will they be able to raise that weight?" Chase asked, thinking it would be so much easier to weld each section on the tower as they climbed.

"Pulleys and hoists," Rob said. "Mexican ingenuity."

Black let Chase and Wen get a lead on the way down. He hung back, watching through a small pair of binoculars as the workers straightened the bent sections. *This is a big deal*, he thought. *And I'm going to have to stop it.*

He moved swiftly through the jungle, finding heading downhill much easier, and soon caught up with Chase, Wen, and Rob. The whole time he was trying to figure out how he would sabotage the tower.

As soon as I get down, I'll call in and see how soon they can get me explosives.

Chapter Forty-One

Once they were back in town, Chase and Wen split from Rob, as he needed to organize the crew for the following morning when they would weld and test the tower. Meanwhile, Chase and Wen would go to meet with Juan about the Telmex equipment.

Chase steered the golf cart while Wen read from the directions, which were written in Spanish. "It feels like we're in some kind of third-world country club," Chase said as he took a turn and two more golf carts passed them.

"Apparently it's only been a few years since some enterprising entrepreneur introduced golf carts to the area," Wen said. "I bet all the seniors from Canada and the US didn't take any convincing."

"Better than ATVs," Chase said, recalling the narrow streets of Yelapa, in another part of Mexico where ATVs were used as the only vehicles in town. He shuddered, thinking of the friends he'd lost there.

"Yes," she agreed. "Rob told me that Lo De Marcos is

now somewhat crowded with golf carts. Most days they outnumbered cars."

"Yeah," Chase said, as they saw half a dozen more. "What street are we on?"

"I think this is Almada."

"Why don't they name their streets?"

"It's not that they don't *have* names. It's that they don't put up signs."

"Seems like a way to mess with the tourists," he said.

Wen laughed.

They passed a market with cases of Negra Modela beer stacked so high that Chase was concerned they would fall into the street and block their way.

"I hope the Telmex employee can really help us," Wen said.

"If we ever find his house," Chase said, swerving around a sleeping mutt.

"A lot of dogs, several on every block."

"The question is whether the little dogs will run under the golf cart, and if those big ones will *eat* the golf cart."

"They all seem friendly," she said, smiling.

"What about that one?" Chase pointed to a small dog barking at a moped speeding in from another street.

"Take a left up here," Wen said, frowning. "I think we might have company."

Chase noticed a green golf cart followed them on the turn. He step on the 'go' pedal.

Wen took the pistol out of her pack. "I wish our groceries had been delivered," she snapped, frustrated to only have the gun she'd taken from the man in San Pancho.

"More shadow people?"

"I don't know, want to pull over so I can ask them?"

"That's probably not a good idea."

"We could wait until they start shooting at us," she said.

"Rob told me he upgraded the controller, added a heavy-duty forward reverse switch, beefed up the motor, installed a solenoid . . . hopefully we can outrun them."

"Outrunning bullets isn't easy."

"It is still a *golf cart*."

They bounced over a speed bump as a rusted red Subaru went by. Wen momentarily considered carjacking it. Chase turned down a rutted dirt road.

"We shouldn't go this way," Wen said. "I think the only reason they haven't fired at us yet is they don't want to do it on the public streets."

"Isn't this a public street?"

"Not *as* public."

A bullet suddenly hit the front of the golf cart's frame.

"You were right." Chase said as two old horses crossed in front of the golf cart, forcing him to brake.

A full barrage of bullets followed, spooking the horses. Chase pushed the pedal down hard, with anticlimactic results. The golf cart took substantial hits, but somehow Chase and Wen avoided injury.

"Lose them!" Wen said, as if Chase were driving a muscle car.

He couldn't help but laugh.

"We're getting ahead, but we've got to go faster." Wen watched the green golf cart. "Keep the lead, keep the lead."

"I'm not sure speed should be our biggest worry," Chase said as he widened the gap. "I have no idea how fast the batteries drain."

Now well into the back areas of Lo De Marcos, the dirt streets were crowded with roosters, old cars, abandoned structures, and half-built buildings. The distance between the two carts narrowed and the golf cart's heavy plastic roof was suddenly shredded by apocalyptic machine gunfire.

Chapter Forty-Two

At one of the most remote pieces of wilderness in America, situated in Washington State, a remarkable structure sat perched on a snow covered cliff. It was the safest of safe houses.

But not anymore.

The six men and two women assigned to protect Tu and Zǔ mǔ—all ex-military, CIA, or FBI—had encountered just about every kind of situation, including tours of duty in combat zones and hotspots around the world. They were agents of Sepio, an elite, private security force utilized by the rich and famous around the globe. Chase liked to say that Sepio's exorbitant fees matched their skill level.

"Teaberry-Four, this is Teaberry-Leader, check-in." The Sepio agents had taken their codenames from the tiny red mountain berry that grew nearby.

"Teaberry-Four, all clear."

The Sepio crew had been alerted that Tu and Zǔ mǔ had to be moved because of an imminent threat. Another Sepio team was on their way to assist in that operation.

Until then, the Teaberry unit needed to keep them secure in their current location.

"We have just received new information," Teaberry-Three reported to Team-Leader. "They want us to move out *now*."

"Without reinforcements? Why, what's going on?"

Teaberry-Three relayed the instructions. The Leader opened up the radio channels.

"Everyone listen up," Teaberry-Leader said. "Change of plans. Apparently the exporters know our location."

Everyone knew "exporters" was code for the Chinese, and everyone knew that if the MSS hit them, there was a good chance some of the Sepios would not walk away—especially if their reinforcements didn't reach them first. Teaberry-Leader knew that Tu was a high-value target, and the MSS would commit resources that would exceed his own in the effort to obtain him. He was baffled at how the Chinese had located them.

"Take up positions," Teaberry-Leader said. They all had snow gear and the latest tech. "Teaberry-Two and Three get up on the deck with the sniper rifles. Teaberry-Four and Five secure the guard stations."

The concealed guard stations had been built between the gated entrance and the house. Advance military construction techniques had been utilized, making the stations highly rated defensive positions, and their best chance to stop any incursion.

"Copy that."

"Teaberry-Six and Seven, I want you in the opposite diamonds. From there, keep an eye on the air. We have no idea how they're coming in."

The diamonds had also been outlined as strategic areas and a hardline hold to the house.

"Watch the perimeters of both directions. The front road and the smaller back road out."

"Copy that. We're moving."

"I'll remain at the residence," Teaberry-Leader said. "To provide a last line of defense."

"ETA on our backup?"

"Still three hours out."

"That sucks."

"Factory is working on moving something in sooner," Teaberry-Leader replied, using the code name for Sepio Strategic Command. The secluded nature of their location in the remote mountains of Washington was working against them. No matter what they did, getting more personnel there was time consuming.

Seventy-seven minutes later, the MSS flew down with three civilian helicopters, each holding six men.

"Exporters coming strong," Teaberry-Six reported from the diamond. "Three choppers, six panthers in each." 'Panthers' referred to the MSS black ops agents, outfitted in black and green camo.

"Coming fast," Teaberry-Leader said. "Eighteen to eight. You each take two, and I promise I'll get the last four."

They all knew the Leader was not joking. He'd faced greater odds than this in many situations during his thirty year CIA career. Now in his late fifties, the Leader might not have the mobility and agility he once had, but his experience made up for it.

At the guard stations, Teaberry-Four lined up a shot, and came out of concealment firing. Teaberry-Five emerged simultaneously, and they each took out two panthers. Several other MSS operatives dove for cover in the surrounding area.

The panthers launched an RPG into one of the stations, blowing it, killing Teaberry-Four. Teaberry-Five brought two more panthers down in an ensuing firefight before a gas canister flew in.

"Teaberry Leader, T-Four is dead, and—"

In the haze and confusion, Teaberry-Five was surrounded and killed before he could finish.

Teaberry-Leader broke his own rule and rushed into the field to help his dwindling men. *My best chance to protect the assets is to stop these hostiles before they reach the house,* he thought, knowing if it was just him that survived to face the onslaught, the outcome would not be good.

Teaberry-Six and Seven fought hard in the diamonds, annihilating four panthers in less than three minutes. However, in less time than that, they also joined the dead.

A fresh snow began to fall.

"Ten remaining," Teaberry-Leader broadcast to his three surviving Sepios.

The odds hadn't changed, but as the panthers drew closer to the house, and their prize, Leader knew his chances were worse than ever.

Chapter Forty-Three

"This guy isn't a very good shot," Chase said after they'd both reported no injuries. The slow-motion high speed golf cart pursuit continued through the dusty streets of Lo De Marcos.

"Hard to shoot if you're bouncing around," Wen countered. "One of the reasons I'm not shooting back. The real question is, why doesn't he have a machine gun?"

"Maybe *his* groceries didn't get delivered either," Chase said. A bullet hit about an inch from his hand, blasting a chunk out of the steering wheel. "Time to shoot back!" he yelled.

"We have so little ammo."

"At least make them think twice about getting too close!"

The carts entered an area with a corner market, a laundromat, and too many people, so Wen held back. Surprisingly, the pursuers also stopped shooting. Wen finally fired as Chase turned right so fast that two tires lifted off the road, nearly tipping the cart.

"Did we get anything?" Chase asked.

"Nothing that *counts*!"

The golf cart stayed behind them, following like a magnet. A shot tore through the side, and another blew into the back seat.

"Sooner or later they're going to hit one of us," Wen said. "You need to lose them."

"You think?" Chase whipped around another corner. "Damn . . . dead end."

A high brick wall painted in faded colors of a long ago forgotten political candidate loomed in front of them. Wen leaned out onto the back of the cart, lining up her pistol as the green one barreled toward them. Seeing her, the driver veered left, and Wen's first shot went wide. The injured passenger returned fire, but Wen's second round found his chest. His bullets chipped into the brick wall several feet above and beyond their cart.

Wen almost fell out as Chase made a last second turn into what wasn't much more than a narrow courtyard, invisible until they reached the dead end of the alley. Chase navigated through the incredibly tight space, metal and paint scraping against the wall until they squeezed out the other end.

"Here they come!" Wen yelled. "And I'm almost out of bullets!"

An oversized Tecate beer box van steamed toward Chase and Wen. She stole a quick glance back to see how close the shadow people were. Less than twenty feet separated them.

Chase swerved onto a crumbling sidewalk to avoid the truck and sideswiped a crate of bananas and several bins full of avocados at a small vegetable stand. Rattling back down onto the cobblestone, they had their first real lead from the shadow people.

"We're lucky our cart is faster than theirs," Wen said.

"I don't call that luck." Chase turned around to check their lead. "If they had less ammunition than us, *that* would be luck."

"Watch the horses!" Wen yelled as two Mexican guides leading a group of five gringos on a horseback tour that would take them through the pretty sections of town and onto the beach—assuming Chase didn't plow into them first—crossed the road in front of them.

Chase steered the cart into the narrow space between the horses and a row of parked cars, but got too close. One of the horses spooked, reared, and threw its rider, a lanky Mexican in blue jeans and a cowboy hat. The horse dragged him along the cobblestone for ten or fifteen feet before the experienced hand was able to pull himself back onto his ride. The stunt would've gained a round of applause at any rodeo.

By then, Chase had already turned another corner and scattered a couple of American tourist families. Two young boys were the last to jump out of the way, cussing and yelling about nearly being run over by a crazy man driving a golf cart.

"Lots of obstacles," he said. "And we might run out of battery any second."

A minute later, they were back onto Universad, a street with a sign, and filled with newer gringo mansions. Unapologetic wealth, not trying too hard to blend in. The street was smoother, except for the potholes, and let them make some real "speed."

Chase hung a hard right onto a main drag, Camino Las

Minitas, and nearly had a collision with a gas truck that was continuously broadcasting "El gas, Global Gas." He sped past the La Jungla restaurant and a series of RV parks, including the one where Rob stayed, and headed on through the section of restored homes parallel to the beach, drawing closer to the center of town. Pushing the golf cart as hard as he could, Chase further widened the separation between them.

Wen looked behind them. "We may have lost them. Let's go!"

They rode up the main drag when the green golf cart shot out of a side street and pulled in right behind them.

"What the hell?" Chase snapped. "How did they do that?"

With the distance between the two golf carts now gone, the injured passenger fired directly at Wen.

Chapter Forty-Four

Inside the safe house, Tu and Zǔ mǔ were well aware of all the commotion. "Tu, you have to stay calm," Zǔ mǔ warned him as she saw the panic in his eyes. "Those security people are experts. They will protect us."

"We need to call Chase."

"We can't reach Chase and Wen right now. They far away, and can't help us."

"But—"

"That's why these men and women are here. To help us."

"But there are too many of the MSS. Maybe they will get all the people protecting us. They will take us, they will *hurt* us."

"These men from China, trying to hurt us, are bad men. We are good. We have that on our side."

Tu grimaced as more gunfire erupted nearby. "But the good do not always win."

"Tu, listen to me. You are smarter than all these people put together. If you are calm, you will be able to find a way to stop them." She took his hands and held his gaze with her ancient eyes. "If all those people out there died to save us, we must honor them by surviving this. Chase and Wen are counting on you and me to survive this."

An explosion interrupted her, but she held his eyes, even as he blinked.

"It has come to this," she went on. "This is more important than just you and I. Remember, in life, *never* be controlled by your fears."

Something in Zǔ mǔ's tone, in her eyes, worked like one of the old grandmother's magical herbal tonics.

Tu responded with a calm look of his own. "Okay, Zǔ mǔ. I will find a way. Those men will not win."

"Good boy."

"I will think like Chase and Wen," Tu said, beginning to look around their rustic, million-dollar lodge for ideas.

"Remember," Zǔ mǔ said. "They aren't all going to get into the house. There are eight warriors out there doing everything to stop those men from reaching us."

Two more explosions shook the house.

"We must hurry," Tu said. "We can beat them, but we must start now!"

The bullet from the injured golf cart passenger came nowhere near Wen. It didn't even hit their cart.

"He's weak!" Wen yelled.

"The driver is obviously well enough," Chase said, still marveling at how they had caught up. He took another turn down an angled side street, past a giant yellow triangle-shaped overpriced souvenir shop. Chase had been there earlier looking for a hat.

"This is crazy—where are you going?" Wen yelled.

"The only straightaway around. Heading to the highway."

"No," she said. "Let's get back out across to the other side of town."

Chase took the next turn, the green golf cart right behind them. Utilizing their advantage, Chase broke out across the busy main road coming in from the highway without slowing, barely missing a local Compostela bus. Their pursuers weren't so lucky. The big bus slammed into the green golf cart, sending it crashing over onto its side as the powerful vehicle pushed the tiny cart, scraping against the cobblestone before it finally came to a stop.

Wen jumped out and ran back to the accident scene. Bystanders were already gathering. She pushed through to check on the green cart's occupants. The passenger was dead, having hit his head and been caught in the front of the golf cart, then taken a bus tire to the face.

"He's a revolting mess," someone said in Spanish.

Wen found the driver laying a few feet to the side of the wrecked golf cart, still breathing, but gravely injured. She cradled his head. "Help is on the way, but you must tell me who sent you."

He moaned.

"*Please*, who sent you?" she repeated.

"Jekyll," he managed to say, his voice hoarse and strained.

"Jekyll?" she repeated.

"Yes," he moaned.

"What is Jekyll? Who is Jekyll?"

His eyes closed. His breathing ceased. Wen might've dropped his head on the road had there not been so many witnesses. Instead, she laid it gently down. Many of the witnesses were making the sign of the cross. Wen looked up and saw Chase standing in the crowd. She shook her head, indicating they were dead, and had given up no answers. Then she rose quietly and slipped into the crowd herself. The two of them melted away.

Chapter Forty-Five

Tu looked out the window. The snow-covered ridges looked like a fortress, but he now knew their safety had been compromised. "We must protect the house," he said, turning to Zǔ mǔ. "You must help."

"Yes, I help," she said.

"I think you should fill pots with boiling water."

"Why?"

"Men with guns cannot shoot well if their face is filled with boiling water."

Zǔ mǔ smiled, and quickly went into the kitchen.

"I think another place where we can stop them," Tu said, now talking to himself, "is on the dangerous deck."

The deck, one of the highlights of the luxurious-rustic lodge, had a million-dollar view. Perched above a seventy foot drop, other than a small patio carved out beneath, the sweeping overhang jutted out from a near vertical rock face. It had always made Tu nervous, even though Zǔ mǔ loved the view. He could not bring himself to go to the edge of the railing.

Now I must do what Zŭ mŭ told me. I must turn my fear into strength.

Tu stepped onto the snowy deck. From there, he could see much of the property, glistening in white. He spotted three Sepios, dug in, defending Zŭ mŭ and him. Then, right before his eyes, one of them fell, his body ripped apart by bullets, the pure white snow splattered red.

Tu couldn't even tell where the attack had come from. He wanted to run, but the action, so far below, was riveting. A Chinese invader went down, and then another, but then one of his Sepio heroes was blown apart. Tu began to shake.

"I don't know what to do," he said out loud, suddenly a little boy again.

The third Sepio killed another MSS agent. Even though it was one of the bad guys, it still scared Tu. He screamed as the third Sepio died in a violent rampage.

Tu ran back inside. "Zŭ mŭ!" he shrieked. "They are killing us all!"

Juan, an eleven-year Telmex employee, had lived in Lo De Marcos all his life—except for three years when Telmex had sent him to Guadalajara. He much preferred Lo De Marcus, not only because it was home, but because Juan loved the sea.

Chase and Wen arrived at Juan's door exhausted and shaken. The front walk and porch were creatively crafted from river rock laid out in a mosaic-like design. The house, painted sunshine yellow and turquoise, seemed quite inviting, while the neighboring house was made of rough gray concrete and in need of much work.

"Is everything okay?" Juan asked after opening the door and getting a look at them. A little Chihuahua scurried from behind him and barked. "Don't bother our guests, Patitas," Juan told the dog.

"Yes," Chase said unconvincingly. "What's his name mean?" he pointed to the dog.

Juan smiled. "Patitas means little leg."

Chase laughed. "It fits."

"Si." Juan looked at Wen still concerned. "Are you sure it's okay, you seem upset."

"Crazy day," Wen said.

"If I can help . . . let me know."

"We did have a little trouble finding the place," Chase said, waving a hand. "That doesn't matter now, we're here. Can we talk about 5EX?"

"I understand the problem," Juan said. "I have been concerned about 5EX myself for some time. I have to work there, and so many people say the health issues are serious."

"I believe they are," Chase said. "But you understand this is about more than that."

"Si, pero. I think I can help."

"It could be very risky," Wen said.

He nodded and shrugged. A concerned smile hid behind his bushy black mustache.

"Why are you willing to do this?" Chase asked. "Why jeopardize your career, maybe more?"

"I'm a member of *the* family," he said, as if it should have been obvious. "The head of our family asked me to help, and when the head of the family asks you to do something, you do it, because you are part of the family, and they are the head of the family."

"At the expense of your safety?" Chase asked.

"They have earned the respect and obedience from

members of the family. I would never question that. In this case, it is simply extra that I am concerned for my own health. Anyway, I think I can help without causing problems for me." He gestured for them to follow him out to a back courtyard.

Chase liked Juan immediately, and trusted his reasoning for helping. "Did you talk to Rob about our situation? I mean *specifically*?"

"Si, he filled me in on most of what I think you want to do. That is why I can say I think I can help." Juan disappeared for a moment and returned with a pitcher of water, thick, blue-rimmed Mexican glasses, and a plate of cookies.

"Is it possible?" Chase asked, reaching for a cookie, raising it in thanks before devouring it.

"Si, I think we can do this. I don't know all the specifics, if it will actually bring down the network, but I know that we can do what you want. Get the signal out."

"Is there time?"

Juan laughed. "In Mexico, time is a funny thing."

Chapter Forty-Six

Teaberry-Leader's real name was Dan Naurock, but over the course of his three decades in service, he'd earned another nickname. His buddies, subordinates, and superiors alike, called him "Rock" because he was unyielding, steady, and powerful in the face of any enemy. Now, after monitoring the action on the radio, Rock knew he was the last man standing, that seven deadly panthers were coming for the boy.

They'll have to go through me.

Rock had no time to warn or prepare Tu and Zǔ mǔ. He had already given them a heads-up just before the siege began, and advised on precautions they should take. The dusting of snow wasn't going to make things easier, but there were some advantages, and Rock would always take any edge.

"Hide," he'd told them. "Stay away from windows and doors." There should have been a safe room where they could barricade themselves inside an impenetrable space.

There would be one in the place they were going next, but he knew they would likely never get there.

The odds are that whatever they've done to prepare, or wherever they've hidden, will not be enough, he thought. *Stopping seven MSS assassins without a team . . . This is a suicide mission.*

However, Dan Naurock couldn't think of anything more worth dying for than to protect the little boy and an old lady from killer Communists agents.

I can do this . . . I'll take them all out. Barring that, I'll be damn sure I take as many with me as I can. The more down, the better the chance the kid has of surviving.

Of course, he had another pulsating reason to kill all the MSS agents; they had just massacred his buddies, men and women with families.

No more time for thinking. Ol' Rock still has some tricks up his sleeves. You panther pigs are about to find out how we do things in America.

Counting on having far more experience than his opponents, a little luck, and even some divine intervention, Rock mumbled a quick prayer, shoved a fresh magazine in his gun, grabbed the RPG, and moved out, knowing that even if he caught all possible breaks, it still might not be enough.

Juan showed Chase and Wen a map of the central Mexican Coast and pointed to the ridge above Lo De Marcos. "We are lucky that there is already a tower on top of the peak."

"But it is currently broken up," Wen said.

"Si, pero, it is nothing to repair. My cousin is a welder. He will go up, and uno, dos, tres. Pero, we hope the concrete sets today, tomorrow it may rain. And I think some cable would help."

"Like a guy-wire?" Chase asked.

"Si. We anchor into the trees up top. They are very strong."

"What about the QAMEX?" Chase asked. The quadrature amplitude modulation extender was the magic of 5EX, setting it light years ahead of all the next-gen mobile networks that had come before it.

"I can get it, no problem," Juan said, smiling as if it were a silly question.

Wen was distracted, watching the street through the windows, waiting for more shadow people, the police, or worse, agents for the consortium.

"Really?" Chase asked, surprised such a valuable piece of equipment could be so readily attainable.

"Si, is no problem," he repeated.

"And then receiving the signal?" Chase asked.

"Rob has a good idea. We use a shrimp boat, take it out to the horizon."

"We'll need receiving and transmission equipment."

"I can get, no problem. Pero, the big thing is a waveGrader. That's what tends the signal and processes the QAMEX."

"Where will we get that?"

"There is one in Lo de Marcos." Juan showed a toothy grin. "Inside a secure Telmex storage shed. We can borrow it." He sat at the edge of a handmade, leather bound, wooden framed chair, pontificating with stout arms and expressive hands, like a raconteur telling a story of long ago. He embodied a strange calmness, as if he were a wise old prophet.

What an interesting man, Wen thought. *So real and unpretentious. I could listen to him all day.*

"I'll be right back," she said, stepping outside before Chase could ask her if something was wrong.

"We'll pick it up in the truck and drive it out to launch," Juan continued. "When the fishing boats go out, we can connect with the shrimp boat . . . that is the easy part."

"The tower is the trick?" Chase asked.

"Si, pero. Once the tower is back up, it will broadcast our signal to the horizon and the ship will send it from there."

"The 5EX network relies entirely on continuity," Chase said, looking out the window, trying to see where Wen had gone.

Juan nodded. "And for their test, there will be no redundancy. Of course, in the final set up, there will be redundancy for multiple places, so if they lose one or two, even four, no problem, that stays. Pero, in this case for trial, there is no redundancies."

"Meaning if we interrupt the signals, the network will crash."

"Just like that!"

"You make it sound so simple," Chase said.

"It is what I do. It *is* simple, and I hope it works because if the transmission fails, we get a *long* delay. Isn't that what you want?"

"We'll need more than a long delay, but we've got to start somewhere.

"Si, the journey of a thousand miles begins with the first step. We take that step today."

"Gracias," Chase said. "Don't you have to get people to help us?"

"It has been all arranged. It is Saturday, so there are extra people."

"Okay. You let me know how much we need to pay them," Chase said.

"You can discuss that with my grandfather."

"Of course."

Wen came back in. "We need to go."

"Everything okay?" Juan asked.

"Yes. I'm sorry, but we're late for a meeting." She stared into his eyes for an extra moment, reached out her hand, and warmly shook Juan's. "Muchas gracias. Another time, I hope we meet in different circumstances. And the recipe to those cookies, maybe?"

"Thanks for all your help, Juan. We'll see you later," Chase said, knowing there was no meeting.

Chapter Forty-Seven

Rock knew the RPG could only be used once. After he fired, they would know where he was, and they would kill him.

I've got to take out as many as I can with it.

A few minutes later, when the seven agents split up, he discovered that luck had laughed at him.

He checked his "scopes," the cameras eyes that were scattered around the property and the exterior of the house and several out buildings, but it wasn't constant coverage. Just enough to tell him he was screwed.

I'm gonna have to burn an RPG on one lousy panther . . . damn, he realized as he looked to see which one was the most heavily armed. Rock sent the rocket and began running, his boots giving him good traction in the slick terrain. He didn't see the result of the blast, but heard it as the ordinance annihilated its target.

One down, six to go.

Seconds later, incoming fire obliterated Rock's former

hiding place, but he had moved fast, knowing the property, the shortcuts, and where every one of his opponents were.

He caught the next panther from behind, slitting his throat and dashing toward the next target.

Two down, five to go.

Rock had not wasted time searching for communications on his victims. He knew there would be none. Experience told him MSS assassins arrived as units, yet worked as individuals. They did not carry communications so operations could not be compromised by a fallen friendly. Their exacting training and precise tactics meant an agent could anticipate what each one was going to do, where they would be.

The same regime had given Wen the advantage through the years when facing her former comrades. However, she wasn't there that day. Even though she would've moved all of the earth and killed anybody in her way to get there, she could never have made it in time.

Chase looked at Wen as they walked out of Juan's home. "What's going on?"

"Tu . . . Zǔ mǔ . . . they're under attack."

Chase swallowed hard, stomach dropping into a pit of acid. "Who?"

"I don't know," she said, jogging now. They had abandoned the bullet-riddled golf cart in a deserted overgrown courtyard before arriving at Juan's. Rob would have to get it later and sell it for parts. Chase would make sure he got a new one.

"Where are you going?" Chase asked.

"To our place. The groceries will be there."

Chase could see that Wen wanted to go back to the States, to save Tu and her grandmother, but it would be impossible. "Did you try calling them?" A ridiculous question, Chase knew.

"Yes," she snapped. "As soon as I received the panic report text from Sepio, I tried, but nothing will go through. *Tu and Zǔ mǔ!*" Her words came out quietly, but he knew she was screaming within.

"Sepio will protect them," Chase tried to console her, but he didn't believe it himself. He dialed Dez's number at the same time Wen was calling the Astronaut.

"We're too far away," Dez said, looking at the map. "He's in the middle of nowhere. *Everyone* is too far away."

"Helicopters? A corporate jet with paratroopers? *Anything*?" Chase asked, desperate.

"I don't think so," Dez said. "I'll call Sepio, but . . . "

"The Astronaut thinks he can get a satellite to see the safehouse," Wen interrupted.

Chase had a flash of watching the footage of his father dying. He didn't want to repeat the torture of seeing MSS agents or shadow people kill Tu. "What good does seeing do?"

"We can get a drone there."

"A military drone?"

She nodded.

"How? Tess will never help us."

"The Astronaut doesn't need her permission," she said. "He can take control of one through Heaven."

Chase knew about the extremely classified computer network of the US Intelligence services, but had no idea it interfaced with the military. "Really?"

"Command and Control can be accessed through Heaven."

"A precision hit? In time?" he asked, wanting to believe, but his logical mind was already calculating the impossible odds.

"It's all we have!" Wen yelled. "It's going to work because we have *nothing* else!"

Chapter Forty-Eight

Rock left the MSS agent's weapons behind. He already had more than he could use. Running through the trees, Rock knew his next strike would bring attention to himself, but he had no choice.

I can't get close enough to use my knife. I've got to reach the house before they do.

Rock opened fire with his machine gun, easily cutting down another panther since the man had no idea Rock would be there. "Three down, four to go," he whispered as he continued running.

I told my team I would get four. I've gotten three for them, but now I have to get my four.

He knew two agents would be coming for him, and two more would be going to the house.

He stole glances at the tablet strapped to his wrist as he moved quickly, stealthily, through the brush, checking the panthers' locations and guessing which two would be coming his way. Fortunately he had the visuals, because he'd been wrong about one of them. Adjusting his route, Rock decided on a hand grenade to take out the two coming for him.

I just need you two scumbags to get close enough to each other to eat shrapnel.

Realizing he was close to part of the perimeter defenses, he went toward them, making sure to make noise, breaking branches on the way.

A fire trap will be perfect, he thought, tapping the tablet. *And it's on the way to the house.*

Once the two were near, he remotely triggered the trap. machine guns fired as expected, knowing it wouldn't reach them, but would distract and draw them closer. He waited, counted to three, then lobbed a hand grenade.

Four and Five down, two to go.

Rock bolted straight for the house, knowing the last two agents would make their defense in the residence and prioritize their objective to capture or kill the boy.

Checking his wrist tablet, he saw the real-time image of only one of them.

Damn, it's from one of the house cams. He continued moving faster while circling back around, hoping to get there first. "I might even be able to intercept you," he hissed to the image on his tablet. *If that happens, there could be a chance to win this thing . . .*

The timing will have to be perfect.

His thoughts were agonizing as he reformulated his plans yet again. Rock had to intercept one of them fast. If not, the other one could get to the house before him and reach Tu. He recalled doing a similar maneuver in Libya twenty years earlier.

I've got the angles.

The house was now visible through the trees and on his

wrist. *It's an easy sprint, old man. Panther should be coming to me in about fifteen or twenty seconds.*

He checked again and saw that the second agent was still farther from the house. Rock silently thanked Chase for letting them strategically prepare the property with blockades and traps so anybody would have to take a far more convoluted approach.

Silently he mouthed, "Ten, nine . . . "

Still camouflaged.

"Eight, seven . . . "

The shot was almost there.

"Six, five . . . "

He wanted to fire blind, knowing where the panther was, but couldn't risk it. Not for the little boy.

"Four, three . . . "

He aimed his submachine gun, checked his wrist. Saw both men.

"Two, *one* . . . "

The gun felt good as the bullets flew. He knew it was a kill. Rock could always tell by how the gun felt firing, sort of like how a baker listens to a cake for doneness before pulling it out of the oven. He allowed himself a brief smile, remembering his grandma's words as the man crumpled.

He was back on his feet, moving toward the house, when the burning, tearing, agony of lead entering his back sent Rock into the ground. He rolled over and fired wildly, hoping to get whoever had hit him, but his shots only went into some trees.

He knew it had been an armor-piercing round since it had penetrated his Kevlar vest, but he had no idea who the shooter could have been. "How the . . . " He glanced at his wrist and saw the second man was still a safe distance away from him. "Who else is there?"

Playing the past fifteen minutes over in his mind, Rock remembered he hadn't waited after he'd thrown the hand grenade. He cussed, figuring that obviously one of those two had survived.

He tried to get up. *Not happening.* He tried to crawl. *No.* He strained for any real movement and tasted metal. His chest felt tight, like the pressure as if he were underwater, as it pumped out blood. *Everywhere.*

"Sorry kid," he said, knowing there were only seconds left.

Rock raised his gun, blurry eyed, trying to find a target. *The bastard who shot me might come this way, or might already be on his way to the house.* He tried desperately to see the screen on his wrist, but couldn't raise his arm, or his head. A breath later, he was dead.

Rock had taken out five. It had almost been enough.

Chapter Forty-Nine

Tu looked out from the deck, unaware that Rock had just died, his last defender gone. "I have a feeling it's not good, Zǔ mǔ."

"We are not fighters," Zǔ mǔ said. "But we will fight."

Tu looked into the old woman's eyes and found so much strength there, he almost believed she could single-handedly defeat a battalion of MSS agents. "And my brain can be used as a weapon," he said fiercely, as if realizing it for the first time. "That is why they are coming after us, they want to use that weapon . . . But *I* will use the weapon *against* them."

Zǔ mǔ nodded, a weak smile on her face. "Yes, but we must be . . ."

She hesitated, wanting to caution him, to remind him that these men were trained killers, with every advantage and weapon at their disposal. She wanted to save him from harm, but in that instant she realized *he* was their best chance. If he failed to stop them, if he died trying, it would be better because if they got him, Tu's life would be over anyway.

"I am the grandmother of Wen, the great warrior. She has *my* blood running in her veins." Her face turned into a determined, forceful expression. "These men came to the wrong house."

"We don't have much time," Tu said. "I think our traps will work, but we need some kind of weapon, just in case." They had used the time Rock had bought them rigging up traps for their unsuspecting guests, some simple, some ingenious. Zǔ mǔ was skeptical they would do anything but slow their attackers.

While Tu dumped the contents of his large marble collection inside the front hall, Zǔ mǔ went to the downstairs cedar closet. It was the place where Wen had told her to hide if there was ever any trouble. "*The last resort.*" Some of the places they had stayed had elaborate, nearly impenetrable safe rooms. This one had no such space. Instead, there was a walk-in cedar closet. On the top shelf, in a locked case, Wen had left a gun she hoped Zǔ mǔ would never have to use—a Glock 19 pistol, 9mm, with a fifteen round magazine.

Zǔ mǔ knew what she had to do.

Tu ran in from the deck. His hands were shaking. "Here they come."

"How many?" Zǔ mǔ asked, carrying the third boiling pot.

"Two so far."

"Show me." She put down the pot and followed him back out onto the deck.

"Careful, not there." He pointed to the side of the deck where he had finished pushing fresh snow.

"Okay. Remember, bring in that saw," she said quietly, as the men got closer.

They went to the edge and looked over, careful to stay hidden behind the railing's thick beam.

"The men will go right under here," she said. "Help me with this."

Tu looked at the heavy redwood chaise, its cushions stored for the winter. "It's too heavy," he said.

"Heavy for me, too. We can do it together."

They braced it against the railing, and kind of half pushed, half rolled it up to the top.

"Don't let it go yet," she whispered, trying to anticipate the men's steps.

"I think three more seconds," Tu said, so softly that she barely heard.

"One," she mouthed holding up a single finger.

He held up two fingers.

"Three," they whispered together, and then let the chaise fall. Zǔ mǔ dashed back inside quickly to finish her work. Tu could not resist watching from behind the railing slats as the chaise plunged seventy feet, crashing into the back of one of the MSS agents.

The man let out a terrible, animal sound as the heavy patio furniture flattened him into the snowy ground.

The other one immediately began firing his machine gun up at the deck. Tu rolled away and jumped back into the house, squealing, "We hit one, we hit one!"

"Good, but there are more. We must finish," Zǔ mǔ said.

Emboldened by his success, Tu ran to the small, detached garage to implement a phase of his scheme he'd been too afraid to attempt earlier. He grabbed the heavy, five-gallon can of gas and headed back to the house. Heaving the big red poly can upstairs to the master bedroom, he positioned the container, then climbed the narrow flight of steps that led into a small attic bedroom, where he sometimes played.

Tu looked out the high dormer window protruding from the steep third floor roof, and to his dismay, saw two agents running up the driveway. He could not tell for sure, but was fairly certain they were the same two, although he did notice one was limping slightly.

"I guess my lawn chair bomb did not stop him," he muttered, out of breath. "They got here sooner than I thought."

Tu waited until they were close enough to the house. The broad edge of the eaves, lined with eighteen-inch long icicles, were only part of his attack plan. The roof was packed with six-inches of thick snow, also a weapon.

"You may think it is only a little snow," he mumbled to himself, as if talking to the men, "but I did the calculations in my mind. There is sixteen feet of snow between the window and the edge, and if a six foot wide section falls, that snow will weigh more than a ton! Two thousand, four hundred, eighty-seven pounds . . . approximately. All falling on your heads."

He had also estimated the velocity and overall force of the impact by taking into account the pitch of the steep roof, the twelve foot drop to the ground in free fall, and a number of other factors. It would be a brutal hit, but he secretly hoped the icicles would impale them first, although he knew that was not really possible.

"Either way, bad men, it will hurt . . . a *lot*."

Chapter Fifty

The Astronaut had exhaustively worked every contact, tried every trick, called in every favor, used every secret to gain access to a satellite that could view the safe house, while knowing none of it would matter if he couldn't figure a way to wrangle an armed drone to use on American soil.

Chase and Wen paced the open concrete roof of the building where they were staying. "How soon until we get visuals?" Chase asked.

Wen shook her head, as if unable to speak. Chase imagined she was trying to use her mind to somehow fight the battle thousands of miles to the north. Her concentration reminded Chase of his meditations, only she wasn't trying to clear her mind, she was searching it, delving into all her experience, desperate to find a solution. But Chase knew there was nothing they could do, and fought his own losing battle against the choking frustration.

"He got it though, right?" Chase asked, trying to engage her.

"Yes, and he'll ping us when pictures are live." At least

Chasing Mind

Wen was speaking, but it obviously annoyed her to do so. They'd come to the roof because it was their best chance to get coverage. Chase was pleased to discover that from one corner, if he leaned out far enough, an ocean view could be found. Needing something, anything, to look at, he walked back over there again, and wished he could fly.

Still triumphant over the patio furniture attack, Tu hoped this one would do more damage. All it took was a simple push broom, hit at just the right spots, and the roof avalanche took off. The sharp icicles came down like freezing daggers, followed by more than a ton of heavy, wet snow.

The icicles did not make a direct hit on either agent, but did graze the side of the face of the chaise victim. However, the snow slammed down on its targets with the projected crushing force of Tu's earlier calculations, leveling, and then burying both men.

The snow had been fast and heavy, but not deep enough to permanently remove the threat. The furious MSS agents came up shooting. Tu was already gone, running off to set the next trap.

The two panthers rushed the front door, shot out the locks, and kicked their way in, only to slip and land flat on their backs again. This time, Tu's collection of 1,278 marbles, bunched inside the door, had been the weapon. He actually owned 1,282 marbles, but had held onto his four favorites, which remained in his pocket for safekeeping.

As Tu ran through the house, he could hear the men yelling, and realized that had Wen been there, she would have been in position to shoot the men after the avalanche, or the marble incident. He wished she had been there.

But if Wen were here, these bad men never would have gotten this far. These men would be dead.

Back on their feet, the agents gave silent hand signals, cautiously heading down the hall. They each stood before a closed door on opposite sides of the hall. With guns ready, they timed it to open the doors simultaneously. Instantly, pots of scalding water fell down on each of them. Screaming in Mandarin, they backed into the hall.

"It's acid! I think it's acid—my eyes are burning!"

"This hell house!" the other said, clawing his back. Not much had hit his face, but the concoction had burned his neck and back. "I'm going to kill you all!" he shouted wildly.

It wasn't acid, but Zǔ mǔ had loaded the boiling water with all the cayenne she had in the house, and added several Chinese herbs that would cause burning and itching to the skin.

"Obviously there is no security left protecting the old woman and little kid," the agent hit by the chaise said, still trying to clear his eyes.

"Yes," the other hissed, "but even these amateurs have taken us down *three times*. They are getting the best of us."

"Not for long," chaise-agent whispered.

A loud noise rattled from upstairs. Chaise-agent motioned to himself, then pointed up. The other indicated he would stay down.

Chaise-agent cautiously climbed the stairs. The scowl on his face had a tentative hint of fear, as if he knew a vicious dog or poison darts could be awaiting him. There were two rooms upstairs, and another narrow spiral staircase leading to a loft. He quickly surveyed the areas, seeing one door was closed, the other open. He went to the closed door.

Slowly opening it, he extended his arm in first, in case something fell on him. Nothing. Beyond the door was a large master bedroom.

Where would a kid hide?

He saw a small shoe sticking out from under the bed and smiled. The man leaped onto the bed, quickly grabbed the shoe, and yanked the kid out. Only it wasn't Tu. The shoe and sock were attached to a pair of pants stuffed with rags. He moaned, then realized, to his horror, the entire room smelled of gasoline.

Chaise-agent turned to flee. At the same moment, a large flaming ball of wadded up newspaper landed on the bed. Almost instantaneously, the mattress and entire room erupted in flames. The man, already on fire himself, dove for the door. The flames overtook him, and he dropped and rolled, but the entire floor was engulfed. Crawling, he finally reached the door, but it wouldn't open. Something had jammed or blocked it from the other side.

Chapter Fifty-One

The Astronaut clicked the switch reluctantly. Having seen an advanced overview of the scene, he knew how upsetting it would be to Chase, and especially to Wen.

"It's . . . it's . . . Oh, no . . . it's worse than I thought," Chase said.

Wen, surveying the scene less like a parent and more like a trained intelligence operative, first looked for any sign of movement, of life. Seeing nothing dynamic, she recreated each battle, every step of the MSS agents. Knowing their tactics, she systematically replayed the events in her mind, picturing with startling accuracy the details of how everything had happened.

"It looks like it's over," Chase managed.

Parts of the property were heavily treed, most of it sloping, rocky terrain, which was what had first attracted them to the area. The topography was ideally suited for a safe house—remote, inaccessible, concealed—yet those same qualities made it difficult for them to see certain aspects of specific battles.

"Guard stations," she said, pointing, knowing what had transpired there. She traced the images from the live feed. "Diamonds." She knew Rock would have told his people to defend from there. Wen recalled meshing her experience and ideas with the team from Sepio. She'd been especially impressed with Rock, and believed he would die to protect Tu and her grandmother.

Wen's finger found Rock's fallen body. Her heart sank. "No," she said, her voice pained and scared.

"What?" Chase gasped, afraid she might have seen Tu severely injured or dead.

"Can we zoom in more?" she asked the Astronaut.

Then Chase could see it, too. He recognized Rock, and felt her grief. Rock would have been the last line of defense, and would have fought to his final breath.

Chase joined her frantic scanning of the area as the astronaut zoomed in and out, canvassing for more bodies, more evidence. Nothing. The trees hid too much.

Wen, frustrated that the cameras could not see inside the house, pleaded with The Astronaut to get as close as he could.

"Smoke," she barked.

Chase saw it too, at first thinking it was from one of the wood stoves or fireplaces inside.

"Zoom on the smoke," Wen demanded.

"There's too much," Chase whispered.

Then all three of them saw the flames breaking through the sidewall.

"I think that's the master bedroom," Wen said.

"The roof," Chase said, as the fire reached it. "That means it's burned through Tu's play area on the floor above."

Wen preferred the agony of watching to not knowing

anything. Somehow, Chase, too, felt a little stronger, and less helpless, while witnessing the scene. He was enduring a separate hell as memories of his father's death flooded his mind, yet he could not turn away, willing the camera to find Tu, to show him alive.

Zǔ mǔ heard the burning man screaming upstairs and prayed that meant Tu had escaped. But she knew there was at least one more threat left.

I must protect Tu.

The gun scared her. She had never fired one before, never even held one, but she knew it was their best chance, perhaps their only chance. Having no idea where the other man was, or if more were coming, she knelt behind the center island and moved around until she was in front of the opening to the great room and the hall beyond. From her concealed spot, she could see the door to the deck and approximately a third of the way down the hall. From this angle it looked clear, but she wasn't sure.

Zǔ mǔ steadied her nerves and stood up. Her knees popped. She thought it sounded like the loudest noise in the world, and hoped nobody heard.

If I can get behind the couch, I might be able to shoot him when he comes down the hall. She shivered. *Can I really shoot a person?* She nodded instinctively. *These men are here to kill us or to take Tu. I will not let that happen.*

The shadows shifted in the room.

The time is now.

Zǔ mǔ took a deep breath and quickly climbed onto the couch. In one motion, she rose above its upholstered back.

The black and green clad agent seemed gigantic in the opening to the hallway.

A monster, a horrible creature.

Their eyes locked.

She pulled the trigger.

He fired.

The three 9mm bullets that escaped her gun's chamber embedded themselves into the wood paneled wall almost two feet from the agent. His single shot penetrated the flesh just above her thigh.

It was the most painful thing she'd ever felt. Zǔ mǔ fell backwards off the couch. Her head slammed into the floor, but she hardly felt it. The excruciating pain from the gunshot stole the attention of every nerve in her body. In the moments it took her to focus, panic ripped her consciousness apart.

The gun! I dropped the gun! Where is the gun!

Through fuzzy eyes, she saw the monster coming toward her.

Did I scream?

The cloudiness took over her vision, her mind.

Am I still screaming?

She reached out, trying to find the gun.

He's coming! Where's Tu?

She continued grappling for the gun, her only hope.

It kicked back so much when I fired . . .

She tried to see her wrist, sure it had snapped from the force of the weapon, but Zǔ mǔ could feel nothing. Nothing but the gunshot wound.

Having taken care of the "old woman," the panther went to find the "sneaky kid."

Chapter Fifty-Two

Tu darted past the last panther in the hall. He ran to the great room. "Zǔ mǔ!" he yelled as he caught a blurring glimpse of her blood-covered body. Knowing he could not stop, and the sight of her laying upside down, lifeless . . . the blood . . . suddenly his resolve, his confidence, all collapsed into terror. He wiped the tears welling in his eyes, desperate.

Still moving, Tu pinched his cheek. "Focus!"

After nearly crashing into the sliding glass door, he threw it open as he had dozens of times before, but a fleeting thought told him this might be the last. He slid across the snow-covered deck, not knowing if he was brave enough to handle the moments to come. Fighting every urge to cry, he positioned himself against the heavy wooden railing and turned to face the evil man following him out the door.

The MSS agent aimed a submachine gun at the little boy and spoke in Mandarin. "I should shoot you *right now*. All your nasty little tricks. What do you say? You are not so smart now."

Tu said nothing, just stared doe-eyed at the panther.

"Yes, they say you are supposed to be so smart, but you ran out here and trapped yourself like a little pig in a pen."

Tu looked from side to side, as if trying to find a way to escape.

"There's nowhere to go little piggy. But lucky for you, you are worth more to me alive than dead . . . quite a bit more."

Tu continued to look around, a panicked expression on his face.

The agent shook his finger at Tu. "But don't think that means I won't shoot you if you do anything crazy. In fact, get over here right now!" The man reached into one of his pockets, pulling out heavy duty nylon restraints. "Going to hogtie you, piggy."

Tu shook his head. At the same time, he began fidgeting with something in his hands.

"You get over here! Don't make me tell you again, or I might just take a pay cut and bring back your severed hands for proof of my kill."

The words, in Tu's native language, frightened him more than anything he had ever heard. He thought he was about to die. He wanted to run. He was so scared he even considered surrendering to the agent's demands. Instead, he looked at his hand again. This time the action caught the panther's attention.

"What you got there? What are you hiding? Show me!"

Tu shook his head again.

The man fired his machine gun, sending rounds flying barely above Tu's head. "You tell me boy, or next time I won't miss!"

He shook his head slowly, as if thinking it over this time.

"Show me what's in your hand!"

"No!" Tu said in a firm voice that enraged the panther.

"You are going to regret that, you little pig. I'll come over there and *take* it from you. I might toss you over." The MSS agent advanced, leading with the machine gun, his finger caressing the trigger, eyes filled with fury. He reached for Tu's hand.

Tu opened his hand and threw the contents into the panther's face, stunning him just enough so that he froze for an instant. Then Tu pushed the entire weight of his little body against the panther's legs.

The man flew backwards, crashing into the wooden railing that Tu had so carefully sawed earlier, left within a fraction of separating. For a seemingly endless slow-motion moment, it felt as if the railing would hold, but as the man shifted, trying to recover from the blow, the wood broke through, sending him off the deck, cascading backwards into open air. Flailing wildly, the panther realized his plight, but his feet found nothing, and his hands couldn't reach anything.

He plunged seventy feet, landing in a heaping pile on the hard, cold, snowy ground.

The momentum and force of the stunt carried Tu, sliding in the snow, to the edge of the deck. Too slick to stop, at the last instant he reached out a hand for the post he knew was solid and caught it even as his legs went over, feet dangling above the same abyss that had swallowed the enemy. He screamed silently, as if knowing to do so out loud would cost the strength he needed to hold on. Yet it was absolute fear that had stolen his voice.

I'm going to fall, he thought, his cold fingers weak.

He looked for someone to rescue him.

No one came.

Chapter Fifty-Three

Wen and Chase sat riveted, unable to take their eyes off the screen as they watched Tu run out on the deck. "There he is!" Wen said, as now half the house was in flames.

Chase laughed with relief at the sight of their precious boy. "He's alive!"

"Oh no," Wen said, as the MSS agent appeared on the deck.

Chase clenched his fist as the man pointed his machine gun at Tu.

"Where are we with the drone?" Wen snapped.

"It's not looking good," The Astronaut reported. "I'm having trouble accessing the authorization codes. Nothing is working."

"Maybe Zǔ mǔ is still . . . I mean she could save him," Chase said.

Wen looked at the wide shot of the burning house and shook her head. "I don't think so."

"He's yelling at Tu," Chase said. "What's he saying?"

There was no sound, but enough detail to see the rage on the agent's face.

"No!" Wen yelled as the man move toward Tu.

"We have two Sepio helicopters approaching," The Astronaut said.

"How close?"

"Eighteen minutes."

Chase swallowed hard, knowing it wouldn't be soon enough.

Wen screamed. It all happened so fast. Suddenly Tu was hanging on for his life.

"Come on, Tu, pull yourself up! You can do it!" Wen said

Chase's hands involuntarily moved, as if reaching out to grab the brave little boy.

The Astronaut realized he was holding his breath.

The seconds seemed endless. The collective silence only broke as Tu appeared to be slipping. All three of his guardians let out desperate sounds.

"Tu, you are strong!"

His grip weakening, Tu closed his eyes, not wanting to see what awaited below.

Then he thought of Wen, as if he could hear her.

He opened his eyes, focusing on the deck. *Wen would do this . . . she could do it . . . and so can I.*

Finding the last ounce of courage and strength, Tu reached his other arm around, took hold of the post with both hands, and, struggling against his own weight, gravity, and pure exhaustion, he somehow pulled himself up.

"Oh my god," Chase mouthed in relief.

Wen wiped away tears.

The Astronaut smiled so big it hurt, and then remembered to breathe.

Tu lay on the snowy deck, catching his breath. Then he saw his favorite marble, one he called the Eysen, because it looked like a special artifact from one of his favorite books. He held it up to the sun, looked at the colors swirling in the tiny sphere, and smiled. The four marbles had saved him.

"You wanted to know what was in my hand," he said, as if talking to the now dead agent. "Now you know." Tu was sorry to have lost the rest of his favorites, but throwing them at the man had been his only choice.

"Zǔ mǔ!" he suddenly yelled, scrambling to his feet as he recalled her bloody body. It was then he realized the house was an inferno, and he was not going to be safe until he got through the raging fire.

Chase looked at the screen. "How is Tu going to get out of the house?"

Wen was realizing the same thing. They both knew the structure. There was no way off the high deck other than to go inside. "The fire's too big!" Nearly every part of the home was constructed from wood. "The place is like a giant campfire!"

"How did it start?" Chase asked.

"What does it matter?"

"I don't know."

They could see that the front door was completely engulfed now. "The back door," Wen said. "He may be able to get there through the great room."

As she said it, Tu disappeared back into the house. Then, as the three of them watched, and time stood still, the other side of the house, where the back door was, collapsed as if bombed from the sky.

"There's no way out!" Wen screamed, the guttural sound of maternal instinct.

Chapter Fifty-Four

Two helicopters appeared in the sky above the burning home. Sepio agents dropped down by ropes, two to the deck, four more on the grounds around the front of the home.

"The Calvary has arrived," The Astronaut announced.

"Are they in time?" Chase asked.

Wen, so caught up in the action at the safe house, actually jumped at the sound of Chase's voice. She so desperately wanted to crawl through the screen and rescue Tu.

Less than a minute later, two Sepio agents carried Zǔ mǔ's body out onto the deck and secured her to a gurney suspended from the chopper.

"Zǔ mǔ," Wen whispered, holding back tears.

A few seconds later, a woman brought Tu out a first floor window, through what appeared to be an impenetrable wall of flames.

They watched as he was raised up into one of the helicopters.

"Can we talk to him?" Wen asked.

"Already working on it," The Astronaut said. "It may take a few minutes."

Almost five minutes after they lost the satellite feed, they received the go-ahead.

"Tu, it's Wen," she said.

"And Chase," he added.

"Are you okay?" Wen asked.

"I'm fine, but Zǔ mǔ . . . "

"I know, but—"

"She's alive," The Astronaut broke in. "I just spoke to the other chopper. They have a medic onboard. She is alive, and they are flying her to the nearest hospital.

"Did you hear that?" Wen asked Tu.

"Yes. But she is hurt bad . . . too much blood . . . I don't know."

"Let's see what the doctors say," Chase said. "As soon as she gets to the hospital."

"We're so proud of you," Wen said. "You are so brave."

"I was scared," he said, sounding ashamed.

"I know," she said. "That's why you were so brave."

Mumford Grimes sat on a rickety porch of an old beach house on the coast of Belize, positioned so that the table and his laptop computer were in the shade, but his left arm and both his legs were in the sun. The house, a generous term to describe the structure, stood little more than twenty feet from the high tide mark. It would be illegal to build today, but it had been there a long time.

Just off the porch, in the full sun, on the soft white sand, a beautiful woman in a bikini sat in a low chair. They looked like a pair of typical vacationers, except wedged between her towel and a folded newspaper, Lena Shelby hid a Beretta 9mm semiautomatic pistol. Grimes had a matching one hidden in an empty cardboard six-pack container.

"Are we going?" Shelby asked casually.

"Not yet," Grimes said, studying a map on the screen.

"Why not?"

"It's a mess."

"Tell me something I don't know." She stood up and moved over to sit on the edge of the porch to be closer to him. "For as long as we've been pursuing Chase Malone, it's been a mess, and it keeps getting messier."

"Yeah, but this is a whole new level of mess. There's a group called the consortium."

"And?" she asked, looking down the beach, always alert.

"Now *they're* after him."

"How do you know?"

"I know a guy who knows a guy."

She smiled slightly, taking a sip of mineral water, understanding better than most that Grimes always knew someone. He knew everybody. "And what's the consortium's business?"

"I'm just getting into that now," he said, rubbing his eyes. "On the surface, they're doing this big wireless network roll out—you know, the next generation 5EX—but they're tied up with Chinese tech giants, CIA, I think there's even a link to Belfort's group."

That surprised her. Belfort, their contact to the secretive cabal that had employed them for more than two years, was all they knew, and that was almost nothing except endless amounts of cash and incredible, almost supernatural intelligence. "I thought we didn't know *who* Belfort's group is."

"I might have some ideas."

"I'll bet you do." Shelby tried not to be annoyed, not to be hurt, but she wished Grimes would trust her. Although they'd only started sleeping together a few weeks earlier, they had worked together a long time. She loved him, and was sure he felt the same—in as much as he was capable of something as soft and warm and dangerous as love—but he sure as hell didn't *trust* her. Shelby believed love and trust went together naturally in a basic human nature kind of way, but Grimes held trust as a whole separate category, unrelated to anything else. She didn't agree with him, yet understood that's how he'd stayed alive so long.

Shelby had seen dozens of her associates die. Grimes was legendary—mostly because he was still alive. There were rumors that he was some kind of a magician. Many in their field didn't even think he existed, others were convinced he was an advanced DARPA android and not human at all. However, Shelby had seen him bleed, and knew he was very real.

Chapter Fifty-Five

Tess frowned when her assistant told her Chase was on the line, then easily shifted to a smile. "Chase Malone, how nice of you to report in."

"Have you forgotten *again*?" Chase asked.

"Forgotten what, exactly?"

"That I don't work for you."

"No, I haven't, but remind me one more time—who *do* you work for?"

"I'm self-employed."

"That's because you're often working for the other side."

"And who's the other side?"

"Whoever is not doing what I want."

"That's about it."

Tess sighed. "To what do I owe this rare honor?"

"I'm calling because I need your help."

"Of course you do," she said, sounding bored. "What would you like me to do for you now?"

"Are you familiar with the consortium controlling the new 5EX rollout?"

Tess glanced at the monitors in her office, filled with data on that very subject, and wondered, *What the hell is my karma with this guy? Chase Malone seems to stumble into every important crisis I'm involved in.* "Yes, I've heard of it. Let me guess, you're opposed to 5EX because you think it's going to give the world cancer and neurological disorders."

"As a matter fact, that *is* true, but there are other, far worse reasons why this rollout needs to be stopped."

"That's not going to happen."

"It *has* to be stopped. This is extremely dangerous."

She assumed that if it wasn't the health concerns, then he must be upset about the Chinese involvement. But it was also possible Chase might know about INSIGHT. "The consortium is working with the US Government. They've brought together a broad coalition of industry players, and—"

"Why are so many bankers suddenly involved in telecom? Are you telling me you don't know what they're *really* doing?" Chase snapped.

"Don't know what *who* are really doing?"

"What the *consortium* is doing," he repeated with exaggerated slowness, unsure if she was playing him, as she often tried, or if Tess was really behind in the game this time.

"They're trying to set up the most advanced global wireless network we've ever had. Higher speeds, better connection of more devices—industry and consumers will benefit."

"No, they're trying to snatch the last remaining bit of privacy humanity possesses."

"How are they doing that?" she asked, thinking he sounded like a fringe conspiracy theorist.

"I have a hard time believing this is news to you Tess. I

know what they're doing. I know about INSIGHT," he said, hoping the word "INSIGHT" alone would shock her into admitting CIA involvement or her knowledge.

"What's INSIGHT?"

She typed the word into her screen, searching for the latest updates from her analysts. Then she added "Chase Malone" and cross indexed it against all known data with the consortium and its related projects and affiliated companies. Instantaneously, it would review Ennis Cavanaugh, and the other principals in the same query. Nothing new came up. That was curious because of Chase's track record of injecting himself into the center of some of technology's most significant global controversies. But Chase had done such a good job at making himself invisible, and his massive SEER program could seemingly create new realities . . .

"You've baffled me," Tess went on dryly.

"Really?" he said skeptically.

"Chase, for once you know more than I. Why don't you enlighten me."

"If you really don't know, then I'm even more terrified about INSIGHT than I was to begin with. If they've managed to keep *you* out of the loop, then damn it, they are playing *big*."

"I can tell you don't believe me, but I'm telling you, I have no idea what you're talking about, at least by that name. If you think I'm lying, let's end this call now, because you're wasting both our time. However, if you *sincerely* want my assistance, just tell me what the hell you're talking about." She sensed the urgency in his voice, and had worked with him enough to know he was truly worried, and she understood why. INSIGHT was potentially horrifying—unless she could somehow get control of it for CISS. Either way, Tess was determined to find out what Chase knew, and use it to her advantage.

"Okay," he said, pacing the rooftop beneath a shaggy palapa. "INSIGHT is your worst nightmare. The bankers' final takeover of the last thing they don't own—our *minds*!"

Chapter Fifty-Six

Otis and Ennis were placing the last few dominoes in a new run. "Along the ramp," Ennis said, pointing.

"Got it," Otis said, filling in a gap. The initial chain would go uphill, ending with a domino dropping into a tank of water. As the black and white piece fell into a submerged shipwreck, the impact would cause the ship to move and start a group of toy divers floating over to a coral tunnel. Upon reaching it, the last diver would hit a treasure chest. As it opened, a new domino would release and float up to the surface, where it would collide with a boat, sending it to shore, where it would start a new chain.

"This is a brilliant series," Ennis said enthusiastically.

"One of our best," Otis agreed. "I've got some news on Malone." Ennis had relayed the news he'd received from their man in Mexico about the young billionaire's plans to disrupt 5EX.

Ennis looked at his son, then to the dominos, and finally back to his son, as if to say, *"Don't you want to see the latest?"*

But business was business, and there'd be time for dominos later. "Tell me."

"You were right. They have help from a Telmex employee. He had to sign in to get access to parts. It's a security measure to prevent unauthorized use or distribution of 5EX equipment in Mexico."

"Seems in this case it was necessary, and very helpful."

"Yeah. The man's name is Juan Medina."

"And do we have an address or contact number for Mister Medina?" Ennis asked, scoping the dominoes, looking at different angles. He rubbed his hands together vigorously and rearranged a few pieces.

"Yes in Lo de Marcos, a beach town. Not only that, but Thaxton is already on his way there."

"How close?"

"He's already in Mexico. I think he'll be in Lo de Marcos soon, that's the same town where Chase Malone was last reported."

"How very convenient."

"What do you want Thaxton to do?" Otis asked tentatively, as if he was afraid of the answer. He put back the dominoes his father had just rearranged.

Ennis smiled. "Don't worry. We're not the Mafia. We're not going to have this poor Telmex character offed or anything . . . We're bankers . . . We're going to *bribe* him."

"Bribe?" Otis looked up, well aware of how loaded that word was.

"Obviously, Chase Malone isn't going to succeed. And more than likely he's counting on Telmex Juan, so we'll use that to our advantage."

"How much?"

"Find out what a Telmex employee makes. Triple that amount. I can't imagine it's more than fifty-thousand pesos, that sounds like a place to start the offer," Ennis said, flipping a domino in his pocket.

"What if he doesn't agree—"

"Hear what I'm saying. Just keep offering more pesos. Eventually he will say yes. It's a poor country, and the man works for Telmex. Once he accepts our offer and this messy business is done, Juan Medina will be able to do what he wants." He patted his son on the back. "We're talking about a multi-trillion dollar venture here. And Chase Malone, or his penny-ante friends, aren't going to stop us."

"But we don't know *what* they're doing."

"Thus the donation to the Juan Medina retirement fund."

"Got it," Otis said, relieved that his father wasn't going to order a hit on Chase or the Telmex man.

"Now come look at this next section," Ennis said. "The dominos are going to jump over this waterfall."

"How many?"

"All twelve go over. And when they fill up the pool on the bottom, it will overflow. That water will flood the next run of dominoes and trip this line."

"Really nice," Otis said. "I love the colors. It's a true water theme." His father had ordered dominos in multiple shades of blues, clear, gray, and white. He pointed to a large platform in the center of the display. "What's that over there?"

"It's going to be a geyser."

Otis laughed gleefully. "That's *incredible*." He looked up at the ceiling, which was twenty feet high. "How far will it shoot?"

"I'm hoping all the way to the top."

"Is it the grand finale?"

"When the water comes down, it hits another place and stops that." He pointed to an open channel.

"You mean like a damn?"

"Exactly. And that'll all be filled with water falling from the geyser, which causes this to shift, damning the river."

"And then what?"

"I'm not sure yet. Got any ideas?"

"How about it sinks the ship?"

"Yeah . . . I like it." Ennis studied the setup, as if considering the latest ideas. "Mexico . . . are we ready."

"We are," Otis said, sorry they weren't discussing dominoes anymore. "Full launch?"

Ennis smiled. "Thirty-six. Don't worry, it's gonna work out." He tossed his son a domino. "We're making a better world."

Otis caught the domino. It was a new one, with the holes going all the way through. "It's going to change things, Dad, but I don't think you understand just how much it's going to *affect* them."

"You're probably right. Anytime there's innovation on this scale, there are unforeseen consequences, and I'm sure there'll be some difficult things we'll have to handle that we haven't considered enough. But we can do it. We have the tools, the expertise, the people. Don't worry so much."

"You're assuming Chase Malone isn't going to get in our way."

"What can he do? Steal some equipment? You get the Telmex guy under control. Malone is just another tourist."

"Why does he want to stop it?"

"There's always somebody who doesn't want change. You know what Gandhi said: 'Be the change you want to see in the world.' That's what we're doing. Look around.

There's so much misery. So many horrible people. We're doing away with all that. *We* are the responsible citizens, not trying to screw things up, but *building* things up. It's going to be an amazing new world, Otis. Just imagine how it will be without criminals, crime . . . "

"I know. But my concern is still *who* gets to decide."

"It's not us. No single person," Ennis said, as if this were the greatest concern. "It's the algorithms."

"Algorithms can be wrong. They can be biased." He looked out the large windows onto the power of Washington, important people who all thought themselves more important than they were, few who were actually important at all.

"Depending on who set them up."

"That's what I'm worried about."

"If that happens, we'll fix it." Ennis walked over to his son and lay a hand on his shoulder. "You have to trust me."

"I *do* trust you, I'm just not sure you know." He turned to look into his father's eyes.

Ennis didn't return the gaze. "We'll know when we get there."

"We probably only get one chance."

Ennis shook his head emphatically. "We can fix it."

Otis smiled as he looked away, back out the large windows again. "But the public can be an awesome power."

"By the time they find out—or care—they'll be loving the results."

After Otis left his office Ennis called Thaxton. "You're going to hear from Otis in a minute. You haven't talked to me."

"Okay," Thaxton said.

"Telmex Juan, Chase Malone, anyone else down there

even looks like they might be a problem . . . make sure they aren't."

"Roger that."

Chapter Fifty-Seven

A Sepio team stayed with Zǔ mǔ at the hospital and soon reported to Chase that she was expected to make a full recovery, but would need to remain hospitalized for at least ten days. If things went well over the next forty-eight hours, she could be airlifted to a hospital closer to where Dez and Bull would be keeping Tu.

Dez also talked to Chase, asking him if it was okay to let Tu watch James Bond films.

"Why did you suggest Bond to him?" Chase asked, thinking it wasn't good timing.

"Bull told him he was a little 007, and he got interested," Dez said. "How about we stick to the Sean Connery flicks?"

"I guess, but if it gets intense, turn it off and put on Bugs Bunny or something."

Dez laughed. "He's kind of in charge, but I'll do my best."

Tess, now deep in the horrendous scenarios about INSIGHT that her top analysts had been running, made a surprise order.

"We need to find every connection to WOLF and protect them."

The IT-Squad commander gave her a stunned look. "Tess?"

"The Cause—"

"Is the *enemy*," the commander finished.

"Friends, enemies, you know in our business these labels are transitory."

"Okay, but—"

"WOLF is our best hope to contain INSIGHT. They're way ahead of us on this."

"The lesser of two evils?"

"Something like that." She handed him a flash drive. "Keep them safe. Feed them intel."

"And what about our surveillance and objectives?"

"Get everything WOLF has. Double that for the consortium." She glared at something unseen in her thoughts. "As soon as Ennis Cavanaugh is dead, and 5EX is stalled, we'll close in on WOLF."

"About time," the commander said.

"Yes," she nodded. "Everything is about *Time*."

Juan opened his door, smiling warmly. His expression quickly turned to concern once he saw the strange man standing on the other side.

"Leer Thaxton," the man said, extending his hand.

Juan shook it with a puzzled look on his face.

"I guess I should say hola," Thaxton said, forcing a smile.

"What can I do for you?"

"You have a little problem I'd like to help you with."

"No problem," Juan said, staring at the American. "I don't know what you mean."

"This is about your position at Telmex. We don't want that to be in jeopardy, do we?"

"Pero, why would it be in jeopardy?"

"It seems you made an unauthorized entry to utilize some equipment for an operation that is not only against Telmex policy, but Juan, it is also *illegal*. Do you recall this action?"

"No, no . . . I don't. I have no idea what you mean."

"Really?" Thaxton asked, a confused look on his face as he checked his tablet. "Yeah, actually I think you *do* know. I don't think I'm being unclear here, do you think I'm being unclear?"

Juan shook his head, concerned.

"Listen, Juan, I am not here to try to destroy your life. Quite the contrary, I've come to help you keep your job, *improve* your life. You want to keep your job, right?"

"Si."

"Of course you do. Now listen, there are people who are aware of what has happened. They know what you've done. They're well-connected to Arino, Ruiz, even Slim. You know who these Tex-Mex officers are, don't you?"

"Si." Juan thought of his conversations with Rob, Chase and Wen, and of the plan.

"They wish to discuss it, but you see, I don't want them to have that conversation with your supervisors, or with the Mexican authorities. The federales would not take kindly to a major industry being sabotaged by you, and there are extra penalties for being an insider. You're an insider by the very nature of your employment and your work."

"Pero . . ."

"It is safe to say that you will be spending most of the rest of your life in prison. You will lose everything. I don't want that to happen."

Juan could feel the swelling anger. He thought of calling his grandfather. Perhaps he could make this problem go away.

"But maybe there is another way. Hear me out, por favor." Thaxton gave his best attempt at an authentic smile. "May I come in so we can discuss this further?"

Juan stood to the side and motioned for Thaxton to enter his home.

"Here's the proposition. You are not paid very well by Telmex. I see that you make one hundred forty thousand pesos a year. That's roughly twenty thousand American dollars. I'm willing to give you *triple* that amount for a short time's work."

"What is a short time?" Juan asked, imagining a prison sentence.

"Perhaps only a few days, maybe a week or two, that's it. And then we give you the full amount."

"That kind of money for a few days' work makes me very suspicious. Perhaps like trading one illegal act for another."

"Oh no, I assure you I would never ask you to do anything illegal."

"Juan looked at him. "And *who* did you say your employer is?"

"I didn't," Thaxton admitted. "It's a delicate matter. But I assure you that we are *quite* serious. In fact, twenty thousand American dollars has already been deposited into your bank account." Thaxton checked his smart watch. "About thirty minutes ago. More will follow shortly."

Juan seemed surprised.

"If you'd like to check, please go ahead. I'll wait."

Chapter Fifty-Eight

Chase and Wen rode borrowed bikes into town that night to try the chile rellenos at a small restaurant highly praised by Rob. Sitting out on the roadside patio, they tried to relax and pretend they were just like all the other tourists.

"How do they find us?" Wen asked as Chase sipped a cold Mexican Coke. She enjoyed fresh coconut water.

He shook his head. "If The Astronaut can't figure that out, I doubt we ever will."

"We *have* to."

"I know," he said, turning serious, thinking of Tu. "We will. Are you surprised we haven't heard from Shelby and Grimes yet?"

"No," she said, but he could tell she was surprised, or at least disappointed.

A Lo de Marcos Policia pickup truck, with four officers inside, drove slowly past them.

"Did you see those police look at us?" Chase asked.

"They're looking at everyone tonight. A couple of dead gringos and two golf carts racing through town shooting at each other doesn't happen too often around here. Not to mention you almost running that man off his horse. Probably one of their brothers."

"Let's hope not."

"Tess will know right where we are."

He took another swig of his favorite drink. "Why?"

"Local authorities have to report deaths of Americans. It goes up the food chain, eventually the American Embassy ... CIA ... Tess."

"And she'll know it's us?"

Wen shot him an '*Isn't that obvious?*' look and drained her coconut water.

"Yeah, I guess she will," he said, looking down the street as a group of loud gringos stole his attention.

"I guess they haven't heard," Wen said.

"What?"

"That someone's hunting Americans."

Chase laughed, but her joke made him a little uncomfortable.

Not far away, Doug Black also sipped a cold drink. His was a Mexican beer, and he was happy that his targets were finally sitting still.

After dinner, Chase and Wen mounted the somewhat battered bikes that were, despite appearances, kept in good working order. "Let's ride around a little," Wen suggested, as the sun set into the ocean.

Chase was enjoying the ride until they turned onto the

cobblestone streets.

"This is sort of like getting beat up while riding," he said.

"Quiet," she said. "Just enjoy the sites."

As they wove their way back to where they had been earlier, Wen scanned the area.

"These cobblestones are beating the hell out of me," Chase said.

"Shh. Ride standing up," Wen said.

Chase was amused by the simple solution. It didn't hurt at all. "I'm free!"

Wen didn't answer.

"I swear we're going faster on these bikes than we were on the golf cart."

"Not quite, but it's definitely easier to weave in and out on these narrow lanes."

Another police truck passed them.

"Was that the same one?" Chase asked.

"I couldn't tell. But it doesn't matter. They didn't give us a second look."

"Maybe Rob has a contact with the local police. We might be able to find out if they've identified the shadow people."

"It's worth a try," Wen said. "But you know they're just as likely to come up empty."

"Too bad there wasn't time to get any identifiable parts or DNA from them," Chase said, remembering the time she'd *cut off* one of the shadow people's fingers. "What do you think *Jekyll* means?" he asked as they rode past some sort of pineapple farm.

"I have no idea, but I sent it to The Astronaut. He'll run it with everything we know about Finale, Grimes, etcetera."

"Dez will put it through SEER and see if it gets a hit. We might get lucky."

"We need to get *something*."

They turned down a dirt road full of huge puddles. Horses freely grazed on the side, and chickens ran around squawking.

"Are you sure the dying man was answering your question?" Chase asked,

"Yes," Wen said. She knew it the moment he'd given her the word, and had thought about it a lot since they'd fled the accident. "He was definitely telling me something."

"Why? I mean, these people have always seemed willing to die to protect whoever was behind it," Chase said, steering around piles of horse manure in the road while also trying to avoid a series of muddy potholes. A little girl shooed the chickens into a yard and then stood and stared at the gringos. Wen said something to her in Spanish. The girl giggled and ran off.

"We'll never know why he decided to answer the question," she said. "Unless . . . "

"What?"

"Unless *Grimes* is Jekyll."

Chapter Fifty-Nine

In the morning, rain began as a mist, but quickly became thick waves of water, the drops strung together as if thousands of hoses were spraying simultaneously. Chase and Wen waded through the street. "It's more like a flooded river," Chase yelled to Rob, recalling the dry, dusty streets of yesterday. "I thought it didn't rain here in January!"

"Dude, it's Mexico. It rains whenever it wants."

"Can you believe what the rain has done?" he shouted.

"It's unrecognizable," Wen responded.

"It's not a normal rain!" Chase barked. "It's a damned hurricane." Chase knew it wasn't a hurricane, but it sure felt like one, with rain falling more than an inch an hour for the last three hours, and no letup in sight. "How are we going to get up that hill?"

"The horses can make it."

"Can we weld in this stuff?"

"I doubt *you* can, but *those* guys can," Rob said, smiling.

"I thought there'd be more."

"We've lost a lot of the others," Rob said, looking back. "Many are needed to help in town with the flooding."

The bridge was already partially underwater when they crossed, and was now acting more like a combination dam and waterfall. The horses still cleared it easily, and the guide kept them going at a good pace.

"It's going to take longer to get up this time. We need to be as fast as we can down here in the flats," Rob shouted as they urged the horses to a full gallop.

At least we got the heavy supplies up the day before, Chase thought. *The concrete had had enough time to set, but how much water's filling in the ground around the base?*

When they reached the shipping containers, Chase now understood why the concrete foundation had been put in place. "It looks like they're floating in the middle of a lake!"

They fought to get the horses to stay on the trail as the winds pushed heavy rains from various directions.

"We'll get a little relief in the jungle!" Rob yelled back.

Chase strained with his horse's reins. Wen continued scouring the area, but could not imagine anyone out there doing surveillance in the torrential downpour. Visibility was much lower than normal, but that same feeling came to her from the day before, and now she wondered if it was just the eeriness of the jungle.

"I still feel like someone's watching us!" she yelled to Chase.

"If they're crazy enough to be out in this and they're not shooting us, then I don't care what they're doing," Chase shouted back.

Wen felt differently. If anyone was out there watching, it was a problem, even if they *weren't* shooting them. They were trying to get information, or waiting to attack at just the right time.

As she continued steadying her horse, keeping it on the watery trail, she also played with the riddle in her mind. *Why would they be watching and not striking?*

None of the answers she came up with were satisfying, or good. She hadn't seen anything, but knew enough to know that wasn't always necessary.

There's someone out there, and they are collecting information. The fact that she could not see them and yet still knew they were there told her they were pros. She considered doubling back at one point and wished she had done it the day before. Now, in the storm, it didn't make sense, and they didn't have enough time.

There never seems to be enough time . . .

They still had a whole day of work before the test, one more long, critical day.

How are they even going to get the antenna up?

Then she would have to defend that peak and the mountain and the tower against whoever was lurking out there in the woods, more shadow people, and whatever the consortium was going to throw at them.

Doug Black crouched in the soggy weeds, grateful for his waterproof pants and rain jacket, but his waterproof boots were doing nothing. Somehow the water had gotten in, and immediately wicked up his socks, making his legs wet. It was surprisingly chilly, the warm humid air having vanished with the cold rain.

It didn't matter to him that he was getting wet, though. He was doing a job for which he would be well-paid, and he expected there wasn't much more than twelve hours remaining before he was through.

However, it was harder to navigate the jungle in wet conditions. He was naturally camouflaged in mud and green outerwear, but Black still kept his distance. He could afford to, since he knew where they were going. He'd considered getting to the peak before them, but that would be reckless. There was always a chance they would change plans, and he couldn't risk losing them.

He *had* lost them when they'd been on the golf cart, and unfortunately missed the final blow when the bus took out their two pursuers, but he knew it'd been Chase and Wen. He had watched them, and knew who was after them.

The town was still abuzz with reports of gunfire and the fatal collision between the Compostela bus and the golf cart. That kind of violence was rare in the sleepy town, which had thus far escaped crime related to the drug cartels that had hit so many other areas. Many gringos in the community relied on golf carts, so it shook them even more. Most of the rumors were pinning it on drug-related disputes, as the cartels had recently been expanding their territory and influence into the Riviera district. Black was not about to dispute any of the talk, since *he* had helped fuel it.

In the hours since, he'd been trying to collect more information on Chase and Wen and the man they were with. Black was increasingly frustrated that no one seemed to know Rob's last name. In fact, no one seemed to know much about *any* of them.

But now that two men have died, and shots have been fired in Lo de Marcos, the information will begin to flow.

Time is running out . . .

Chapter Sixty

Tess looked at her deputy with an expression so grave and serious that Linda realized this was the most important order she'd ever been given, but it didn't stop her from questioning it.

"Is it illegal?" She handed Tess a green apple, knowing she hadn't eaten in at least twelve hours.

Tess rolled her eyes, clearly disappointed. "It's illegal only in the conventional sense. *Those* laws apply to the general population. We operate under a different set, and you very well know that."

"But it *is* immoral. I mean, you're talking about an American citizen who's done nothing wrong. We have the—"

"*Nothing* wrong?" Tess shot back incredulously. "I have a *list*. He's done countless things that warrant this." She bit into the crunchy, juicy fruit.

"But are those things illegal?"

"There you go again. You've been here long enough,

seen enough, that I don't understand why you're questioning these things. I have the authorization. Thanks, this is delicious."

"I know, but this just seems different," Linda said. "We're not talking about a terrorist or someone threatening the security—"

"What we *are* talking about is most certainly a threat. We can't allow this—"

"But the history," Linda insisted. "Are you forgetting when Chase was in China? Are you ignoring all of that?"

"I'm not forgetting anything, Linda. I don't forget things. Have *you* forgotten?"

"It's just ... it's so extreme."

"Yes," Tess agreed, trying to regain and maintain her patience. "I have issued a COD, and whenever I do that, it is *not* an easy decision. The authority to do so has been given to me because I weigh every possible alternative to taking such action."

"The CISS of Death, in this case, I don't—"

"You know me, our work here. It is not easy, nor is it trivial. We are the last defense, the balance of power. If there was any other way . . . but this situation is potentially catastrophic and irreversible. We *cannot* allow him to be successful."

Linda nodded, knowing she'd already pushed too far. There was no sense in arguing any longer, and although she had worked in intelligence and been Tess's right hand for several years, killing did not come easy to her.

Of course, she would not be physically pulling the trigger, and Tess had been the one to give the COD order. However, Linda would be the one making sure it was carried out. She would be *part* of killing a man, an innocent man, and even though Tess said there was no such thing as a truly innocent man—certainly none of the ones that crossed their paths—Linda felt guilty.

She already had trouble sleeping at night. There had been others . . . the faces from those files haunted her, but for some reason this one was different. This one seemed a much dirtier act, because the target seemed much cleaner.

"So you will have no problem seeing this through?" Tess asked.

Linda knew this would be the last conversation on this topic. "I will make sure the COD is carried out."

"Good," Tess said. "Now get me Holt Gatewood over at HITE. I'll take the call in Secure."

Linda's head suddenly ached. Tess wanting a call with Gatewood, combined with the CISS of Death, told Linda she was right. As hard as Tess was working, the world was probably going to end anyway. Maybe not today, or next week, but within a few years, today's way of life would be but a distant memory . . . back when things were still good, and people believed they were free.

Higher and higher they climbed. With each new foot of elevation, the more difficult the gains became. The slippery, uneven trail, now at its steepest, was losing itself to the storm. Rain-rivers, heavy with mud, formed from the newly exposed earth created by the fresh cut roads and building lots. Rutting channels brought vast brown water ripping down against them. The horses increasingly faltered in the thick currents.

"This is my worst nightmare!" Chase yelled as his horse slipped. Never having much luck with horses, he was now trying to convince his ride to charge up a treacherous mountain during a veritable tsunami from the sky. They rounded a curve in the trail as it opened into a waterfall. Frothy, muddy water forged new gullies and deeper trenches as the rivulets raced down the mountain toward the ocean.

"It's impossible!" Rob yelled.

Rocks began tumbling loose with the heavier deluge as the construction-scarred jungle allowed the mountain to erode away beneath them. Chase's horse went sideways, slipping down, throwing him clear an instant before it rolled.

"You okay?" Wen shouted.

"I was almost killed by that horse!" he said, knowing she would get the irony with his history of horse issues. He was relieved to see the horse, having survived the tumble, galloping onto firmer ground in the forest.

A group of five Mexicans, on horseback with most of the equipment, were out front, and apparently had the experience to make it through. "Keep going!" Rob yelled to them as he dismounted.

Leaves swirled, and the wind worked its wrath as branches snapped, unable to withstand the combination of forces.

"Watch out!" Rob shouted as another section of the trail collapsed and the earth wall beside them slid away, the water and steep terrain creating a lethal landslide.

Francisco, another Mexican, riding behind Chase, screamed as flowing debris swept him and his horse down. Chase, already on the ground, ran to his aid.

The lead horse, carrying the welder and his equipment, turned back, but Rob waived him on. "Keep going! We need you up there. We'll get him."

"I try!" the man shouted, as his group kept pushing on.

Chase looked over the edge of what was left of the trail to the eroding cliff below. "I see him, he's about thirty feet below," Chase yelled. "His horse is farther . . . hard to see how badly the horse is hurt." He couldn't imagine things getting much worse as he looked back at Francisco.

Then the first tree fell.

Chapter Sixty-One

In the pounding rain, with their horses revolting and the wind bringing leaves and limbs down with such force it was nearly impossible to tell which direction was which, Chase stared down at what was now a waterfall, trying to figure out the best way to rescue Francisco.

Juan rode up and jumped off his horse.

"Where were you?" Chase asked, worried.

"I got delayed back in the muck." He pointed over his shoulder. "Who is it?"

"Francisco."

"Oh no."

"I can get him. You help Pedro with the tower."

"I'm not leaving until we get him out of there," Juan said.

"I'll get Francisco, we need you up there!" Chase tried again, knowing Juan's Telmex expertise with the sensitive equipment was crucial.

"No, Francisco is more important than the tower."

Chase wanted to argue that point, having been in too

many situations where a single life could make the difference for millions. This was definitely another one of those instances. However, when Juan stood next to him, overlooking the abyss, Chase saw the determination in the man's eyes, and knew he wasn't going to win the argument.

"I think I can get down over there," Juan shouted above the storm, grabbing a rope from his horse.

"No, you stay up here. I'm a climber," Chase said.

Juan handed him one end of the rope and tied the other around a large tree.

"Chase," Wen shouted, "it's too dangerous!"

Chase agreed with her as he went over the edge and began lowering himself into the chaos of the explosive storm, the mountain collapsing around him.

Juan began feeding the slack down as Chase quickly discovered this was no normal descent. "It's impossible to get any footing," he said to the wind. The ground under him continually washed out, muddy rocks tumbling, bouncing into him. The pull from the downward current was like nothing he'd ever fought through. It seemed the rope was swaying and flying in every direction. "Hold it steady!" he shouted to Juan.

Both Wen and Juan were gripping it tightly. They'd snaked the rope around a second tree and retied it to lend more stability. "We're trying," Juan yelled, "but the currents keep taking it!"

Even with that reassurance, the rope twisted as Chase slipped through a gulley, the mud and rain on his hands prevented a firm grip on the line. He slid five feet, screaming in pain as a large log caught him hard across the chest. The vibration of the impact reverberated up his spine, leaving him immobilized for an instant, until a torrent of water gushing over his face brought him back.

He felt the tug as Wen and Juan corrected the slack and tried to give him more stability. Soon he had the man in sight. At the same time, he saw the horse slowly get up and drop again, this time rolling down the remaining slope. Chase knew the horse would not survive the fall.

"Do you see Francisco?" Juan shouted, sounding more like a distant voice calling him from another part of the mountain.

"He's not moving!" Chase yelled.

"Can you reach him?"

"I need to work my way over!" Chase's response was lost in a loud clap of thunder. The jungle had darkened considerably, the mood shifting as the storm closed off the remaining muted light. Only the lightning gave true visuals, but the strobe effect left him constantly misjudging distances.

Chase could not see Wen and Juan anymore. Rain and muddy runoff filled his eyes, making it difficult to see. He wiped his eyes. "Damn, I've lost sight of Francisco's body," he muttered.

The slack in the rope faltered, then gave way as the roots of the second tree they'd been using as leverage lost its battle with the storm. Chase barely heard Wen and Juan's distant screams as the giant tree slid off the cliff, bringing a mass of debris heading right for him.

"Pull! Pull!" he shouted, having no way to know if they could hear his desperate cries.

Chapter Sixty-Two

Chase's feet found a rock ledge under the sliding mud and vegetation. *A chance for survival!* A giant tree stood a few feet away. Chase dove through the muck, reaching it at the same time the incoming trunk hit. The massive log swung sideways, pivoting against the standing tree, then shot over the cliff, propelling itself into the canopy below.

He spotted Francisco again. "Getting to him is the easy part," Chase grumbled, not realizing he was talking out loud, "but stopping without taking him over the cliff with me, then figuring out how to get us both back *up* in a landslide . . . shouldn't be too difficult."

His sarcasm was met with several softball-sized rocks smashing into his shoulder.

The only thing stopping Francisco from going over the edge were two saplings perched precariously on a narrow shelf. As Chase got closer, he had little faith that the young trees were going to stand much longer.

If I can keep hold of the rope, Wen and Juan will be able to pull Francisco up. Unless the whole mountain collapses on top of us. He knew he'd never make it without the rope. *Pretty sheer drop.* Chase inched down. *Sort of an endless fall . . .*

He tried yelling up to Wen and Juan, but got no response.

Suddenly, his steady descent became a fast, slick fall. He flailed about, trying to slow himself, but there was nothing to grip. The gooey mud and wet leaves made everything feel like oil-coated seaweed. He hit the saplings going too fast. There was nothing but more movement as everything slipped away.

Landing waist-deep in the cascading mud, the slide carried him further down the mountain, sinking him even more. The weight of cold, wet earth pressed in, now up to his chest. Chase realized he was about to be buried alive. With that final fatal thought, the mud went over his head.

Holt Gatewood was the powerful administrator of HITE, short for Hidden Information and Technology Exchange, a government entity so classified that most US presidents usually didn't learn about it unless they got a second term. HITE had been established after World War II to handle captured Nazi secrets, technology, and even metaphysical data and artifacts. If a UFO of extraterrestrial origin really *did* crash in Roswell, New Mexico, during the summer of 1947, HITE would have wound up with the wreckage, and whatever it may have contained.

The name was a bit of a misnomer because the hidden technology and/or information was never exchanged. Instead, a select committee made up of top US intelligence leaders—with security clearances *much* higher than that of the President of the United States—decided who, where, when, and *if* the information would be released. HITE was the ultimate strategic advantage because its members could ignite huge shifts in power and wealth via the introduction of new technologies—be it nuclear weapons, computers, satellites, pharmaceuticals, etcetera.

Gatewood, Tess, and Dr. J. W. Skyenor, Director of Defense Advanced Research Projects Agency, were in charge, and the three most influential people in US Intelligence. They were also rivals of sorts, who only worked together during the most dangerous of crises.

"Tess, leave this one alone," Gatewood said over the encrypted line. It was unusual they ever spoke on the telephone, instead favoring in-person meetings only when absolutely necessary. Those rare conferences took place at "Bunker W," an ultra-secure underground facility on the grounds of the CIA's Langley, Virginia campus.

"I can't," she said, trying to pretend she didn't dislike him.

Gatewood sighed. "Damn it. Why not?"

"You know why."

"You're trying to start a war."

"I'm trying to *prevent* one. That's what I do, remember?"

"We need 5EX to happen."

"You need INSIGHT to happen."

Gatewood said nothing for a few moments.

"It still can," Tess continued. "Just not this way."

"You don't—"

"Yes, I do," she interrupted. "This is going to go very badly unless you let me in."

More silence. However, Tess knew he was going to acquiesce, because she was using the most important asset she had—her reputation. Gatewood might not like her, but he *trusted* her.

"Tell me what you have in mind," he finally said, setting his square jaw tight, a resolute grimace familiar to his stocky stature. He liked to be right all the time.

"How much time do we have?" Tess asked.

"The eleventh hour was fifty-nine minutes ago."

Chapter Sixty-Three

Desperately holding his breath in the mud, Chase's mind flooded with panic. *No air!* The closing earth strangled the dwindling life from his body until a jolt vibrated through the mud. Another downed tree trunk hit against two big ones that were still standing. Like a tractor-trailer sliding into a bridge abutment, it stopped the flow.

Still buried, but not moving, he fought to get some kind of traction. *I refuse to surrender.* He thought of Tu . . . *Dear, beautiful Tu.*

Not knowing which direction to go, he started peddling as if on a bike, trying to move the soggy earth before more piled up on top of him; pushing, almost swimming through the mud, trying to escape his would-be grave as the ooze continued to avalanche in on him.

Finally, his hand broke out of the slime and he felt the rain. Chase gulped air as if it were the first breath of a dead man. But before he could pull his body out, the mud came in, pulling him back, sucking him down again. Finding a seam, then a gap, he pushed, keeping his head up in the realm of oxygen, of life.

As he clawed his upper body free, he heard Wen screaming his name. His eyes were plastered shut with mud. He might as well have been blind. But he realized why she had been screaming. It wasn't *her* that was coming, it was the water, its sound overtaking her shouts.

Somewhere up above, a storm-made dam must've given way, releasing a wall of raging, muddy water. The unyielding surge hit him with explosive force. It felt as if he would snap in two, and it *kept coming*, a relentless river, a churning waterfall, pounding, ripping. He still couldn't move until the gushing flood began washing away his muddy bonds. If it didn't drown him, the water might just save him.

However, the force also meant he was taking in more muddy water than air, and there was another problem.

My god, once it erodes the mud's hold on me, it's going to send me off the mountain.

His mud prison was the only thing keeping him from the sure end that awaited over the side of the cliff.

I still have the rope, he remembered. It had been buried with him. Chase clung to it, quickly looping it around his waist, and tied it off, unconvinced he could hold it once the waterfall tossed him away.

The water took the remaining earth and rocks from around his ankles. Chase rocketed off the ground, harder and faster than he'd anticipated, like being pushed out of an airplane. Spinning, twisting on the wave of angry water, he caught a glimpse of Francisco's body. Miraculously, it was out of the path of the torrent.

The rope ran out with a bone-jarring jerk, as if falling

from a bungee cord without the elasticity, saving him from going over the cliff, but grinding him into the muddy river. *I'm alive . . . I'm alive!* he thought, gasping, beaten, but smiling in the sheer exhilaration of surviving the cataclysm.

Until the rope snapped.

Chapter Sixty-Four

Chase flew backwards, the frayed end of the rope gripped in his hand, sailing through the air like a recurring nightmare of falling, plunging endlessly, never hitting the ground. He screamed, yet no sound escaped his lips.

The moment of flight lasted forever. His mind, unable to focus, could only find one thought: Wen. In the seconds —or years—that followed, Chase desperately wondered where she was.

He found a new kind of pain when his body slammed into something so hard it had to be concrete. Disorientated, believing he must be on the ground, he tried to roll over, but it had been an upright tree that had caught him. In its release, he fell again, this time about nine feet straight down through a tangle of branches and leaves. Landing sideways, the soggy ground captured him once again, and the mud kept coming. He tried to lift his neck because this time, lying flat, there were no other options.

I'm going to be buried alive . . .

Struggling, stretching, trying to keep his chin and face

out of the endless mud that followed, Chase yelled, "Wen! I'm here! Help!"

A second later, the mud entered his screaming mouth. A second after that, it covered the rest of his face, then everything went dark.

Chase didn't feel the strong hands ripping him from the clutches of death, digging and yanking him out of the mud, then dragging him through the river onto a higher part of the slope, a section of firm land surrounded by tall, strong trees.

He did feel the fingers pulling the mud from his mouth, opening an airway.

Breathe!

Still unable to hear, and blinded by the mud caked over his eyes, he didn't see who threw him across a sturdy shoulder and carried him as he coughed and choked, sucking in precious air. Several dizzy minutes later—maybe longer, he couldn't be sure if he'd blacked out again during the blurry, wheezing climb—he was deposited on the trail.

Chase lay on his back, trying to clear his eyes and ringing ears. His lips were bleeding, his hands shaking. Everything was wet and heavy with mud.

"Hello? *Hello?*" he asked, unsure who was there.

No response. He couldn't quite figure out what had happened, why he found himself alone again. He staggered to his feet. *Which direction? Can I even get through?*

"Wen?" he tried to yell, his voice weak and cracking, but soon he got some volume. "Wen!"

He looked ahead and saw that enough of the trail remained. The avalanche was worst in the steep section below, down where he'd almost died. Chase found walking strange. His legs worked differently than before—clumsy, squishy, slow.

Then he remembered Francisco and looked over the edge. "Whoa!" he exclaimed upon seeing Francisco wedged in a high section of earth against two sturdy trees just off the trail. "Francisco, you're alive. They saved you, too . . . Are you okay?"

Francisco stared at him, dazed. "I don't know."

Chase could see Francisco was weak and in pain. "How did you get here?" he asked, still with the unanswered question about his own rescue, looking around for Juan and Wen and answers.

"I don't know. I think my leg is broken, it hurts like hell."

"I'll be right back." Chase, somewhat more energized by Francisco's miraculous return, walked determinedly on a still-intact part of the trail, calling Wen's name.

After rounding a bend, he saw her. She was still staring down into the raging waters. He called her again. This time she heard him, her expression instantly transforming from fear to miraculous amazement.

Chapter Sixty-Five

Juan collected the horses, and then he and Chase helped Francisco onto one before leading them through the final washed-out area. Once back on the relatively undamaged section of trail that wound to the top, the three horses made good time, even though the torrential rain never let up. The welders were finishing up when they arrived, and agreed to help Francisco get back down.

"You ready to go up?" Rob asked Chase, who was wiped out, soaking wet, and looked way beyond horrible.

"Yeah."

"Are you sure?" Wen asked.

"What can go wrong?" His weak smile suggested even *he* didn't care for his own idiotic joke. Chase knew he was in no condition to climb the fifty foot tower, but Rob and Wen had no idea how to do the install or hook up, and Juan was terrified of heights.

The storm brought the night early. The hard rain washed most of the surface mud from Chase. He rested as long as they could afford. After two energy bars, and drinking as much fresh water as he could handle, it was time.

Still shaky, Chase slung the antenna and a heavy pack on his back.

"Are you really *sure* you're up to this?" Wen asked again.

He shook his head no, but answered, "Yes."

"We could wait."

"No. I'm not going to get any less tired. It's now or never."

While unspooling cable behind him, Chase climbed the shaking structure in the dark. Wet hands on slick rungs; it looked like a suicide mission. The wind picked up considerably, and it seemed as if the rain was drawing extra water from the ocean hundreds of feet below.

Ten feet up the tower, branches from nearby trees bent at impossible angles, hitting him with their heavy leaves. It was then that he wondered if the concrete really could have set up in so short a time under such conditions. *Did they have enough? I would think it would need to be at least four feet deep.* His engineering mind began computing the odds and probability of imminent disaster.

Five feet more and it already seemed as if he'd climbed a ten story building. He paused and rested for longer than he wanted, catching his breath.

The rickety tower, which twenty-four hours earlier had been a twisted heap of wrecked metal, had been brought back to life, but it wasn't pretty. Stray stands and unconnected cross supports showed the haste and inexperience of the workers. Even though Rob assured him the men were competent, Chase felt the thing could collapse any second.

A gust of wind hit him with the impact of a kick to the gut. One of his hands lost its grip, swinging wildly in the air, trying to reach out for something to hold onto again.

Another gust could take me. How crazy was the idea to mount the antenna in a hurricane!

His climbing skills notwithstanding, it was an insane exercise. He heard Rob yelling from below, but had no idea what he was saying.

I sure hope it's not shadow people . . .

There came a fleeting thought of Shelby perched under some thick palms, aiming her sniper's rifle, getting the perfect shot, ready to kill, mockingly saying, *'You should've killed me when you had the chance, because now it's my turn.'*

The thought helped him get his hand back onto metal. Still unsteady, he started up again, the entire tower shaking violently.

Are these damn welds going to hold?

Chase cleared the tree line and, for the first time, felt the full force of the storm, having lost the protection of the jungle's canopy. The winds slammed him into the narrow metal frame. Unspooling the cable became increasingly more dangerous. It tangled around his feet, and for a moment he felt as if he were being pulled back down, imagining the tentacles of some gruesome monster wrapping around his legs, attempting to strangle him.

He climbed back down several rungs and fought to open the twisting loop. Finally freeing his foot, he moved up again.

I wonder if Wen has found any of her mystery people, because the only two things that could make this climb any worse are lightning or someone shooting at me.

He knew with Wen down below, no one was going to get

a good shot off, and so far the lightning remained in the distance.

He placed his hands and feet deliberately, ascending slowly, yet his feet still slipped often. Chase fought the winds and slippery metal until he finally reached the top, drained. He rested for a moment, clinging to the tower, before summoning the strength to hook on a makeshift harness that would hold him on the top and allow his hands free to work. He felt dizzy, and for a moment he thought he might pass out.

Breathe Chase, breathe.

As the metal creaked and swayed, getting the gear from his pack was almost as challenging as the climb had been. Dropping one of the precious parts would mean going back down and coming back up again. *That's not going to happen,* he thought, clicking on the LED light which had been hanging around his neck. Now illuminating the top of the tower, he wondered how far away his light could be seen, and imagined his enemies—shadow people, the consortium—zooming in on the tiny beacon, ready to take him out. But he pushed all that from his mind and set about working to secure the antenna and the Telmex transmitting equipment that would link up with the WaveGrader and intercept the 5EX transmission.

Chapter Sixty-Six

Chase screamed as the wind, hitting so hard, caused his harness to slip, dropping him three feet, before it ran out of slack and caught. The incident added to his wooziness, but he kept pushing. He took out the two-way and turned it on.

"Anybody still down there?"

"We've been wondering about you," Rob said. "Wen thought she might have to come up there."

"She's good at that," Chase said. "I need some slack on the cable."

"How close are you to connecting?"

"Not very. I just got here. It's not exactly like climbing a ladder on a sunny day. Give me a few minutes." Chase signed off, needing both hands and full concentration. He put on a brighter headlamp to supplement the light around his neck.

It took almost twenty-five minutes before he'd finally finished.

"I think we're good," he radioed back down.

"We can't turn it on until you're off," Rob said. "Too dangerous. Radiation, electricity, water—that's a bad mix."

"All right, I'll let you know when I'm halfway down."

"We'll do it when you get *all* the way down."

"I don't want to climb the whole tower again if something's wrong."

"What could be wrong? Didn't you tighten all those screws?" Rob asked.

Chase unhooked his harness and started back down.

It's always harder going down . . .

"Okay," he radioed when he was halfway down. "Turn it on."

He waited almost a full minute before Rob radioed back. "We got it. Everything is operational."

"Great!" Chase said, relieved. "Now we just need to launch a boat in this mess."

"We've got all night to do that."

"What about sleeping?" Chase asked, not sure he could make it back to the ground, let alone down the mountain and back to the beach to help get a boat out.

"I'm going to turn it off now. I don't want them tracing us."

"Wait, someone has to come back up here in the morning?" Chase asked. "To turn it on again?"

"No, they can do it from the office building."

"Huh?" Chase said.

"You know, the shipping containers."

"Who can we trust with that?"

"Don't worry, Juan has someone who can do it."

"Are we getting a signal?" Chase asked, as they started back to the trail.

"Yes," Juan said. "It's a little weak, but we got the link."

"So we're going to block it?"

"If it holds."

They already knew the potential issue was the stability of the relay and receiver out on the shrimp boat, but they had used stabilizing Bennington circuits stolen from the Mexican Navy.

"I'm still worried," Wen confided to Chase quietly.

He knew her fears, but believed they would be okay. "No one is going to blow that ship out of the water," he said, smiling slightly. He found her battle-weary PTSD almost charming. "Yet, at the same time," he said, "the stakes are high enough that there's a good chance some corporations have probably employed mercenaries who could easily take out the ship. I'm counting on the fact that the consortium doesn't know about it."

He was not yet aware of Thaxton's presence in Lo de Marcos.

Wen had been on the phone near-constantly, trying to get some sort of protection for the ship in between calls to Tu.

"You still don't think we should tell Tess about the plan?" Chase asked.

"Do *you*?" It was a difficult decision. While they needed her assistance, she was also a major threat.

They might have done things differently if they had known what Tess already knew.

Doug Black had managed to avoid the avalanche and catastrophe that befell Chase and Francisco. He'd been hiding ever since they'd stopped, concealed in a higher and somewhat stable section of the jungle. His chosen high ground had actually acted as the bank of one side of the raging river and waterfalls that had engulfed the side of the mountain. That same piece of topography had made Chase's situation worse, as it created a funnel channeling the flood into a narrower, more violent run.

Black had barely gotten out of sight without Wen seeing him. It had been a difficult, albeit instant, decision to not allow Chase to die. His thought process had been helped along by Francisco's plight. Black had already determined that he would try to save the innocent, hard-working man. Once he'd gone that far, saving Chase was a natural progression. He hadn't thought far enough ahead to realize his cover might be blown, or how he was going to get out of there, and definitely not that his own life would be at risk.

Just another day at the office, he thought.

Still, the unusual feeling of saving lives left him a bit confused, but he shook it off as the effects of the storm. He was cold, exhausted, and ready for this freak deluge of rain to *end*. Black just wanted to be back on the warm sunny beach, with an icy beer in his hand, but he still had targets to track.

Chapter Sixty-Seven

Although getting down from the tower was harder than climbing up, taking the trail down the mountain was much easier than their trip to the peak. A brief let-up in the severity of the storm, coupled with lighter loads and a better understanding of the transformed terrain, allowed for a quicker descent. The complete darkness that now shrouded the jungle was the main thing that slowed them, as they didn't have enough lights for everyone.

Sticking close together, they made their way down the wet, winding trail. The rain kept things slick, occasionally returning in random bursts to its full strength.

The river near town was their greatest challenge, swollen to four times its normal size, spilling over its banks as it raged toward the ocean. Rob circled back to Medina's home and arranged to borrow a boat equipped with a powerful outboard motor to ferry them across. Chase never thought he'd be sorry to give up a horse. However, the animal had proven durable, indispensable, and even heroic.

After they reached the other side, the walk would only

take fifteen or twenty minutes, but in his exhaustion, that felt like hours.

Rob told Chase and Wen to meet him in five hours to finish the job.

"That's not a lot of sleep," Chase said. "But I'll take it."

He spent ten minutes in the shower to get all the remaining mud off, and soon he and Wen were sound asleep.

Waking before dawn, after only four hours of sleep, Chase felt like a new man. He marveled once again that Wen rarely ever seemed tired.

"It's a combination of good genetics and MSS training," she explained as they walked out into the rain.

"At least it's not raining as hard," Chase said, pulling his jacket close and pushing away thoughts of the muddy nightmare he had lived through hours earlier.

"Streets are still flooded," she said, pointing her light toward the high water that pooled on the streets closest to the beach.

"I can't figure out how Francisco and I got up to that trail," Chase said as the two of them pedaled their bikes toward El Pequeño Paraiso to meet Rob, careful to stick to the still navigable side of the road.

"Somebody was out there," Wen said in a preoccupied tone as she scanned the dimly lit streets, waiting, as usual, for someone to emerge from the shadows.

"Whoever it was, they saved us. Why didn't they kill me, or just leave me?"

"I don't know . . . That question has been bothering me ever since you told me about your rescue."

"The mud . . . " Chase began, "I was buried. I was dead."

She shuddered, not wanting to think about it.

"Who?" Chase asked again. "And why?"

"The only thing I can think is that maybe somebody wants us to stop the consortium, and they're making sure it happens."

"A competitor?" Chase asked. "That would most likely be—"

"The Chinese," Wen finished for him.

"Then why don't they just stop the consortium?"

"They could have many reasons. Too risky if they get caught, and they are more than likely working with the consortium."

"Betrayal," Chase said. "Then it's even more important that we stop them."

Rob was already waiting when they arrived, and within a few minutes they were on the beach. The rain had picked up considerably. "See it does rain in January," Rob said. "More than a foot of it fell yesterday."

"I remember," Chase said. "I drank a lot of it."

"Where is Juan?" Wen asked.

"He's meeting us at the Telmex shed," Rob replied.

"How are we going to get the waveGrader out? It's too heavy," Chase yelled through the torrent.

"I got an idea. The lagoon isn't that far from the surf."

"What are you talking about? It's at least fifty feet."

"I talked to a guy. They dug a trench before, when the RV park flooded, to drain the lagoon."

"We've already checked. There's no heavy machinery or earthmoving equipment."

"Don't need it man. Cheap labor, strong guys, good work ethic. They've done it before."

"When it was raining like this?"

"No, they waited for the rain to stop. But on a dry day, it took seven guys seven hours—"

"By hand, with *shovels*?"

"Yeah." Rob smiled. "Impressive, huh?"

"Sure, but in case you don't know, when it rains like this, and sand gets wet . . . it's not very stable digging six or eight feet down."

"Right."

"And with the swelling surf, the walls will cave in on them."

"Right."

"Also, we don't *have* seven hours."

"How about fourteen guys, three and a half hours?"

"Maybe twenty guys would have a chance, depending on if it caves in . . . but what good—"

"Don't you see?" Rob insisted. "Once a channel opens up, we get a boat through there."

"A boat?"

"We can load the waveGrader onto a boat, water comes in, takes the boat, goes through the channel. Takes the boat right out to the shrimp boat, like we planned. Done. Easy solution."

Chase frowned. "Not sure I'd call that a solution, where I come from."

"Yeah, where *you* come from, the land of permits and regulations. But here, you get enough men together, they can do anything."

"I think you've been here too long," Wen yelled. Her

feet sank almost a foot into the water covering the cobblestone street as they exited the beach.

"Or not long enough," he replied.

"There has to be a better way," Chase yelled, sloshing along.

"If you've got a better way, let me know. Otherwise, we're running out of time to get the waveGrader out."

"What do you think?" Chase asked Wen as part of a palapa collapsed, dumping untold gallons of water right next to him.

"I don't have a better idea," she said, trying not to laugh.

"You know twenty people to call?" Chase asked Rob.

"I don't, but I know a guy who does."

Chapter Sixty-Eight

Chase looked out to the ocean. With the binoculars, he could just make out the shrimp boat on the horizon before turning his gaze to the sky behind them. He knew the consortium was going to bring 5EX online in the next thirty or forty minutes.

"Let's try it," Chase said, wondering how things could possibly get worse. All their work yesterday would be wasted and the consortium would succeed in launching 5EX if they couldn't get the WaveGrader out.

Bags of garbage floated by. The storm had done real damage, and could still destroy their plans. The winds had died down, and the rain was lessening, but it might be too late to help. They ducked under a sagging canopy near the Telmex storage trailer while Rob made a call.

"They're sending twenty-five guys," Rob said triumphantly.

"When?"

"I told him we needed it to be instantly. He said they would be down as quick as they can."

"It's Mexico, as you keep reminding me," Chase said. "Getting here 'when they can' means mañana, or even *mañana* mañana, especially with this kind of storm."

"No man, you don't understand. The guy I called, he's a powerful dude. Those guys will be at the lagoon before we are."

"Isn't the lagoon just over there?"

"Okay, so I exaggerated a little. Don't worry . . . It'll happen."

Sure enough, a few minutes after Chase, Wen, and Rob arrived at the lagoon, they saw the first few men arriving. By the time they waded across the trailer park and got to the storage shed where Telmex kept the waveGrader, there were at least a dozen men already digging.

"Now we're talking!" Chase said, excited. "All we need now is Juan with the codes, a way to load the waveGrader, the seas to calm, and the tower on top of the ridge not to fall down."

Rob laughed. "Mexican Magic."

Wen smiled while wondering who was watching them, where they were hiding, who else was coming . . . how many guns they had.

Through the mist and swirling rain, Chase could barely make out their silhouettes against the raging ocean. Yet as the sand started to fly, he believed it might just happen.

"See man? These guys, they can do it," Rob said. "My buddy said these guys have done this many times. Maybe not in the rain, but they know what they're doing all right."

"Good, but we still have to get the waveGrader here with no heavy equipment."

"No heavy equipment? What's that?" Rob pointed to an ATV half buried by a collapsed, corrugated metal roof.

"You think it still works?"

"I think everything works here, unless it's broken."

The three of them went over and pulled back the metal, unleashing a new deluge of water onto Chase. This time Wen laughed, but Chase was already so soaked he hardly noticed.

It took Chase a couple minutes but he got the ATV started. "A miracle," he said.

"Mexico," Rob corrected.

Chase drove it over next to the shed holding the wave-Grader. "We still have to get it lifted on."

"We may not have to, man. Little more rain, we can float the boat right over here."

"Little more rain, and we'll have even more problems," Wen said.

"I'm serious. It might be safer to wait."

"There's nothing safe about any of this," Wen said. "We can't afford to be safe right now."

"I agree," Chase yelled. Water ran down his face in a steady stream. "We need some people to help us lift it. Got any more miracles in that phone of yours?"

"No man, I think we've used up all the manpower I can get to dig that trench."

Wen stared across the parking lot at a partially submerged gate. She pointed. "What about that?"

"Maybe," Rob answered, catching on to her idea.

Chase looked around and found a couple tools in the shed. He and Rob ran over to the gate. "I think it'll work." They managed to remove most of the bolts until they came across too much rust. "Got a hacksaw?"

"No. Want me to run down to Home Depot?"

Chase looked up. "Do they have one here?"

"No."

"Then let's pry it off."

After wrestling with the gate for a few more minutes, they were able to get it off and configure it as a combination lever and ramp. After five long minutes, that they didn't have, the WaveGrader was loaded on the ATV and heading to the lagoon. Chase drove straight into water deep enough to get close to the boat where they could use the gate to transfer it safely on board.

"Where's Juan?" Chase asked. "We need the codes to unlock this thing."

"He'll be here," Rob assured him.

Wen looked back into town, worried something might have happened to him. "I'll go look for him."

"Want me to come?" Chase asked.

"No, you help dig," she said, motioning to the huge trench they were trying to make and keep a navigable channel.

Chase thought it looked like quicksand. "Good luck," he said, looking up at the sky. "We're almost out of time."

Chapter Sixty-Nine

Shelby looked over at Grimes, wondering what he was thinking. It was one of her favorite pastimes, one she seldom got right. "So we're *not* going to Mexico?"

"No. Chase and Wen are going to have to wait for our happy little reunion," he said, making them breakfast.

"Then you've decided?"

"Yes. You win." He looked at Shelby with a kind of *'don't you know I would do anything for you'* look, then smiled, looking like the self-satisfied rogue he was. That expression drove her crazy. It was the first thing that had made her fall in love with him. There were probably dozens of women who could make the same claim, but she was with him while the others were just broken hearts scattered around the globe. "We'll meet with them," he continued, "assuming they get out of Mexico alive."

"You said meet. *Not* kill."

"At least not yet." He shrugged. "Call it a truce, or, rather, a pause. I'll hear what they have to say."

She nodded, trying not to smile, happy he had finally

agreed. Yet Shelby knew that when the meeting *did* occur, it would be fraught with danger, not just for Chase and Wen, but for her and Grimes as well. If Belfort, or any number of intelligence agencies, caught wind of their little gathering, it would be the last move on the metaphorical chessboard they were playing on. And Grimes knew it, too. That was one of the reasons it had taken him so long to agree.

However, they both also understood that, after two years of pursuing Chase and Wen, it was time. She thought of the old line, '*The definition of insanity is doing the same thing over and over again and expecting different results.*' Trying to kill Chase and Wen had certainly been crazy. Trying to save them might prove crazier.

With the waveGrader precariously perched on the small boat, Chase, Rob, and a few men that weren't digging, tried to keep it from falling as they pushed and lifted the craft through the makeshift channel. The other men continued digging and dredging, fighting against the collapsing sand. Chase couldn't help but recall trying to steer another boat through another hand-dug channel in Yelapa, but that time people had been shooting at them with machine guns.

The sky lightened every second in spite of the rain. Chase knew the sun was rising behind the thick clouds. "We need more of your Mexican magic," he yelled to Rob. The consortium's test launch was less than half an hour away, with twenty feet left to the ocean. "If we're going to make it before the consortium fires up 5EX, we have to . . . "

"We might just get it," Rob shouted back, pointing to the men breaking through.

Chase could see it happening now, but they still had to

dig down several more feet in the last twelve foot run to the surf.

A couple minutes later, that Mexican magic arrived. A swell from the incoming tide lifted the boat in the channel and swept it out into the surf.

Chase, not able to hold on, went under. As he came up, sandy and soaking wet, Wen was laughing. "Are you okay?"

"Let's just say our next vacation should be in a desert. A hot, dry desert with no water around for a hundred miles."

"Deal."

"Where did you come from?" he asked. "Any sign of Juan?"

Before she could answer, another large wave sent Chase back under. The two men still holding the waveGrader were having a tough time keeping it from capsizing the boat as it negotiated the large, breaking waves. However, the expert captain managed to get through.

"How long will it take them to get there?" Wen asked Rob as Chase was shaking off the sandy water.

"They said fifteen minutes."

"It's going to be close," Chase said. "They've got to unload the waveGrader and hook it up to the receiving equipment."

"They've got a hoist on that shrimp boat," Rob said. "They're ready and waiting."

"What about Juan?" Chase asked Wen again.

"I've got the codes, but he's a little shaken up."

He frowned. "What happened?"

"Consortium sent an assassin," Wen said.

"They were going to *kill* him?"

"If he didn't sabotage our efforts. The guy is still out there somewhere. I've got Juan stashed at our place for safekeeping." She gave the Telmex codes to Rob, who relayed them to the tech on the shrimp boat.

"It's a waiting game," he said.

"Not a fun game," Chase muttered.

"Unless we win," Wen added.

They continued to pace the beach, unwilling to leave until the waveGrader was set up. Twenty minutes later, they saw the signal from the boat to the tower.

"Yes!" Chase exclaimed. "They're ready."

Wen instinctively looked to the sky, checking to see how high the sun was, looking for threats. The rain had almost stopped, but the clouds were still thick.

They headed back to their rental to get some dry clothes and check on Juan. There wasn't anything left to do except wait.

"Let's get cinnamon rolls from La Flor," Chase suggested. "Rob keeps saying they're the best in all of Mexico, but he really just means Lo de Marcos."

Chapter Seventy

Ennis and Otis Cavanaugh sat with the other thirteen members of the consortium and watched the Mexico rollout of 5EX from a special control and monitor room of the Gold Building. The mood was tense, yet celebratory. It had been a long road, years in the making.

"This is it," Ennis said, raising a bottled water. There was no alcohol in the room, as Ennis was a recovering alcoholic. Some people had bubbly water, and assorted fruit juices supplied the rest. "To INSIGHT, and the new world."

Everyone drank to the toast. The men and women gathered had no doubt that their actions would change the world. The consortium consisted of twenty-nine corporations. Baidax was the newest, but they were not represented there today since the Chinese firm had no idea about INSIGHT.

Ironically, it had been a Chinese student at MIT who had first brought the technology forward.

"How's this going to go?" one of the attendees asked.

"The big screens over there will show us the reach of

5EX," Ennis said, cautioning, "There are definitely some pockets where we won't have full coverage yet."

Otis pointed to the different spots on the digitally enhanced satellite map. "These areas will be coming hopefully by the end of the year."

"We'll see these areas light up," Ennis said, gesturing. "Green for good, and if there's any problem, there will be yellow or red sections. We don't expect to see any of those today. And over here, we've got split windows where we'll be able to see actual shared screen devices from the field in real time, with speed tests. Any latency issues—"

"What about the storm?" someone asked.

"Yes, there was a major rain event along the pacific coast in the central region," Otis replied. "We were concerned, but it has cleared off as of late last night."

"We're ready to begin," Ennis said, noting the countdown clock had clicked to zero. "Telmex will be throwing the dish controls switch . . . and it's open," he announced, relief visible on his face, as if years of pent-up strain from the work and difficulties had finally been released—which they had.

As the lights began going green, Ennis walked around the table to briefly visit with each member, shaking their hands and exchanging a few words. Everyone smiled as the maps continued lighting up. Ennis saved his final congratulations for his son, Otis, hugging him tight.

"It's just the beginning," he whispered in his ear. "Not the end."

The reports began coming in from Telmex personnel:

"It's all looking good. Everything's green."

"We're seeing fabulous results."

"It's all working perfectly."

The green continued to spread across the maps. Finally,

the shared device screens began popping. "The speeds are incredible," one man said. "I've never seen anything that fast."

They kept spreading and moving.

"It's like lightning," another said.

"The storm didn't cause any issues," a woman said. "We're getting astounding results."

"Look at all that beautiful green," Ennis breathed. The map had no red or yellow areas. The grays were changing systematically to green, as planned. Any remaining tension in the room melted away. The mood was jovial, and growing more positive with each expanding green section.

"*Dad*," Otis said, quietly but firmly.

Ennis could tell by his tone that something was wrong. He looked at his son, whose eyes moved toward the corner of one of the screens. A yellow line had crept in north of Puerto Vallarta. Ennis assumed it must just be a small glitch, but the yellow grew until it went red. And then the red became a swatch up the coast.

"Why the red?" one of the members asked, concerned.

"Not certain," Otis replied. "Getting Telmex on the phone right now."

"Some of the shared screens are showing error messages," someone said.

"It's beginning to look like the red is going to sweep across Northwestern Mexico."

A Telmex technical head soon assured him that they were looking into the matter. "It appears, if early indications are correct, there is a stray signal interfering."

"From where?"

"Somewhere between Sayulita and Minitas."

"What could it be?" Ennis asked. "I thought everything

had been validated, secured, triple-quadruple checked." He was trying to not sound as worried as he was.

INSIGHT and 5EX's first major test, and with the Chinese on board . . . this has to work, he thought in a panic. *If we don't get first mover advantage, we could lose not just the 5EX standard, but INSIGHT as well. INSIGHT is the prize, the entire package.*

INSIGHT is everything.

He smiled, attempting to look in control.

5EX is simply the carrier, but INSIGHT is the future itself.

"Everything was fine," Otis said. "I confirmed each station myself. As of midnight last night, we were clear and band tested. All posts reported 'still green' this morning . . . an hour before the test. I can't explain it, but it's a very strong signal."

A bad feeling hit Otis as he listened to the Telmex technical head relay more information.

At the same time, Ennis texted Thaxton on another phone, wondering why Chase Malone wasn't already dead.

Chapter Seventy-One

Ennis got on the call with the Telmex man. "Could this be sabotage?"

"That is a very strong possibility," the technician replied. "I know of no accidental glitch that would give these readings. It's almost like somebody jamming our signal. One of the vulnerabilities of the test network is that if an open signal crosses the grid in the right frequency, it can bring down the entire connected section."

"And we can't account for that?"

"Once the full grid is set up, it's not a risk, but you wanted the test fast, we thought . . . "

Ennis had never been big on the technical aspects, he was a money man, a deal maker. He couldn't recall exactly, but someone had told him this could happen, but that it was incredibly unlikely because it required triangulating three towers, specific equipment, code overrides, and a lot of other details. "A perfect storm."

"Yes."

"They could only have done it with someone inside Telmex," Ennis said, thinking of Juan and Chase.

"I'm afraid to say that is probably true," the man said. "I'm getting the same question from our people in the field. Forgive me, my first priority is to get us back to green and stop the encroachment of the dead zones. I'll be back in touch when I know more."

Ennis thanked the technician. There wasn't much more they could do. The red continued to finger inland toward Guadalajara, and the consortium members were rumbling. Ennis squeezed the domino in his pocket, fearful he was about to see the dominoes fall on the Telmex 5EX status satellite maps.

The red expanded.

Otis was torn, as he had been all along. He wanted his father to be successful. He *believed* in the importance of 5EX, but Chase Malone had more than likely discovered the inclusion of INSIGHT, which would explain the aggressiveness of the attack.

Ennis informed the others that they believed the 5EX test rollout had been the victim of sabotage, either by activists or corporate espionage related to competitors.

Thaxton, still in Lo De Marcos, looked at the text from Ennis authorizing him to spend whatever was necessary, hire whoever was needed, and obtain any other resources he thought he would needed to make sure Juan and Chase did not see another sunrise in Lo de Marcos.

Thaxton knew just what to do.

While still dealing with a barrage of questions from the consortium members, Ennis looked at his phone. "Mexico," Ennis announced.

"Excuse us, we will return shortly." He and Otis quickly slipped from the room before the protests could grow.

"The first tests are coming back," Steve Sykes, their INSIGHT point man in Mexico, told them on speaker once they were back in Ennis's office. "Well, 5EX may have had some glitches, but . . ."

"That's an understatement," Ennis snapped.

"INSIGHT did not," Sykes added.

"You mean we got it?" Ennis asked, allowing himself a little bit of excitement while suppressing the feeling a child has on Christmas morning when he's unwrapping the final gift, the one he believes may finally be the one he wanted most.

"It's incredible. We couldn't have asked for better data," Sykes said. "We are reading minds!"

Chapter Seventy-Two

Ennis smiled at Otis. His dream had come true. The INSIGHT system was operational. *It's working*!

"Beyond the data," Ennis said cautiously, "are we getting the results?"

"You'll be astounded. Are you at your computer?" Sykes asked.

Ennis opened up a large-format laptop he used just for INSIGHT and began scrolling through profiles of users. "I'm in."

"You can see it for yourself."

"My god . . . just look at their thoughts." Ennis began reading through . . .

A Mexican real estate agent wondering how he could charge buyers more.

A waitress thinking about how much she hated her job and the group of gringos at table four.

The excitement was growing even more as he watched . . .

Chasing Mind

A mother of four, contemplating whether her husband was cheating on her.

The husband, thinking about his mistress.

The next "captured" thoughts Ennis saw were the ones he'd been dreaming about.

A man thinking of committing a crime. Not just any crime, but rape.

INSIGHT would follow the man and see if he did it. It would prove their point for good.

"The man is deviant," Ennis said to Sykes.

"Yes, but nobody knows it. He's a regular office worker in the insurance industry. Married, three kids. Seems normal, but he's not."

"Clearly," Ennis said.

"Then it brings up the point," Sykes said. "Do we *let* him do it?"

"He's going to do it anyway."

"One day . . . *maybe*."

Otis shot his father an annoyed look. "He may just think about it and never do it."

Ennis stared at him as if this were a strange idea that he had already dismissed. "It's going to be exceedingly difficult to convince people this works . . . There needs to be a few victims so that we can demonstrate its power and protect everyone else. Otherwise, it's all theory."

"You don't have to convince me," Sykes said.

"It's different once you're facing it in real life," Otis said. "A person's most private thoughts on your screen . . . their hopes, desires, fears . . . someone's *fate* in your hands?"

"I don't want to see anyone get hurt, but if this man's victims have to suffer a little so that millions more are spared, it's worth the price," Ennis said. "It's the same debate over privacy. How valuable is privacy if it allows evil to fester?"

"There's a chance something worse than anticipated happens," Otis said.

"We'll be able to tell in advance," Sykes replied.

"Maybe not," Otis countered, looking around at the seemingly endless stacks of artfully arranged cases of dominos in every color, trying to find some grounding for this insane conversation.

"Things can always go worse than we expect," Ennis said. "That's the way it is. We can't base what we do on 'what ifs.'" Let's keep him monitored."

"You're forgetting we're not fully up yet. He could act *anytime*. It could take us another few weeks, particularly after today's problems, before we are at full capacity."

"Right, but we can still watch him."

"He could act *in that window*," Otis insisted, beyond frustrated.

Ennis nodded, resigned to the fact and still bitter about the morning's failure. "We'll do our best. If not, there's no shortage of bad people in the world. We'll find another insurance clerk with fantasies of rape. Or maybe we'll get *really* lucky and find a murderer." He said it offhandedly, not thinking through how the statement would sound read in court one day.

It even made Sykes shiver a little. He believed in the overall concept, but now that they were getting down to implementation, he had to hope his thoughts weren't going to be read every minute.

Otis scoffed. "Callous. These are real people."

"Don't worry, it's the details that are messy, even ugly, but this is a noble fight," Ennis insisted. "Something to be proud of. Something that will make the world a far better *and* safer place."

"Keep us posted, Steve. Once we're back up, make sure we don't lose the rapist," Otis said, ending the video call.

Otis and Ennis stared at each other silently for several moments. Otis looked out the large picture window onto a cloudy, dreary world and walked over to a work table to set up some dominoes.

Ennis joined him.

"The symbolism," Otis began. "One domino sets off a chain reaction. The results are permanent. Everything in their path falls . . . "

"Exactly, but like the dominoes, we can tell where the changes occur. It follows *our* path. The plan is good."

Otis looked at him skeptically. "Are you willing to push the first domino?"

"We already have," Ennis said. "Too late to turn back now."

Chapter Seventy-Three

Otis dropped the dominoes. "I'm out of here."

"Wait," Ennis said. "This is the *future*. Look at the *good*."

"The tradeoff is too great."

"Thus the dilemma. If you *know* someone's going to commit a crime, do you let them?" Ennis asked. "Even if it will prevent others from being able to commit more crimes?"

"No! There's repulsion. You cannot let any single person do any single thing wrong, knowing harm will come."

"And yet it is a fair question."

"One that belongs to the victim. Do you allow *them* to have a choice? What if they don't want to be the hero or the martyr?" Otis blasted. "Why do *you* get to decide?"

"Why do *you*?" Ennis fired back. "Hypothetically, what if the victim was your daughter?"

"It's not that easy."

"For any of us?"

"No. I'm not the one doing this, you are. You are going

to let some innocent woman be raped, maybe killed. She'll die so you can advance your utopian cause."

"It's worth it."

Otis shook his head. "I really can't believe that."

"You keep ignoring the thousands, or *millions*, we'll save."

"Who made you God?"

"Somebody has to decide.

"But why you?"

"Can you really not see it?" Ennis spoke calmly. "If we allow someone to suffer once, we can save so many others. Do you know how many rapes take place here in the United States alone? What about all those women? What if we asked them?"

Otis shook his head.

"We can stop all of them from suffering, from dying," Ennis continued. "The algorithms will identify perpetrators *before* crime happens."

"Then there's no trial, there's no chance for those perpetrators to change their mind, to get help?"

"*We'll* get them help. There'll be programs for those who have been identified as having these thoughts. Then they can be saved, if possible. If not . . ."

"If not, *what*? Are you going to put them in prison for having bad thoughts? Is that fair?"

"There will be review boards that—"

"Or maybe we should just have anybody with impure thoughts executed. But first don't forget to make him wear a scarlet letter."

Ennis sighed. "This isn't as simplistic as you're trying to make it."

"That's just my point. It's not easy, it's incredibly, *outra-*

geously, complicated, and that's what you don't get. There's too many gray areas in your master plan to make it the way you want."

"So this isn't just about this one victim? You really think my whole vision is wrong?"

"This one victim is just one issue. One time where the philosophical dilemmas are too great to be easily solved."

"But after that?"

"There'll be a million others. Many of them will be much harder than this one."

"We'll form committees, panels of judges, groups of psychologists, who can resolve all these issues."

"Who picks the deciders? Who determines what their criteria is, how—"

"They will take all the questions one at a time. Creating a new reality is never easy. But the old one sure isn't working. What do you want me to do?"

Otis stared back at his father. "You know what I want. I want you not to let that woman get raped, and then I want you to rethink this."

"I can't do that. You may not understand, Otis, but we can eradicate evil for good. Yes, it comes at a cost, but in the end, the world—which is hard to even imagine at this point—will be so wonderful that it will be unrecognizable. Everyone will be better off."

"Except this woman."

"Maybe not."

"You want to know what I want? If you let this happen, then I want you to go to that woman's hospital room and say *you* could've prevented this. Or if she gets killed, I want you to go to her family. Maybe she has children. You look them in the eye and say *you* could've saved her life, but *you* chose not to because it was better for your plan to give proof to your theory that bad people exist."

Ennis looked at his son. "I'm sorry, but don't you see? It's already too late. Privacy is gone, one way or another. AI algorithms are going to determine who is good and who is bad. INSIGHT is only one method. The evolution of intrusion isn't coming . . . it's already here."

Chapter Seventy-Four

Doctor Pān and Doctor Lei were surprised to be in the United States so fast. They had been unable to save Chun, but used what they'd learned from peering inside his mind to contact the Cause.

"Welcome to the United States," Holt Gatewood said to the two Chinese scientists.

"Are you with the Cause?" Pān asked in excellent English, since it had been that group who had gotten them out of China.

"Yes," Gatewood lied. "We are grateful you've decided to help us."

"I'm sorry we were unable to prevent Chun's execution," she said. "I know he was important to WOLF. Did you know him?"

"I did not, but he did provide valuable resources to us. His sacrifice will have a lasting impact on our work. Chun made a difference."

Lei smiled and bowed slightly, as if this pleased him. "If

not for him, we would still be there," he said in equally good English.

"I understand," Gatewood said, still impressed with the HITE team for being able to pull off the trade with the Cause. One way or another, HITE would end up controlling INSIGHT. Although the Chinese program wasn't a direct connection to the consortium's plan, it was as Gatewood had told Tess: *"All part of the same beast."*

Chase and Wen retrieved their bikes at Rob's, then got back to their rental to find no trace of Juan.

"Where is he?" Chase asked.

"We have to find him," Wen said.

"Where do we start?"

"His house."

"Let's go!"

The residents of Lo de Marcos were busily cleaning up after the storm as Chase and Wen biked through the wet streets, heading to Juan's. The early morning hours were usually busy with tourists heading to breakfast or to the cinnamon roll place, but this was not a normal morning. All the streets near the river or the beach were flooded, water and debris everywhere. Chase was starving, and looked up the street toward the bakery as they passed, but there was no time.

"Text," Wen said. Thinking it might be Juan, she slowed to a stop in front of a second-hand clothing store.

"Is it Juan?"

"No," she said. "You'll never guess."

"Not in the mood," Chase said, still in damp clothes and exhausted.

"Shelby."

"Really?" Chase asked, not sure they would ever again hear from the sniper who they released after she tried to kill them. "How did she get that number?"

Wen looked at him as if that were a silly question, since Shelby and Grimes had been tracking them for years.

"What does she say?"

"She and Grimes want to meet. In the Caymans, after we finish in Lo de Marcos."

"So they know where we are?" Chase asked, looking around for an incoming bullet.

She nodded, tapping away at the screen. "Don't they always?"

"What are you doing?" Chase asked.

"Telling them we'll be there."

"We're going to meet the two people who have been trying to kill us *in person*?"

"Not today."

"Oh, well, *that's* a relief."

Thaxton walked into Juan's home and found him eating breakfast.

"What are you doing here?" Juan asked, startled.

"You have to tell me how to undo this, or I'm going to have to undo you."

"Pero, Chase Malone is in the next room. You should ask him."

Thaxton pulled out his pistol, thrilled at his luck to have both his targets in the same place. He walked cautiously into the adjoining room where four men with machine guns were waiting for him. "It's over," one of them said.

Two more entered behind him. The show of force quickly convinced Thaxton not to fight. "Who are you?" he asked, giving up his weapon.

"You'll be able to ask all the questions you want once we get back to Washington."

"Washington?" Thaxton was fairly certain they were CIA, but he didn't know that a secret division inside the spy agency, known as CISS, even existed.

Tess Federgreen saw Thaxton taken into custody via the chest cams on the IT-Squad agents. At the same time, she was reading the file of Doug Black. Hours earlier, she had "transferred" the DEA informant to CISS after she'd gotten wind of the DEA operation that had mistakenly assumed Rob, Chase, and Wen were trafficking drugs for a Mexican cartel. She noted in the report from his supervisor that Black had saved Chase and Francisco prior to the transfer because he thought it was the right thing to do.

He had no idea that one day in the future he would end up working with them on the same side.

By the time Chase and Wen arrived at Juan's, the IT-Squad and Thaxton were gone. They found the Telmex man finishing his breakfast.

"You're okay?" Wen asked, looking around suspiciously.

"Si, I was hungry."

"It's not safe," Wen told him.

"Pero, men came from the government and took Thaxton away."

"What men? Who's Thaxton?"

"Thaxton was a thug from the consortium. Threatened me. Not sure who the men were. US CIA, I think. Said to tell you Tess says hello."

Chase and Wen exchanged a glance.

"Want some?" Juan asked, pointing to a plate of pancakes.

Chase happily accepted.

"My friend called me," Juan said while pouring a mixture of melted butter, piloncillo, and toasted pecans over a stack of pancakes for Chase. "The blocking worked. 5EX collapsed."

"Gracias amigo, muy tasty," Chase said. "You helped save the world, my friend."

"Pero, they'll just do it again. The consortium will take what they learn here, run another test, and bring 5EX and INSIGHT back to life like a scary monster."

"I know," Chase said, "but we'll also use the time wisely."

Back at CISS Mission Control, Tess nodded. She was happy that Chase and Wen had survived. She cancelled the COD on Ennis. Linda would be relieved. She had convinced Tess that after what Chase and Wen had learned about the genetic manipulations and mind reading ambitions of the Chinese government, that mining Ennis's brain, recording his thoughts could be more valuable in their fight.

"That's right, Chase," Tess said to his image on the screen, "we're always just buying time."

Even though she knew he couldn't hear her, she paused, as if waiting for his reply. When none came, her expression turned to a bittersweet smile. Her job grew more difficult and complicated every day. She felt as if she'd made a thousand deals with a thousand devils, and the tangled web would one day smother her. But for now, everything was good again.

She looked back at the screen and saw Chase and Wen laughing, and she almost allowed herself to join in. Her smile faded as she spoke to the screen again, this time more softly.

"The end is going to come eventually. All we can do is slow it down. And maybe, just *maybe*, we'll get to define which form it takes."

Epilogue

Although a bit slower than before, Zǔ mǔ did recover from her injuries. She and Tu were moved to a more fortified safe house in Washington DC, with a vault-like safe room. Chase and Wen knew the MSS would come for him again, and they continued to work for a permanent solution. They chose DC so Tu could work with a Think Tank whose main objective was containing the Chinese Communist Party.

As usual, Gatewood and HITE "the invisible agency" pulled off the biggest victory of the ordeal by winding up with the two lead scientists of the Chinese Mind Project as well as all the 5EX and INSIGHT files. Gatewood would ride out the public relations crisis in anonymity and continue to consolidate HITE's power.

Grimes and Shelby had the greatest challenge ahead, preparing for the ultra-covert meeting with Chase and Wen. Hoping to finally come face-to-face with the couple they had been hunting for years. However, Grimes and Shelby would also have to avoid their own employers, the ruthless and incredibly wealthy cabal that had sent them and the other shadow people to kill Chase and Wen.

"Perhaps Grimes can fill in the blanks," Wen said, thinking of the few clues they had, Finale, Jekyll, some dates and times, but little else, to unravel the mystery of the shadow people.

Chase looked at her, still concerned about the risky meeting that might or might not actually take place one day. "Or it will be the final act."

The 5EX Messages

Because of the efforts of Chase, Wen, Rob, Juan, and all the others, full implementation of 5EX and INSIGHT were delayed by twenty-nine days. By the time the system swept over the world, Chase, Rob, The Astronaut, Dez, Bull, and Tu, had developed a brilliant and sophisticated countermeasure. They called it BLINDSIDE. The program was loaded onto every connected device. The day of the much hyped launch of 5EX, BLINDSIDE put a warning message on every device that informed the user of government monitoring:

Your thoughts are being hacked.
The government and the consortium of banks and tech companies behind this will tell you this is just malware. The media will call it a gigantic hoax, a widespread hack.
Don't believe them. They are monitoring your thoughts.

As predicted, the government and the news media announced the biggest hack in history, even coming up with a catchy name—the Hypno-Hack. Headlines and news anchors proclaimed, "Hypnoses-Hack: a hoax," and soon reported that they had arrested the people involved.

The next morning, BLINDSIDE struck again with new messages:

This was not a hack, and is not a hoax.
The only hoax is the government saying we have been arrested.
We have not. We are free.
Here is the proof that they are reading your minds.

The following lines texted to each individual were different, but each began with:

Here is what you were just thinking...

People began talking to their coworkers, friends, and relatives. Soon everyone realized that they had all received unique messages. Word quickly spread that the messages had been accurate accounts of their private thoughts.

A surge of outrage against the government, the banks, and tech giants identified in the texts, swept the globe.

The Consortium had some success in blocking the messages for several hours.

BLINDSIDE finally got another message out five hours later:

They are still monitoring your thoughts. If you want to prove it, go through your list of contacts and friends on your social media accounts, click on their profile, and you will be able to see if they are on a connected device. If so, you will be able to see what they are thinking in real time.

Millions of people began invading the thoughts of their friends, colleagues, relatives, people they hardly knew . . .

The resulting bedlam was a riotous force.

Some people actually liked the feature. However, most others completely disconnected.

Now try it on these people:

Ennis Cavanaugh headed a list of dozens of consortium members and other implicated government officials. The list was included in the messages. Ordinary folks in the general population were able to access the thoughts of everyone of the 5EX/INSIGHT perpetrators, even incriminating thoughts that had been recorded and preserved from earlier.

Criminal investigations were launched. Mobs stormed banks and corporate buildings belonging to those involved.

The final message that appeared included a link to a free application that would show if anyone was monitoring you, and, more importantly, *who* they were. The wording of the message was ominous:

Tech giants aren't always trustworthy.
Governments don't always look out for your best interests.
Politicians, who promise they will protect you and your privacy, lie.
But the BLINDSIDE apps will constantly be monitoring those that monitor you.
Give away your privacy bit by bit, and eventually there is no privacy remaining.

The message and its related discussions were immediately suppressed on all major platforms.

Next in the Chase Malone Thriller series

vinci-books.com/chasing-time

Out of time. Out of options. Who will pay the ultimate price?

With global war looming, Chase Malone and ex-spy Wen Sung race to secure a rare element that could stop disaster. In a world of betrayal and espionage, time isn't their only enemy—sacrifice is the only way out.

Turn the page for a free preview…

Chasing Time: Chapter One

WASHINGTON DC

April 2nd - 2:42 am - Eastern Time

The strong scent of cherry blossoms filled the warm, surprisingly humid night. He pictured their beauty, wondering if he'd ever see them again when they were drenched in sunlight. *They want to kill me,* he thought, looking back into the darkness. Washington in the spring was a beautiful place, even in the middle of the night, but not if you were running for your life.

The Astronaut tried to calm himself, pressed up against the black granite wall of the Vietnam Veterans Memorial. Breathing in the perfume of the trees, he could almost pretend it was going to be all right. Yet The Astronaut knew better. He was an intelligent man; logic, odds, calculating the countless potential outcomes of his predicament, came easily.

The CIA referred to him as an 'Astronaut' even though he'd never even piloted a plane, much less a spaceship. The odd moniker was due to his "out of this world" mind. His brain came wired a little differently than most—capable of extraordinary feats, able to detect patterns and see answers normal folk couldn't imagine.

But as he ran from people intent on doing him harm, The Astronaut felt anything but special. He felt ordinary. So ordinary it was as if he was nothing. For years, he had worked with the CIA and other intelligence agencies around the world, helping them do what even the super computers and advanced AI could not. He—and a few others like him —was able to use his mind in ways that programmers were unable to force machines to do. Something about human intelligence, mixed with human emotions, mixed with instincts and uniquely human experiences, mixed with one other ingredient, perhaps the most magical (The Astronaut was on the spectrum, a neurobiological type, gene variant of autism), had formed a mind that was indeed exceptional.

The math savant did not like to be touched, yet embraced numbers, which to him were a secret language expressed in colors so numerous that even the most talented artist could not conceive of what he saw.

So as he crouched in the shadows of the wall, he knew there were originally 57,939 names at the time of the memorial's dedication in 1982, but now there were 58,318, each etched in chronological order of their deaths on 140 panels. He knew the wall was constructed at a cost of $232 million, he knew how many members of Congress had voted to allocate funds, he knew that it attracted more than 78,000 visitors every month, he knew how high each letter was and the total number of letters on the wall, and The Astronaut also knew that this was where he would die.

But how many are trying to kill me? It drove him crazy not to know that answer to input the critical data into his mind, so he could accurately calculate the odds.

The Astronaut was close enough to the cold, monolithic surface that his warm, panting breaths clouded three of four names. The black granite had been so highly polished that in daylight it acted as a mirror, but at night its ominous structure might swallow him.

His entire life, The Astronaut had known he was "unique." In some ways that had made him fragile and weak, but he'd always believed that in any fight, the smartest would prevail.

I am one of the smartest.

However, on this balmy night, on the National Mall, in the capitol city of the most powerful country on earth, there was no solution that he could see . . . no way out.

What if my mind is not going to be able to save me this time? He scanned the area, sure they were closing in on him. *Maybe it will be my lungs and my legs that save me . . .*

He heard shouts. There were so many of them. It didn't make sense that a single unarmed mathematician could attract that kind of force against him, but nothing in The Astronaut's life made sense. A strange, awkward man outside of his realm, he ran with spies, secret agents, assassins, brilliant scientists, rogue revolutionaries . . . his life had been extraordinary because he had something so rare. And people, both good and bad, were attracted to rare things.

The Astronaut didn't even know who was after him, who was going to kill him. He had been running from them for days, weeks—in fact, it had actually been *months* if he admitted to ignoring the earliest signs.

How did I let it come to this? I am not ready to go. I don't want to leave this world . . . I like it here.

The panic began to take him. He fought its greasy claws, knowing that if he got lost in the terror, there would be nothing left.

Chasing Time: Chapter Two

ANOTHER PART OF THE WORLD

"It's the middle of the night there," a gray-haired man said. His expensive black suit added an appearance of importance. He studied the faces on a giant monitor occupying a section of wall surrounded by rich, red, floor-to-ceiling draperies.

Another man in a bright red necktie nodded. He, too, looked at the faces as though they were pieces on a chessboard. Although the large table could easily accommodate thirty-six people, they were alone in the vast room. An eight foot wide bronze sculpture of a hammer and sickle hung on the opposite wall, mounted on a slab of wood, also painted a deep red.

"Have we heard from Tolstoy?"

"Not since this morning," the gray-haired man replied. "But as I said, it is nighttime there now."

"There is a situation beyond them," the red tie man said, motioning to the pictures on the monitor. "This Astronaut could unravel Blackout."

"Tolstoy's operatives will have The Astronaut soon. This is not a problem."

"But Tolstoy has not reported."

"We have another contact through our embassy in Washington."

"That is risky."

The gray-haired man smiled slightly. "Life is risky. They have full surveillance, and twenty-seven minutes ago they located The Astronaut again. This time he is alone, and he is running. We have also discovered where he has been staying."

"In Washington?"

"Yes. We have people going there now."

"The CIA and the FBI could pick up on our activities."

"Yes, they could."

The red tie man looked at the screen and began to say something, but hesitated.

"What is it?" the gray-haired man prodded. "Speak freely."

"I don't know if we can kill all these people and expect to make each one look accidental."

"Of course not. They will figure it out, but it will be too late."

"Not too late to blame us."

"The blame will fall elsewhere. You worry too much."

Red tie man nodded. "I do, because I am a strategist. I get paid to worry." He frowned. "Worrying is my life. You are in espionage. Worrying should be *your* life as well."

The gray-haired man looked to the portrait of Karl Marx on the other end of the room. "No, my job is to make sure our country, and our philosophy, dominate the world. Our ways during the era of the Cold War were often ignored. We were behind times, even forgotten . . . Ah, but the world has changed so much."

"When do we meet with the full committee?"

The gray-haired man looked at the clock. We are more than forty-eight hours from the removal. Much can still happen. We have a full meeting scheduled for twenty-four hours prior to removal and again at twelve hours ahead of time."

"Two meetings so close?" the man in the red tie asked, still uncomfortable with using the term 'removal' to describe the attack, although he could not argue with the accuracy of the word. In just over forty-eight hours, an American city, along with a million of its inhabitants, would be removed from the face of the earth.

"As I said, things are moving smoothly, but as we get closer . . ."

"And how will the president be able to deny our country's involvement?"

"You forget, our country is not involved."

The man in the red tie looked at him skeptically. "But we are. You more than anyone should know not to underestimate the US intelligence agencies."

"And *you* should know better not to underestimate *our* intelligence agencies."

The red tie man looked back at the screens. Being a diplomat, he was wary of this plan for many reasons, not the least of which was that a good many of his friends and associates were going to die as a result of it. He worried intensely that they would be discovered. Yet it might also work, and then they would have a whole new set of problems.

He had been against this radical intervention from the

start. He was *afraid* of it. But theirs was not a structure where one could voice opposition to a plan that was already supported by one's superiors.

"Don't be so nervous," the gray-haired man said again.

"I told you, worry is my business."

"You will have much less to worry about after Five-Fours. We will clearly be dominant . . . the most powerful country in the world."

The official name for the attack, the removal, the insanity, was "Five-Fours," since the strike would happen at 4:44 am, on the fourth day of the fourth month. The field ops only knew it as "Blackout," but the diplomat in the red tie sitting at the long table in that massive room believed it should be called "The End."

"But you said they will not know it is us," red tie man said. "And if we avoid the blame, how will we get the credit?"

"The United States will be reeling," the gray-haired man replied. "You saw what happened after 9/11. They were never the same again. This is a million times 9/11. Five-Fours will *finish* them." His voice rose. "The United States will be a wreck, a failed state. They will be scrambling to put some semblance of their former selves back together again . . . and they will be missing almost all of their leadership."

"Yes, but—"

"Remember, it's not just Washington DC that will be gone, not just the great symbol of their *perceived* greatness, but all the *people*. The president, vice president, the entire cabinet, your friend, the Secretary of State, most of the members of Congress, all those annoying senators, the majority of their intelligence apparatus—that you tell me not to underestimate—will all be gone. Who will be left to figure anything out?"

Grab your copy…
vinci-books.com/chasing-time

About the Author

USA TODAY Bestselling Author Brandt Legg uses his unusual real life experiences to create page-turning novels. He's traveled with CIA agents, dined with senators and congressmen, mingled with astronauts, chatted with governors and presidential candidates, had a private conversation with a Secretary of Defense he still doesn't like to talk about, hung out with Oscar and Grammy winners, had drinks at the State Department, been pursued by tabloid reporters, and spent a birthday at the White House by invitation from the President of the United States.

At age eight, Legg's father died suddenly, plunging his family into poverty. Two years later, while suffering from crippling migraines, he started in business, and turned a hobby into a multi-million-dollar empire. National media dubbed him the "Teen Tycoon," and by the mid-eighties, Legg was one of the top young entrepreneurs in America, appearing as high as number twenty-four on the list (when Steve Jobs was #1, Bill Gates #4, and Michael Dell #6). Legg still jokes that he should have gone into computers.

By his twenties, after years of buying and selling businesses, leveraging, and risk-taking, the high-flying Legg became ensnarled in the financial whirlwind of the junk bond eighties. The stock market crashed and a firestorm of trouble came down. The Teen Tycoon racked up more than a million dollars in legal fees, was betrayed by those closest to him, lost his entire fortune, and ended up serving time for financial improprieties.

After a year, Legg emerged from federal prison, chastened and wiser, and began anew. More than twenty-five years later, he's now using all that hard-earned firsthand knowledge of conspiracies, corruption and high finance to weave his tales. Legg's books pulse with authenticity.

His series have excited nearly a million readers around the world. Although he refused an offer to make a television movie about his life as a teenage millionaire, his autobiography is in the works. There has also been interest from Hollywood to turn his thrillers into films. With any luck, one day you'll see your favorite characters on screen.

He lives in the Pacific Northwest, with his wife and son, writing full time, in several genres, containing the common themes of adventure, conspiracy, and thrillers. Of all his pursuits, being an author and crafting plots for novels is his favorite.

Acknowledgments

I dictated parts of this book while walking the beach and town where a substantial part of the action takes place in, Lo de Marcos, Mexico. Thanks to Shannon Black for introducing us to that cool part of the world, and to both Kilroy and Shannon for taking us up to the peak overlooking the town and so much beautiful coastline. We had a much easier time getting to the top than Chase did, but during that hike, Kilroy provided many of the background details that made the story more exciting. Also a special thanks to our hosts Miguel and Nancy for making us feel like family, for making our little piece of paradise feel like home, for sharing their happiness and for always being warm and welcoming.

To my wife, Ro, and our Teakki, who help with so many parts of these stories, and our own wonderful story. And my mother, Barbara Blair, who reads these books more times than anyone else. Moms are good that way.

I'm always grateful to Melanie C. Hansen for checking the final version and slaying the occasional sigasaurus, to Gil Forbes for his "Forbes Treatment," and to Joan Osborne who rooted out several misplaced modifiers and provided other helpful suggestions. Thanks to Jack Llartin, my copy editor, for getting the manuscript into its final form, racing (and beating) deadlines, and for always being there.

Thanks to the team for all the fast work!

And, finally, to Teakki, who patiently waited to talk

about his latest script ideas for one of the many films he's planning to make until I finished writing each day. Can't wait to read this one with you!

Most of all, I can never express enough gratitude to my readers. To all the ones that have read everything I've published, to the ones who have just finished their first Booker thriller or Chasing adventure, it means the world to me that you've decided to spend your money and time on my stories. Please drop me an email anytime – responding to reader emails is one of my favorite times of the day!

I'd also like to mention a few fellow authors who are important to me for many reasons: Craig Martelle, Michael Anderle, Mark Dawson, Nick Thacker, Ernest Dempsey, Eric J. Gates, Dale DeVino, Phil M. Williams, Jennifer Theriot, Haris Orkin, Michelle McCarty, and Zoe Saadia.

A special thanks goes out to the following readers and members of the street team for either their support, kindness, reviews (I *love* reviews), suggestions, and/or encouragement (If I left anyone out, I apologize, please forgive me, and let me know, I can fix it!) in no particular order:

Karen Mack, Rob Weaver, Ken Clute, Tricia Turner, Nigel Revill, John Nunley, Linda Loparco, Ernest Pino, Diane Whitehead, Patricia Ruby, Douglas Meek, Kathleen Robbins, Glenn Legge, Glenda Dykstra, Pam Gilbert, Ernest Manpino, Cara Johnson, Carol M, Kat Heyer, Ken Friedman, Joan Osborne, Rob Zorger, Robyn Shanti, Bob Browder, Chis Bond, Melanie C. Hansen, Chet Keough, Sue Steel, Jacky Dallaire, Adam Tanner, Frank Murphy, Gil Forbes, Blake Dowling, Sam Rhoades, Karen Markovitz, Kyle Dahlem, Christine Moritz, Tom Strauss, Irene Witoski, Martha Heckel, Sandie Parrish, LA Dumas, Bob Dumas, John Nicholson, Peggy Gulli, Randy Howerter,

Ingo Michehl, John McDonald, Kathy Creecy, Susan Norlund, Liz Miller, Cheryl Olson, Jan Dallas, Chuck Gonzalez, Justin Lear, Rick Ferris, Janice Gildea, Vivienne Du Bourdieu, Elaine Dill, Sharon Moffatt, Jean Sink, Julie Price, Judith Anderson, Terry Myers, Carl Howard, Chris Tomlinson, Judy Hammer, Satish Bhatti, Christopher Bowling, Michael Ferrel, Susan McGuyer, Bill Borchert, Samantha Jackson, Debra Harper, Dennis Lowe, Cathie Harrison, Marcel Roy. Gerry Adler, Brian Schnizlein, Mike Lauland, Mark Perlmutter, Frank Fusco, Gene Leach, Ron Babcock, Leslie Royce, Michael Picco, Gillian Charlton, Sam J. Rhoades III, Stephane Peltier, Ron Babcock, and a double-extra thanks to whoever the reviewer "Serenity" is! And special gratitude to Grady Harp!

There is a goal among some authors to turn readers into fans, fans into super fans, and super fans into friends. I am fortunate to have been able to achieve that goal on numerous occasions.

Thank you.